MURDER BY THE BOOK

D. R. MEREDITH

WHEELER
CHIVERS

This Large Print edition is published by Wheeler Publishing, Waterville, Maine USA and by BBC Audiobooks Ltd, Bath, England.
Wheeler Publishing is an imprint of Thomson Gale, a part of The Thomson Corporation.
Wheeler is a trademark and used herein under license.

The text of this Large Print edition is unabridged.
Other aspects of the book may vary from the original edition.
Set in 16 pt. Plantin.

LIBRARY OF CONGRESS CATALOGING-IN-PUBLICATION DATA

Meredith, D. R. (Doris R.)
    Murder by the book / by D.R. Meredith.
        p. cm. — (The murder by the yard series) (Wheeler Publishing large print cozy mystery)
        ISBN 1-59722-347-6 (alk. paper)
        1. Clark, Megan (Fictitious character) — Fiction. 2. Reference librarians — Fiction. 3. Group reading — Fiction. 4. Amarillo (Tex.) — Fiction. 5. Large type books. I. Title.
    PS3563.E7355M87 2006
    813'.54—dc22   2006019955

BRITISH LIBRARY CATALOGUING-IN-PUBLICATION DATA AVAILABLE

Published in 2006 in the U.S. by arrangement with The Berkley Publishing Group, a division of Penguin Group (USA) Inc.
Published in 2007 in the U.K. by arrangement with the author.

U.K. Hardcover: 978 1 405 63946 0 (Chivers Large Print)
U.K. Softcover: 978 1 405 63947 7 (Camden Large Print)

Printed in the United States of America on permanent paper
10 9 8 7 6 5 4 3 2 1

To Mike, my husband, former career prosecutor, and present criminal defense attorney, who, in the real world, would keep Megan Clark from making the kind of legal missteps that would land her in jail. However, Megan lives in the world of imagination, so she will continue to be an amateur sleuth in the best Miss Marple tradition.

ACKNOWLEDGMENTS

I must acknowledge the debt I owe to the Grande Dame of Mystery, Agatha Christie. Without her wonderful books, particularly the ones the Murder by the Yard Reading Circle discusses, I might never have been inspired to attempt such a challenging plot. I can only hope that I do justice to dear Miss Agatha, and if I don't, I hope she doesn't haunt me too long.

I also wish to acknowledge another Doris who once owned a bookstore on Sixth Street. Coincidentally, her bookstore was also called Time and Again. Here we go again, Doris, to one more adventure on Sixth Street.

establishments, events, or locales is entirely coincidental. However, Sixth Street and the Route 66 Historical District is real, fascinating, and funky, although the business folk along the Street don't go in for murder. It would frighten away the tourists and is generally bad for business.

1

We live in dangerous times. All one can do is to keep the spear ready, and a feeble thing it is, touch the amulet, and hope for the best.

James Compton in John Bingham's
A Fragment of Fear, 1965

AMARILLO, TEXAS — THE PRESENT
Sacrificing virgins isn't common practice anymore. Neither is doing ritual dances in feathers and masks, or bowing down to graven images. At least not among the general populace in these United States. City living has deadened our instincts, sapped our need to sacrifice virgins or engage in ritual dances to protect ourselves from nature's more destructive aspects, and replaced it with an egocentric belief that nature is fragile and man must protect it. Man is not afraid anymore. He feels at one with the earth, with nature. In his blindness

he won't admit that the earth doesn't care what some two-legged result of evolution may feel toward nature. The earth in all its ramifications simply is. It continues its revolution around the sun every 365 1/4 days; the weather continues its cycle of wet and dry, cold and hot, as it has done for millennia since life crawled out of the primeval muck and began to evolve. Man in the city only pays attention when a hail storm damages his roof, or a tornado blows away both roof and house, or a hurricane hits land and reconfigures the landscape. Or a tsunami washes away the landscape altogether and reveals what has been hidden. Only then does man begin to fear Nature.

Droughts reveal what is hidden also, and perhaps their practice of slowly shrinking the concealment by increments is more ominous than a sudden wall of water which may, after all, sweep away all in its path, so that objects vanish, not to be seen again for centuries. A drought holds an object in place while shrinking everything around it. If man has lost his fear of the elements, if he no longer watches the cycles of weather, no longer fears drought, then those who have guilty knowledge of what has been secreted never think to worry about the three-year-long dry spell that has punished the Texas Panhandle with unrelenting sunshine and hot, dry winds.

The drought sucks up water in what few lakes and streams exist in the Llano Estacado, "The Staked Plains." A shallow stream barely wider than a yard and scarcely half as deep trickles down the middle of the Canadian riverbed, leaving bare wide swathes of sand that stretch to the tall sandstone and caliche cliffs on one side and small weed-covered hillocks on the other. The water level in Lake Meredith near Amarillo drops nearly every day, and the city fathers speak of water rationing. But such indicators of coming trouble never break the surface calm of those in the small group gathered in the used bookstore on Sixth Street. Only one worries about the drought. The others only complain about the size of their water bills without thinking of what else the dry weather may bring about. Each passing day the drought threatens the members of the reading circle although everyone is unaware of it.

Lake Greenbelt near Clarendon, Texas, shrinks as the cloudless skies continue into the fall, until the ruins of the original town site lay exposed to man's sight for the first time in nearly a hundred years, drawing professional archaeologists to direct droves of amateurs who sweat under the unrelenting sun for the privilege of participating in a real dig. And Wild Horse Lake, a complimentary name for an old playa lake bed, squats by Front Street on the edge of Amarillo's original town site, shriveling like a drying piece of rawhide until ugly, garbage-strewn banks rise above the rapidly diminishing water. But more than the garbage thrown in its waters is exposed when the lake recedes toward its center like age-shrunken gums. The water breaks against an obstacle as the wind sweeps across the lake's surface. If the Murder by the Yard Reading Circle's members don't yet sense an ominous threat from what lies beneath the surface of Wild Horse Lake, they soon will.

They will soon wish for an amulet, wish they had performed a ritual rain dance. One might even wish he had sacrificed a virgin.

TIME AND AGAIN BOOKSTORE, SIXTH STREET

Fall was Megan Clark's favorite season of the year. Sometimes it arrived in September; sometimes it put off its arrival until late October. This year it was late October, and fall was in full bloom: mums and marigolds, ragweed, and prickly Russian thistle shorn of leaves, free of its roots, and transformed into tumbleweeds, tossed by the dusty wind to lodge against parked cars, the sides of buildings, any stationary object in its path.

Megan rolled down the passenger-side window and breathed in air as crisp as a newly picked apple, full of the scents of Sixth Street: barbecue from Sam's Open-pit Barbecue, the light perfume of late-blooming petunias in hanging baskets on storefronts and in flower boxes lining the curbs, the musty odors from antique stores with their doors open to air out their establishments, the smell of frying onions and peppers from Jose's Authentic Mexican Cuisine. And dust. With the drought there was always dust in the air.

An explosive sneeze seemed to shake the pickup's passenger cab, followed by a series of smaller sneezes like the aftershocks of a major earthquake.

"Roll up that window!" shouted Ryan Stevens, punctuating his order with another gigantic eruption.

Chastised by her own guilt more than his demand, Megan quickly obeyed. "Sorry, Ryan, I forgot about your allergies."

Ryan turned his head to glare at her out of watery, bloodshot eyes. His nose was approximately the color of a ripe chili pepper. He pulled a handkerchief out of his shirt pocket, wiped his eyes, and blew his nose. "I hate fall. Swollen sinuses, itchy throat. I wonder what the pollen index is? Probably out of sight. And so much dust I can see the air I breathe. My bronchial tubes are probably just little dust pockets."

"You should sleep under a vaporizer."

"Then I'd just have mud pockets. I'm doomed until there's a hard freeze to kill every growing weed in the Panhandle." His voice, usually a pleasant baritone, was nasal and gloomy.

"It's the drought. It hasn't rained in so long that the dirt won't stay on the ground where it belongs. It must be miserable for people like you."

"What's that mean? That I'm some kind of freak because I'm allergic to pollen. Millions of people are allergic to pollen. It's unnatural not to be."

"Ryan, if it grows or blows, you're allergic to it. There's no need to be defensive about it."

"I'm not defensive! I just said it's unnatural not to be allergic to pollen. Why aren't you allergic? You're the only redhead I've ever known who doesn't have allergies. It's unnatural!"

"It's compensation for being short," said Megan with as much patience as she could muster. Usually Ryan was a handsome hunk of wonderful company, but with an allergy attack he was as irritable as a hungry bear. "Why don't you take an allergy pill?"

"I *have* taken a pill!" He sneezed again.

"Here's the bookstore — finally. Listening to Rosemary lead the discussion about *The Murder of Roger Ackroyd* will take your mind off your allergies — if we aren't so late that the program's over."

Ryan made a sound like a pig rooting in a trough. He turned left into the alley that ran along one side of the Time and Again Bookstore and stopped his Ford Ranger, staring in disbelief at the store's parking lot. "It's full. There's no place to park. Those cars don't all belong to the book club members. There aren't that many of us, and only Herb drives an SUV, and there are four other of those gas-guzzlers besides his."

"If you hadn't insisted on driving thirty or thirty-five miles an hour, we wouldn't be late and there might be a parking place," said Megan.

"That was the speed limit!"

Megan didn't bother to reply. She always drove as fast as the traffic would bear, barring the presence of cop cars in her immediate vicinity, viewing speed signs as suggestions rather than limits.

"Park around back by Agnes's back door. There's room, and she won't care."

"It's dark behind the bookstore. It looks like one of the local juvenile delinquents broke the street light again."

"Since when are you afraid of the dark, Ryan?"

She could sense him bristling with indignation. "Since we started finding corpses in the dark."

"Don't exaggerate. We've only found one corpse in the dark. The rest we found in broad daylight. Or in a hotel room," she added, thinking of the mayhem at the International String Figure Association Convention she and Time and Again Bookstore sponsored last spring. After two bodies turned two hotel rooms into crime scenes, the management canceled the rest of the convention by means of locking all the conference rooms, closing down the restaurant and bar, and evicting all those attending from their rooms with some lame excuse that there was toxic black mold in all their bathrooms. Then the hotel chain's attorneys sent Megan and the rest of the Murder by the Yard Reading Circle members a certified letter stating that they were not welcome at any of the chain's hotels. Megan thought the hotel attorneys over-reacted. It wasn't as if she had deliberately included murder on the conference program. Sometimes shit happens.

Ryan parked and turned off the pickup's lights. Darkness settled down like a large, thick blanket dropped from the heavens. Twenty feet away was the alley, dimly lit by a street light at the front of the bookstore. Between them and the alley lay complete darkness. Megan shivered and wished she hadn't insisted on parking back here. Stepping into that darkness was like stepping into a void.

"Be careful, Ryan. It's easy to trip in the dark when you can't see where you're walking."

"I'm not a child, Megan. I can put one foot in front of the other without falling on my a — Ouch!" There was the sound of a falling body followed by an expletive Megan had never heard him use before.

"Ryan! Ryan! Did you trip? Are you all right?" Megan scrambled around the end of the pickup and started up its other side. She stepped on something solid that gave slightly under her hiking boot. She quickly stepped aside before whatever it was bonded to her shoe, but not before she heard another expletive, this time from practically under her feet.

"Ryan, are you there?" She knelt and started feeling the ground. Her right hand felt Ryan's torso. She ran her hands up his torso to his face. He seemed to be sucking on his knuckles. "Ryan, where do you hurt? Do you think you broke any bones? Let me feel your legs. You may have twisted an ankle. What did you trip over anyway?"

"I hurt the hell all over — and keep your hands off my legs. They're fine, but they might not be if you don't stay perfectly still. The only bones that might be broken are my knuckles where you stepped on them with those steel-toed hiking boots you wear."

"They aren't steel-toed!"

"Close enough. Just don't move until I get up and make it to the alley. I think that is far enough away to be safe from you."

"I'm sorry I stepped on your hand, but I hardly think I'm dangerous," said Megan, hurt that he wouldn't let her help.

"I told you it was too dark to park back here. A man can't see where's he's going."

Megan heard him scramble up and walk to the alley faster than Megan thought was safe. He was asking to trip again. "What did you do, turn your ankle on a pebble?"

Ryan reached the alley and turned around. "For your information, those are not pebbles, they're rocks, and I didn't step on one. If you must know, I ran into Agnes's car. To be more specific, I ran into the side-view mirror on her car and lost my balance. My ears are stopped up, and as a result my balance isn't too good. I'd be fine except for a little stiffness from falling on my butt if it weren't for my swollen and throbbing knuckles. But don't worry, I'll put an ice pack on my hand when I get home. I think I still have a package of frozen peas in the freezer from last week's 10 for $10 special at Albertson's. Wonderful ice packs, frozen peas. I've started stockpiling them since you moved back to Amarillo. Now let's get inside the bookstore where there should be hot coffee and cookies, I hope. And light. God knew what he was doing when he said 'Let there be light.' "

Megan followed him down the alley. Men! Why didn't they ever say anything when something was wrong? If Ryan had told her that he felt off balance, then she wouldn't have insisted on parking behind the store in the dark. She refused to feel guilty for stepping on his hand if he was too obstinate to admit that he had a temporary disability.

The Time and Again Bookstore was a

large, one-story, L-shaped, blindingly white stucco building with a solid wooden door painted a shiny ebony at the end of the short wing that faced Sixth Street. A tiny parking lot with spaces for twelve cars hugged the long wing of the L. Each space was marked with a reserved sign, and another sign, visible for two blocks, painted on the short side of the L stated that parking was for customers of the Time and Again Bookstore only. The word "only" was capitalized, half as tall as the rest of the sign, and painted bright red.

"It's the best advertising I've ever done," Agnes Caldwell, sole proprietor of Time and Again, had told Megan one rainy Saturday afternoon when Megan complained about having to park on a side street four blocks away. "Since I have the only parking lot on Sixth Street worthy of the name, all the tourists who can't find a parking place on the street park here. Then, because they're afraid I might have their cars towed, they come into the store to justify their parking. Once I get them in the front door, I can sell them a book whether they originally intended to buy one or not. It's just another way for a small independent bookseller to survive the competition from the chain bookstores."

A mural of old cars from the twenties and thirties, a prominent Route 66 road sign, extinct logos of companies such as the flying red horse for Standard Oil, and a series of Burma-Shave signs were painted on the wall of the long leg of the L. Flecks of paint had fallen from the mural, which rather than reflecting disrepair, instead evoked a sense of history. This was a picture of long ago when television, spaceships, and microchips were dreams of science-fiction writers and a few imaginative scientists. Given the innovations of the last seventy years, the mural symbolized life in Amarillo's past, remembered only by the very elderly, or caught in fading, brittle, black-and-white Kodak photos glued in old family albums or tossed in cardboard boxes and stored in the backs of little-used closets. As an archaeologist/paleopathologist Megan Clark loved the mural.

She loved all of Sixth Street. The buildings mostly dated from the early twentieth century, and when the great Mother Road, Route 66, was built, Sixth Street was part of it. Sometimes, in the late evenings like this under a cloudy sky with only intermittent moonlight, when the dusty air made halos around the old-fashioned street lights, she felt that the modern-day antique stores and little gift and memorabilia stores were just facades that could fade away to reveal the original bustling street lined with the retail businesses that were there in the twenties and thirties. She could close her eyes and hear the labored engines of old pickups with wooden beds — old Chevies and Fords, Buicks and Oldsmobiles packed with household goods and gaunt-faced families migrating to California in search of a fresh start away from the dust-smothered farms abandoned to the banks or to the elements.

Megan shivered as she cut across Agnes's parking lot. Sometimes the past to her was as real as the present, almost as if Time curled back on itself a hundred years or five hundred years to let her glimpse what was. She wondered if Ryan as a history professor ever felt the ghosts of the pioneers and heard the creak of wagon wheels when he lectured on the western migration of the nineteenth century.

She loved the front of Agnes's bookstore, too. A painting of a grandfather clock occupied the space between a small barred display window and the ebony door. A sign saying "Time and Again Bookstore" hung over the sidewalk, like the old signs on English taverns. She followed Ryan as he pushed open the door and walked into the scent of baked apple pie. Not that Agnes had actually been baking apple pies — Agnes didn't cook except at breakfast, and then she opened a box of cereal and peeled a banana. But Agnes did make candles and always had some burning along with tiny baskets of potpourri sitting on the checkout desk and any other empty surface. Agnes hated the musty, moldy smell of most used bookstores and decided hers would smell of spice and "everything nice."

Agnes had hung track lighting down each aisle between bookshelves instead of aiming for a shadowy ambiance. "Most of my customers are over forty and wear bifocals. They want to be able to see what they're looking at. Who wants to squint trying to read the cover copy?" Megan had agreed. There was a feeling of space in the bookstore, and the track lighting cast the soft light of a spring morning rather than the harsh light of a supermarket. The tall wooden shelves that ran from wall to wall and from the back of the store to within a dozen steps of the front gleamed in the soft light. Tall boards in the shape of grandfather clocks printed with subject headings hung on the end of each row, and underneath each board was a footstool with three broad steps. "For the short people who can't see the titles on the top shelves," Agnes once told Megan.

It made sense that Agnes would be sensitive to the needs of the longitudinally challenged. Agnes herself was a short person, a little gnome of a woman with silky brown hair twisted into a knot at the back of her head, who always reminded Megan of her great-grandmother Christy. Except Great-Grandmother Christy wore dresses hemmed just above the ankles instead of slacks and had been married five times. And she was dead. Died at eighty-seven after divorcing her fifth husband. The cause of death was supposedly a heart attack — brought on, Megan was sure, by the shock of finding herself single with no ambulatory prospects in sight.

Agnes, on the other hand, was a spinster. Megan didn't know the reason or reasons that Agnes never married. Agnes always joked that all the good men were married unless she robbed the cradle, and that wasn't seemly at her age. Megan suspected there was more to Agnes's lack of marital status than missing out on the good men, but she never asked. Curious as she was, Megan recognized an out-of-bounds sign when she saw it — usually. Still, spinster or not, Agnes had the same color of faded blue eyes under hooded lids with the same sharp expression of intelligence that Great-Grandmother Christy possessed. Megan's mother always said no one could fool Great-Grandmother Christy for more than a minute, and the same was true for Agnes.

"Megan, Professor, get a cup of coffee if you want one and come meet our visitors."

Sitting in one of the upholstered easy chairs that flanked a couch, Agnes waved them toward the sitting area. "Here are our missing members," she said, leaning toward two women who sat on the couch.

Ryan stopped and grabbed Megan's arm. "Those two women took our spot," he whispered with indignation.

"Just because the rest of the members are nice enough to always save the couch for us doesn't mean we have a deed on it, Ryan. Besides, it's your fault we're late."

"How is it my fault?" demanded Ryan.

Megan ignored him. Sometimes that was the best course of action. "We're sorry we're late, Agnes, but the truck is acting up, keeps dying on me, so we finally had to take Ryan's truck instead, and you know how he drives. A lame turtle is faster," said Megan.

"Just because I don't drive like a bat out of hell —" began Ryan.

"Children, children, are we having a

25

spat?" asked Randel Anderson, teacher of English at Amarillo College, a local two-year institution. Randel referred to himself as "Professor Randel Anderson," but Megan suspected the PhD was either self-administered or awarded by some online university.

"As the Bard says in *Taming of the Shrew,* act 1, scene 1: 'Why will you mew her up, Signior Ryan, for this fiend of hell, And make her bear the penance of her tongue?' "

"My God! The idiot thinks he's a scholar," muttered Ryan.

"Randel! That's a sexist remark, and you promised me that you had changed!" exclaimed Candi Hobbs, who was Randel's significant other, which, in Megan's opinion, demonstrated the young graduate student's severely challenged judgment in men.

"Randel, that was rude, and I won't tolerate rudeness in my bookstore," said Agnes in a commanding voice that any Marine drill instructor would envy.

"Since when is quoting Shakespeare sexist or rude?" demanded Randel, rubbing his goatee with two fingers.

Since Candi had taken Randel in hand, the beard looked less like a goat's chin whiskers, but Megan still suspected he grew it to disguise a weak chin. However, Randel's personal mannerisms, rudeness, sexism, or Shakespeare was not the point of the evening, as she listened to the rising voices in defense of her feminism. Like she needed defending against Randel Anderson. She'd handled worse pests than Randel in kindergarten.

"Randel! Anytime you feel like you're man enough to 'mew' me up, give it a try. Otherwise, put a cork in it and let Agnes introduce our guests."

"Just one darn minute."

Megan looked at him. At five feet, two inches, with curly red hair, whisky-colored eyes, and freckles sprinkled across her nose, she was universally described as cute. She knew it and hated it. Babies and small children are cute. Puppies and kittens, baby bunnies, and fuzzy baby Easter chicks are cute. A twenty-seven-year-old woman with a doctorate in archaeology and anthropology with a speciality in paleopathology or bioarchaeology, whichever term one prefers, is not cute, damn it! In self-defense she had developed a hot-eyed glare that promised a berserker's violence if she was crossed. "The Look," as Ryan called it, had never failed to quell anyone she focused it on.

It didn't fail this time, either.

Randel abruptly closed his mouth and sat down.

Megan turned to the two women on the couch. She wasn't sure she appreciated the amused smile the older woman wore. It made her feel as though she was playing a role in a farce. The younger woman looked unsure, as though she had wandered into a family argument.

Megan walked over to the couch and held out her hand. "Hello, welcome to the Murder by the Yard Reading Circle. I'm Dr. Megan Clark and I autopsy mummies."

"You must not find much work around here," said the older woman, her amused smile growing wider. "I'm Pearl Smith, aka Madam Jezebel, and I read fortunes. I would love to read yours, tarot cards or palms, it doesn't matter to me." She spread her arms palm up to include the rest of the group. "How about a free reading for each of you at my establishment. I'll even wear my turban and purple velvet gypsy clothes and strings of gaudy beads around my neck just so you'll feel like you're listening to a real reading instead of a freebie."

"You ought to sign up for a reading, Megan. Maybe she can predict when you'll find the next dead body," said Randel. He turned in his chair to face the fortune teller.

"Our Dr. Megan finds dead bodies. It's a kind of hobby of hers. Drives the police nuts and leaves them in a quandary as to whether they should arrest her or not. You know that old rule of thumb: the person who discovers the murder victim is likely to be the murderer."

"That's not true!" said Megan. "At least, not all the time. Stranger-on-stranger murders are becoming more common: drive-by shootings, serial killers, psychopaths going postal in the local McDonald's, etc. And I don't intentionally look for bodies; I just accidentally happen to be in the wrong place at the wrong time. I'm walking along and I stumble over a dead body. It could happen to anybody and probably has, we just haven't heard about it."

"Nobody heard of Typhoid Mary either until the bodies starting piling up wherever she went," said Randel.

"That's a terrible analogy, Randel," said Agnes. "And unkind. You're insinuating that Megan is a carrier of murder."

That was such a chilling thought that Megan felt goose bumps rising on her arms and torso. She struggled to think of some pithy comment to end the speculation that she was a freak of nature, an aberration straight out of Stephen King.

Randel tilted his head and studied Megan. "You're right, Agnes. My analogy is incorrect. Megan is more like a human cadaver dog."

There were several outraged gasps, then Ryan stepped in front of Megan. "That's enough, Randel. Any more comments like that and I'll pin you to the wall like a butterfly under glass. How's that for an analogy?"

"Stop it!" shouted Megan. "This is a stupid argument! My finding bodies is just a horrible coincidence!"

"From what I've read in the newspaper, you seem to experience a lot of coincidences," said Pearl.

"No one would pay much attention, including the newspaper, Megan, if you didn't insist on tracking down the murderer. And all of you help her," said Ryan, throwing out his arms to encompass the reading circle. "Once all of you are involved, and Megan actually reveals the killer's identity, then you make good press. Megan 'Sherlock Holmes' Clark and her Seven Little Watsons! My God, it's a PR agent's dream! And it's dangerous."

"There are eight of us, Ryan," said Lorene Getz, "not seven."

"I'm not counting myself. I'm not an

amateur sleuth. I just try to keep Megan from becoming a murderer's next victim. The rest of you can run around pretending to be Miss Maple or Hercules Parrot; I'll be Megan's bodyguard."

"That's Miss Marple and Hercule Poirot," said Rosemary, outraged at his heresy.

Ryan waved his hand. "Whoever. All I'm saying is that all of you, Megan most of all, confuse murder in a book with murder in real life. Sometimes I think I'm caught in a television reality show with Megan both participating and directing. Someone will get hurt during one of your amateur investigations, and I don't want it to be Megan."

"Megan has to investigate, Ryan," said Rosemary earnestly. "That silly Lieutenant Carr always halfway suspects her of being the murderer. If she didn't reveal the real killer, the lieutenant might be forced to consider her a real suspect."

"You can't be serious, Rosemary," said Agnes. "The lieutenant knows Megan would never murder anyone even if she sometimes looks guilty. But that's just the appearance, not the substance."

"Thanks for clearing that up, Agnes," said Megan. "I can't tell you how comforting it is to know that even my friends think I look guilty every time I find a body. I'm grateful that all of you are open-minded enough to believe in the presumption of innocence, particularly when it's my innocence you're presuming."

Herbert Jackson III, the attorney in, and sometimes for, the reading circle, cleared his throat. For Herb, clearing his throat was a verbal punctuation mark preceding a declarative statement usually at least a paragraph long. "We always know that Megan is innocent, Agnes, but Lieutenant Carr is in a different position. He can't refuse to arrest someone, or at least consider him or her a suspect, if the evidence seems to point his or her way. And the number of bodies that Megan has discovered exceeds the statistical probability."

"What's that supposed to mean, Herb?" demanded Lorene. "That Megan will be arrested if she finds another body?"

"No, not exactly. But it does mean that Megan is vulnerable to arrest because of the number of bodies she finds — has found. Fortunately, with the reading circle's help, Megan has managed to prove her innocence thus. Let's pray that her and our investigative skills continue, because eventually the preponderance of her involvement with murder victims may force Lieutenant Carr to seriously suspect her. But even that is not the greatest danger."

"What the devil is, then?" demanded Ryan.

"It is that someone may use her vulnerability to frame her."

Megan felt tiny shivers race up and down her spine. She felt something more; she felt afraid. "Please," she said, forcing the words past her paralyzed throat. "No more."

"I'm sorry if my presence and occupation evoked these comments, Megan," Pearl said. "And I agree with you. No more comments about Megan's past encounters with the dead, please. Personally, I like my murders kept safely between the covers of a book, and I'm sure all of you do, too."

Pearl smiled, clasping her hands together in her lap, satisfied that her request for a change in the direction of the conversation would be granted. And Megan knew it would. Pearl Smith had the kind of charm that always allowed her to gain her way. In her jeans and a white blouse, discreet gold earrings, a gold watch with a narrow band, and a touch of pink lipstick, she looked more like someone's hip grandmother than a fortune teller. The only exotic thing about her was her long, graying hair combed back from a widow's peak and held at the back of her neck with a tortoise shell hair clasp.

And her eyes: slightly oblique and of a pure gray with no tint of blue or hazel. Megan couldn't recall ever seeing that particular shade of gray before, like a misty rain on an autumn day. And like looking through a misty rain, Megan couldn't distinguish what emotional responses those eyes revealed, if any.

Megan hadn't a clue as to Pearl's age, either. She was one of those women who looked old when she was young, and young now that she was old. One thing Megan was certain of: Pearl Smith was not a dotty, superstitious old woman who deluded herself into believing she could read the future. Pearl Smith was a rational old woman who deluded *you* into believing she could read the future. Agnes cleared her throat.

"I'm sure we all agree with you about murder, Pearl. Shall we continue with our introductions?"

Randel's significant other stood up, her hands clasped together under her chin, blinking as she had since she traded in her thick glasses for contact lenses. "My name is Candi with an *i* and I'm a graduate student at West Texas A&M University. I'm writing my thesis on detective fiction, and I'm looking forward to Rosemary's discussion of Agatha Christie. I'm sure she will have some valuable insights." Candi drew a deep breath and gushed, "I'm just so excited to meet a real fortune teller, Madam Jezebel —"

"Call me Pearl, Candi. I'm wearing my street clothes tonight."

Candi blinked, looking confused for a moment. Megan often wondered if the girl composed her conversation mentally, then memorized it before she spoke. At any rate, if you interrupted her midspeech, she acted as if she had lost her place. It was best to let Candi say what she had to say even if she took a long time. Otherwise, she would stumble and stutter until she was back on track. "Uh, well, Pearl, thank you. I just wanted to say that I will call for an appointment. I've always wanted my fortune told. Not that I believe in it, but it will be fun." Megan noticed Randel looking at her like she had lost her mind.

"I'll leave my cards on the refreshment table," Pearl said, smiling at Candi. Megan couldn't decide if the fortune teller's smile was sincere or facetious.

Another member stood up. "I'm Herbert Jackson the Third, but my friends call me Herb."

Megan smiled. Actually, the reading circle

referred to him among themselves as Call Me Herb, but no one would call him that to his face. Everyone liked Call Me Herb, but his stuffy ways amused his friends.

"I'm an attorney as you probably guessed by my attire," continued Herb. "Three-piece suits are required apparel for corporate attorneys."

Ryan leaned over and whispered in Megan's ear, "Like everything he wears isn't in three pieces."

Megan elbowed him in his ribs. "Hush, I want to listen."

". . . have done some criminal work," continued Herb, glancing at Megan. "Even though I am an attorney I like to keep an open mind. I shall book a reading just to welcome you if nothing else. Who knows? Perhaps I'll learn something exciting about myself and my future." The members of the reading circle had identical doubtful expressions on their faces. Call Me Herb was a solid, trustworthy man with a kind heart, but no one would describe him as exciting.

Herb pulled a portfolio out of his briefcase and opened it. "I'm writing a legal thriller and always bring copies of the latest chapter to hand out to the reading circle for their enjoyment. I happen to have some extra, so allow me to give one to each of you."

This time the members' faces wore identical expressions of polite interest. Herb's legal thriller was referred to out of the lawyer's presence as "Herb's Sleeping Aid," since no one could read more than one page without going to sleep. Agnes held the record at two pages before falling asleep in her recliner.

Pearl took the manuscript pages. "Thank you, Herb. I appreciate your thoughtfulness."

"I'll bring copies of the chapters you've missed to my reading," said Herb, sitting down and straightening his vest.

The younger woman on the couch nodded her thanks with a smile, revealing the whitest, most even teeth Megan had seen outside of a toothpaste ad. Her daddy must have spent big bucks on her orthodontia and on her complexion. No one was born with teeth and skin like hers. It was unnatural. Megan decided her hair also owed a little something to artificial enhancement. Not that she wasn't probably a natural blonde, given her pale skin, but not such a perfect platinum blonde. Despite her perfect teeth, skin, and hair, the woman wasn't beautiful. Her face was a little too round and her chin a little too insignificant.

The blonde tucked Herb's chapter into a

red purse of some unidentifiable lizard skin, the size and shape of a tote bag that was big enough to pack a change of clothes, all the makeup she owned, wallet, checkbook, cell phone, umbrella, calculator, and an unabridged dictionary. It was the most ostentatious, conspicuous, *roomy* purse Megan had ever seen. She wondered where she could get one.

The blonde shyly looked around the circle. "I already know most of you. Rosemary, Lorene, and Agnes, of course, I've met at the bookstore at various times. And I've read everything published about you, Dr. Clark. I've even read some of your professional papers published in archaeological journals, the ones I could find in the library. I didn't understand all that you wrote — I don't have the background — but I could follow a lot of it because your writing is so clear. You don't use a lot of long words when short ones will do. I wish you wrote for some of the popular magazines that are intended for the public, like *National Geographic* or *Archaeology Today.* You would be so popular." She stopped and ducked her head, blushing and smiling shyly. "I'm sorry if I sound like some brainless groupie, but I admire you more than any woman I know, and I think calling you a cadaver dog and saying finding dead bodies is a hobby of yours is just plain jealousy!"

Megan always had difficulty accepting compliments, mainly because her mother's were sometimes double-edged, but this young woman's were so extravagant that Megan couldn't believe she was serious. Apparently Randel thought so because he looked like all the blood in his body had pooled in his face — which might be a good thing, because some of it might reach his brain. She had always wondered whether oxygen deprivation explained some of Randel's totally dumb remarks.

The silence finally aroused Megan from her verbal paralysis, and she realized everyone was waiting for her response. She cleared her throat, then grimaced. That was Herb's mannerism. "Well," she exclaimed, and immediately thought how stupid she sounded. A woman with three degrees ought to know how to graciously accept a compliment. "Well," she repeated, then gritted her teeth. She could add stuttering to her social ineptness. "Does anyone know who this person is that our guest is describing, because it's nobody I recognize. If you're talking about me," she said to the blonde, "then I'll have to have my Indiana Jones fedora reblocked, because I can feel my head swelling as we speak — or as I listen, since that's the case. Where were you when I was in first grade, and my teacher said I suffered from a lack of self-esteem?"

"I seem to remember her saying you suffered from too much self-esteem, not a lack of it," Ryan said to Megan in a nasal whisper.

"You're jealous," Megan whispered back while smiling at the blonde. "Thank you, ma'am, but you're exaggerating a little. I'm not that wonderful, just ask Lieutenant Carr. He has a whole list of my faults and will be glad to share it with you."

The blonde flushed and her smile slipped a little. "You don't have to call me ma'am. I'm not *that* much older than you. I'm Maria Constantine, and I do volunteer work at Northwest Texas Hospital. And I'm not exaggerating! You're everything I thought you would be. It's just wonderful to finally meet you."

Megan wondered if she should pat Maria's head or sign an autograph. She'd never had a groupie before.

"You all know her husband, Damian, or at least, you've seen him here on Sixth Street. He's one of our bicycling patrolmen, the very tall, dark, and handsome one," said Agnes, blushing.

Megan nodded. She had seen the police officer Agnes was referring to but had never spoken to him. He was quite a hunk in his shorts and uniform shirt. But he was just a cop, and she couldn't see Maria married to him. Maria Constantine looked too high maintenance to live on a cop's salary. Megan put the mismatch out of her mind for the present time. Ryan was always telling her that she was too cynical. Perhaps it was true love between the officer on a bike and Maria; or perhaps the cop had money and was a cop because he wanted to be. Either way, it was none of her business. Besides, she shouldn't be criticizing her only groupie.

The other members stood and introduced themselves to Maria and Pearl: Randel Anderson, English professor at Amarillo College; Ray Roberts, retired lieutenant of the Amarillo Police Department; and Ryan, history professor and museum curator. Megan noticed that none of the three asked for an appointment with Pearl.

Megan nudged Ryan. "Let's sit down. Rosemary is ready to start the discussion."

"I don't want to sit in a folding chair. It'll give me a stiff back and a numb butt, just like those chairs at faculty meetings."

Megan gave him a push toward two empty

chairs. "You're just afraid you won't be able to sleep through the discussion without sliding out of the chair."

2

A man can shine in the second rank, who would be totally eclipsed in the first.
> Monsieur Lecoq to Fanferlot in
> Émile Gaboriau's *File No. 113,* 1867;
> first English translation, 1875

A head that felt as big as a bowling ball; a hand puffed up to the size of a Little Leaguer's catcher's mitt; eustachian tubes so swollen that my ears popped every time I swallowed, reducing voices to sounds that seemed to issue from a galaxy far, far away; a butt rapidly going numb from sitting in a metal folding chair next to Megan; and I was as miserable physically as I could ever remember being. Not including the time I broke my wrist rock climbing with Megan; or the time I broke my nose water skiing with Megan; or the time I had ten stitches in my head after going canoeing with Megan. Other than fall pollen, do you see the common denominator here? If you guessed Megan Clark, you win the gold ring. I could smoke two packs of cigarettes a day for the next thirty years and not hazard my health like spending thirty days in her company. Staying away from her is not an option, though. Sometime in the past year and a half, since she returned to Amarillo with the ink barely dry on her PhD, I fell in love with her. So here I sit on a butt I can't feel anymore, in the company of a *faux* Gypsy, a *faux* blonde with a Farrah Fawcett hairdo, and a *faux* professor quoting Shakespeare, just so I can moon over Megan Clark like an aging Lothario down on his luck.

My name is Ryan Stevens, and I am Megan Clark's Dr. Watson.

I am also curator of history at the Panhandle-Plains Historical Museum on the campus of West Texas A&M University in Canyon, Texas, some twelve-plus miles from Time and Again Bookstore on Sixth Street in Amarillo. I say "plus" because I've never bothered to check the mileage, but the two cities are close in miles. In another sense traveling from one to the other is like stepping from Wal-Mart into Middle Earth, and you can't measure that trip in miles but in magic.

In Canyon, I am a museum curator, a professor of American history, a *respected,* widowed, aging academic with a sense of humor and passable looks. I teach two courses at West Texas A&M University: *Manifest Destiny and Westward Expansion in the Nineteenth Century,* and *Frontier Life in the American West.* I also teach a seminar on Monday nights, *Custer and the Battle of the Little Bighorn.* My students grew up with slasher movies, so the seminar is very popular. Unfortunately, I always get more questions about what kind of mutilation the Indian coalition inflicted on the unfortunate Seventh Cavalry than I do on Custer's military tactics.

In Amarillo I live in a refurbished Craftsman cottage in an older residential neighborhood and used to lead a lonely, quiet life writing articles for scholarly journals and indulging in my secret passion: reading and collecting Westerns, what my father's generation called shoot-'em-ups. Why is this a secret passion? Because if the Western History Society ever discovered that I not only read Westerns, but *enjoyed* reading them, I would be drummed out of that organization and every other professional organization of which I am a member. The revisionist historians in the society believe Westerns contribute to a mythology that emphasizes racism, sexism, bias, inaccuracy, and numerous other unattractive social traits that I can't remember at the moment. In other words, trash literature no self-respecting historian would read. On a good day the revisionists would make exceptions for the likes of Mari Sandoz and Willa Cather, and on a very good day they might grudgingly accept that books by Larry McMurtry, Elmer Kelton, Richard S. Wheeler, and Loren D. Estleman have a modicum of merit. I didn't know that Estleman also wrote mysteries until Megan told me. You notice that I used the past tense in describing my quiet life in Amarillo? I used to live instead of I live? That's because I live next door to Megan Clark's mother. Once Megan finished her three degrees in archaeology and anthropology, she came home to live with her mother — broke, unemployed, and with a heavy debt of student loans. My life has not been quiet since. I haven't been lonely either.

So what does all of the above have to do with my being Watson to Megan's Sherlock Holmes? Besides fainting at the sight of blood and corpses still in the "seeping" stage, I'm unsuited from an academic standpoint. History is loosely defined as one of the liberal arts, meaning it is not a discipline that relies on physical evidence such as pottery shards, grave goods, or bones. To the historian the word is God. I study words in treaties, government reports, military reports, private letters, journals, memoirs, and eyewitness accounts of events. Oh, I visit battle sites for a view of the topography to better understand the order of battle as described in military reports, but I don't grub in the dirt hunting shell casings to prove whether the military reports are true. Megan also studies the words of history, but with a skeptical, bordering on cynical, eye. Megan wants to see the evidence supporting the written or spoken word. "Where's the beef?" is her personal motto. She studies the artifacts of history, like the placement of shell casings to determine what kind of weapons were used at the Battle of the Little Bighorn and their pattern of fire. The Seventh Cavalry was not only outnumbered, but more importantly, outgunned.

I observe history through the eyes of generals and kings and ministers; Megan digs up the overlay of time and touches the stuff of history in search of the everyday life of the common man. She studies old fiber to see what people wore; old pollen to see what plants grew; old seeds to see what people ate; burial goods to determine what kind of weapons, art, and religious beliefs a particular culture had. She studies pottery shards to determine the trading partners between cultures. She studies trash dumps to determine how people actually lived as opposed to how a society *said* it lived. That's like going through a neighbor's garbage and counting discarded whisky bottles to prove how much he drank as opposed to how much he *said* he drank.

But most of all, Megan studies old mummies and old bones to learn what diseases a culture suffered, and to determine cause of death. Split human femurs indicate cannibalism; scrape marks on bones indicate an individual was skinned either dead or alive; bones also reveal starvation or periods of malnourishment, whether a victim was tortured or mutilated, and his degree of tooth decay. Megan contends that an abscessed tooth is responsible for bad political and military decisions as often as poor judgment. That contention has given me a whole new perspective on history.

To summarize, Megan deals with archaeological artifacts, concrete specifics in other words, to determine actual human behavior. She connects a suspected murderer's personal possessions to his behavior and theorizes how those possessions and that behavior impact his innocence or guilt. She can analyze a crime scene, discover the anomalies, and reconstruct the event. Then she studies the victim's possessions and behavior to determine how that victim attracted the attention of the murderer. Is it sex, money, jealousy, blackmail, obsession, what? Megan is suited to this kind of investigation. I'm not. As I already mentioned, I faint at the sight of blood and guts. Hard to examine a crime scene or corpse while lying in the gutter in a dead faint. I'm also a very law-abiding person. Megan views certain legal statutes as unnecessary impediments to her investigations — the law against breaking and entering, for example.

I have another motive for accepting my role as Watson. I have always secretly dreamed of writing a book. So I write our "stories" based on the records and observations I make during Megan's investigations and her brief jottings in a pocket-sized spiral notebook, her "field notes" if you will. One day I may interest a publisher in my "fiction," and become a well-known mystery writer. I'll keep secret from my future editor that I have read only two mysteries in my life, three if you include Poe's short story,

"The Murders in the Rue Morgue." The other two are Sherlock Holmes and *"A" Is for Alibi* by Sue Grafton, the latter because Kinsey Millhone reminds me of Megan Clark. Kinsey also has little patience with unnecessary impediments, and her best friend is her elderly landlord. Not that I'm comparing myself to Kinsey's landlord. He's ninety-something and I'm only forty-five, nineteen years older than Megan, and still in good shape. I'm not Charles Atlas, but I have my own teeth and hair and no belly hanging over my belt. My wife and I married right out of high school and immediately had two daughters and a set of twins, so my children are grown and following their own path, and Megan wouldn't be faced with raising stepchildren. There is one major impediment. My older daughter, Evin, is Megan's best friend and is liable to think I'm robbing the cradle. From my viewpoint I'm robbing a preschool. Either way I sometimes feel I'm committing incest since Megan spent a good deal of her childhood at our house. Her father died when Megan was five, and her mother is more devoted to causes than she is to Megan. You know the kind of thing: save the whales, save the spotted owl, stop the nuclear waste dump. Megan's mother didn't neglect her exactly, just sometimes forgot for short periods that she had a daughter.

I don't approve or encourage Megan's forays into amateur sleuthing by the way, or her recruiting the reading circle to help her. In fact, I try to prevent it, but bless their eccentric hearts, the members love it. Murder is best left to the police, but since Megan has solved every murder case she has been involved in, while the police fumble around like the Keystone Kops, she ignores my advice. Why stop pitching when your win-loss record is 4 and 0? Megan reminds me of a Jack Russell terrier Evin owned when she was a child: feisty, prickly, small, bull-headed, and with oversized brains. I never had any luck training that dog to come when it was called or to stay out of waste-baskets. I have the same luck with Megan.

I have one consolation, though. It is statistically impossible for the same white, middle-class woman to stumble over any more dead bodies in her lifetime.

My reflections on Megan and her propensity to find dead bodies almost put me to sleep despite my stuffy head and numb butt, when Megan elbowed me in the ribs.

"Wake up, Ryan. Rosemary is starting the discussion on *The Murder of Roger Ackroyd*," she whispered.

I jerked and nearly slid off the slick metal chair. "I wasn't asleep. I was just resting my eyes. They're swollen and sensitive in case you haven't noticed."

She sighed. "You didn't read the book, did you?"

"I'm still working on that book by that Jance woman, *Rattlesnake Junction.* I wanted to finish it first. Can't stop reading a mystery until you know the butler did it." Actually, I was reading my way through my brand new anniversary editions of Louis L'Amour, but I had read the cover copy of Jance's book so I wasn't lying. Just stretching the truth a little.

She sighed again. "That's *Rattlesnake Crossing,* Ryan, and there's no butler in it."

"Just making a joke."

"That's an improvement from feeling sorry for yourself."

I know she meant to sound sarcastic, but I heard an almost infinitesimal break in her voice. I tried looking into her eyes, but she avoided my glance. She only does that when she's trying to avoid telling me the truth — or when her feelings are hurt. I didn't think she was lying.

I lifted her chin until she was looking at me. "I'm sorry I've been such a bad-tempered bear tonight. You haven't done anything to deserve it."

Her smile was a little wobbly. "For a change. You're usually snappish only when I'm investigating a murder."

I smiled back in agreement. "There's not a dead body in sight, and I'm a stinker."

Her smile was stronger. "A stinker. Is that the best you can do?"

I rested my arm on the back of her chair. "Without using profanity, yes. This is Texas, ma'am, and a real man doesn't use profanity in the presence of a lady."

She started to say something, then smiled instead and turned back to listen to Rosemary. I looked at Rosemary, too, but I wasn't listening, I was reflecting. Megan hardly ever took offense at anything I said, but gave as good as she got. What was different this time? Had our relationship shifted in some way and I hadn't noticed? If she was suddenly so thin-skinned toward me, did that mean she was shedding her defensive armor? But that would mean she was opening herself up — and that would mean — could mean — might mean that her feelings were changing from those of a friend, a pal, a boon companion, to those a woman feels when she wants to get closer to a man. I didn't know whether to be pleased or scared.

3

The world is full of clues to everything, and
if a man's mind is sharp-set on any quest,
he happens to notice and take advantage
of what otherwise he would miss.
        Edward Leithen in John Buchan's
                The Power-House, 1916

Megan Clark sipped the coffee Ryan had
brought her, Irish cream for this meeting,
and tried to listen to Rosemary Pittman,
Murder by the Yard's expert on Agatha
Christie, leading the discussion of Dame
Agatha's most unusual mystery, *The Murder
of Roger Ackroyd.* She took another sip of
her coffee and realized she hadn't heard a
word Rosemary said, furthermore she
wouldn't hear a word until she dissected
her own behavior this afternoon. Why had
Ryan hurt her feelings this evening when
she was used to tuning him out whenever
his allergies or her murder investigations

turned him snappish? Why was tonight so different? Why was she so sensitive to his words, his movements, even his smell, for God's sake? He was just a friend. She felt him staring at her profile and kept her eyes on Rosemary. How long had she been able to sense when he was looking at her? She sipped her coffee and thought. A long time, almost since the first day she saw him in his front yard after she returned to Amarillo from college, the first day they had met when she was a woman and not a child with skinned knees. That was the moment, she was sure of it, when she saw him as Ryan, the man, and not her best friend's father. And tonight she had felt exposed to him, like she had stripped off her skin so he could see what was in her heart. That was scary. She had to get hold of her emotions. She didn't intend to let him have first look at whatever was in her heart until she looked first.

She set her coffee cup on the floor beside her chair and tried again to focus on listening to Rosemary and not think about Ryan. She liked Rosemary and her best friend, Lorene Getz. She always felt warm and fuzzy while she basked in their identical unquestioning approval. "The twins" is how Megan thought of them from the very first meeting of Murder by the Yard. Both were of an age, mid-to-late seventies, she guessed. Both had white hair the consistency of cotton candy that shimmered under the bookstore's soft lighting, but Rosemary's hair was professionally done each week, while Lorene, blessed with considerably less in the income department, did her own hair. There was also a discrepancy between the twins in the matter of dress, with Rosemary wearing silk and Lorene rayon. But such differences were superficial, altering not at all the essential "sameness" of the twins. What really set them apart in Megan's estimation was their respective fierce loyalties to the first grandes dames of mystery: Rosemary advocated Agatha Christie as the greatest practitioner of the modern mystery, while Lorene vehemently defended Dorothy L. Sayers as the leading lady of detective fiction's golden age. Megan had once mentioned that R. Austin Freeman deserved a place in the firmament as another star of the period on a par with Christie and Sayers. The twins joined forces and dismissed Freeman as a lesser light, although Rosemary did admit that "he was terribly clever with his invention of Dr. John Evelyn Thorndyke, but all that technical jargon can get tiresome after a while, don't you think, dear?" No one could skewer an opponent so cleanly and skillfully as the twins. Ryan once said that little old ladies were the most dangerous and deadly humans on the planet. Megan didn't go that far, but she did have a healthy regard for the twins' offensive capability. She sat back to listen.

"*The Murder of Roger Ackroyd* is Christie's greatest achievement and is the touchstone of her reputation as the premier mystery writer of the twentieth century," said Rosemary. "The twenty-first century is still too young to determine if another writer will challenge her for the title. Personally, I don't think so." She looked toward Lorene Getz as though she expected her friend to momentarily explode. If eyes could be said to actually sparkle, Rosemary's did.

As Megan expected, Lorene exploded, but in a ladylike manner. The twins' generation didn't scream profanities and gesture with their middle digit at opponents. "Now, Rosemary, you're giving Dear Agatha too much credit and giving Miss Sayers too little. You must admit that Miss Sayers's writing is richer and more stylish than Dear Agatha's, although her simpler style is also effective. But Miss Sayers's mysteries are considered as literary novels by many critics."

Megan couldn't believe it, but Rosemary literally rolled up the sleeves of her sweater. Surely this difference of opinion wouldn't get out of control and sever the twins' relationship.

She stood up. "Now, ladies," she began.

"Dear Agatha's style is perfect for her puzzle mysteries, transparent but misleading. She's not too wordy — like another author I could mention."

"Miss Sayers is not wordy! Her prose is rich and textured."

"But don't you see, Lorene, that Dame Agatha was an innovator. Her use of the Unreliable Narrator is brilliant! It had never been done before."

"I'm not saying Dame Agatha wasn't original in devising her plots, just that she is not superior to Miss Sayers. The sense of place in Miss Sayers's novels is wonderful! The fens in *The Nine Tailors,* for example. I feel the dampness every time I read it. And she didn't need to trick the reader with an Unreliable Narrator either, to solve the mystery. The solution depends on psychology as much as clues."

"I defy you to find a better sketch of insular English village life and the upper-middle class as Dear Agatha draws in her novels. Her . . ."

"Excuse me," said Maria Constantine in a loud voice. She shrank back on the couch as everyone looked at her but modestly held her ground, her face turning a bright pink in what Megan thought must be embarrassment at being the object of everyone's stares. "I don't know which writer is better because I just started reading mysteries, so I can't pick between them, but I would just like to hear about their books and how they can fool readers. I'd like to know exactly what an Unreliable Narrator is."

Rosemary and Lorene both wore identical expressions of surprise that a visitor would challenge them, but surprise turned to embarrassment when they realized the reading circle was staring at them as if they had been caught stealing from the collection plate in church.

Rosemary found her dignity first. "Maria, your question saved us both from making fools of ourselves."

"No, Rosemary," said Lorene, her face the color of an overly ripe cranberry. "We were already making fools of ourselves. Maria stopped us from making complete *asses* of ourselves."

There was a collective gasp from the other members, and Lorene clapped her hands over her mouth and turned even redder. She finally dropped her hands. "My heavens, I didn't mean to say that word."

Randel started clapping. "You're just telling it like it is, Lorene. As the Bard said in *Henry VI,* act 4, scene 8, 'A little fire is quickly trodden out, Which, being suffer'd, rivers cannot quench.' "

"Randel must have bought himself a copy of *Bartlett's Quotations,*" Ryan whispered in Megan's ear, then snickered.

Lorene looked puzzled as if she was unsure if she and Rosemary had been insulted or complimented, but she was saved from her dilemma by Ray Roberts. "Shakespeare sure knew how to use words, didn't he. We better all thank the young lady for putting out the fire before we all jumped in and burned. I was fixing to put in my two cents before she spoke up."

Maria smiled at the old cop, then bowed her head and spoke in a low voice everyone strained to hear. "I didn't mean to embarrass anyone. I just wanted to know what Rosemary meant."

Rosemary straightened her shoulders, a well-bred lady again. "An Unreliable Narrator means that Dr. Sheppard can't be trusted to tell the truth in his account of Roger Ackroyd's murder. No, that isn't right. He tells the truth, but does so in such a way that what seems a straightforward story turns out not to be. The reader trusts him, then at the end learns that he is the reverse of what a narrator ought to be."

"He's a liar is what Rosemary is trying to say," said Ray. "I used to listen to murderers do the same thing, telling a story to make themselves out to be innocent. Old Dame Agatha was clever, stood the whole mystery world on its head with Dr. Sheppard. To my mind she was just as clever in *The ABC Murders.* No one had ever thought up a plot like that one. Again the murderer tried to mislead the reader and Mr. Hercule Poirot. Well, he sure fooled me when I read the book, but he didn't fool Hercule Poirot, not for long anyway."

"I haven't read that book yet," said Maria. "What did the murderer do?"

"I don't want to spoil the book for you, so I'll just tell you a little bit. This killer, see, murdered a bunch of people in alphabetical order by their last names and left a railroad schedule called an ABC by each body. The first victim was a lady named Ascher who lived in Andover. The next victim is Elizabeth Barnard from Bexhill-on-Sea, and so forth. He slipped up on the third murder, though, or so it seemed, killing someone whose name started with an E instead of a

D. The murderer always sends a note to Poirot announcing where and when the next murder will occur."

"That's stupid," said Maria. "If you announce where you will kill someone, the police are sure to stake it out. I would never do that if I were the killer." She turned to look at Megan with an earnest expression. "Would you leave notes, Dr. Clark? Wouldn't notes lead the police to set up an ambush? How would you do it if you're the murderer?"

"Call me Megan. Dr. Clark sounds too formal for a discussion group. And no, I wouldn't leave notes — not for today's technological police forces. Imagine if I sent a note to Jerry Carr saying I was planning to kill somebody on Sixth Street. He'd call in the SWAT team, borrow deputies from the Potter County Sheriff's Department, the Randall County Sheriff's Department, Canyon city police — he would carpet Sixth Street with cops. Then he'd send out patrol cars, send up the helicopters, hot air balloons, high-wire walkers, Boy Scout troops, trained dog acts —"

Maria interrupted her. "You're teasing me" — she hesitated a moment and ducked her head — "Megan, aren't you?" She glanced up from beneath her eyelashes, a mannerism that reminded Megan of Scarlett O'Hara flirting with all her beaus at the Twelve Oaks barbecue.

Megan wondered if Maria was bisexual, or if her very first groupie was just dense between the ears. Either way Megan was beginning to feel uncomfortable with Maria. It was like the woman was playing a part improvised from several different scripts. Two minutes ago she asked pertinent questions about the role of an Unreliable Narrator, then she pretended not to know Megan was teasing her. Maybe she was taking some kind of medication that confused her thinking.

"I'm being flippant. I act that way a lot." *Always when someone irritates me but manners dictate that I can't slice and dice him or her with sarcasm,* thought Megan. "Some of my friends think it's a personality defect."

Maria raised her head. "Oh, no, it's not a defect; sometimes I just don't 'get' jokes. It's my fault, not yours."

Now Megan felt guilty for being flippant, impatient because Maria didn't have a sense of humor, and guilty again over the groupie's blaming herself for not understanding. *Damn, I don't need this. Life's too short to be somebody's heroine, especially someone with no sense of humor and the mental age of twelve.*

"I meant that I agree with you. It would be stupid to send notes. The cops have the numbers and the technology on their side," said Megan. She turned to Ryan for help in dislodging this leech, but his head was down and his eyes closed, sure signs that he was dozing his way through another meeting.

Fortunately, Ray stepped into the breach. "As it turned out those letters were a clue to Hercule Poirot, because — let me look up the exact quote." Ray paged through a copy of *The ABC Murders.* "Here it is. 'When do you notice a pin least? When it is in a pincushion!' Poirot deduced that the killer was emphasizing how many murders he had committed and intimated how many more there would be. The letters were a red herring to lead the police to think of the whole instead of the parts. The ABC schedule was also a red herring. Actually, these days I think those red herrings would still work, maybe even better than they did then, because a reader would think serial killer 'cause the public's got serial killers on the brain, and serial killers often communicate with the police or the newspaper. But their communication is the killer's Achilles' heel in some cases. Look at the Unabomber case.

He wrote an essay about his motives and philosophy, the newspaper published it, and his brother recognized the style and general philosophy and called the cops. Now me, if I was the killer, I'd make sure the red herrings misled the cops by subtly pointing them to another person, rather than announcing the location of my next kill."

Megan thought he looked pleased with himself. He should in her opinion. It was a masterful road map for an organized serial killer, provided the killer's ego didn't lead to carelessness. That was the catch, though. With each successive murder that failed to lead to his capture, a serial killer became more and more convinced that he *couldn't* be caught. He refined his technique and adhered more closely to his pattern because it had worked. That methodical adherence to pattern, provided the police recognized it, would lead to his capture. The serial killer who always picked up his victim prostitutes in a dented white van would eventually be caught because the other prostitutes observed that whoever rode away with a john in that white van never came back alive; in fact, never came back at all. A word to the police, and the killer in the dented white van was arrested. If the killer had driven a different vehicle each time, and hunted in a different location each time, and changed his appearance each time, he might have continued to elude capture indefinitely.

The hair on the nape of Megan's neck stiffened. She was glad Ray was one of the good guys, a retired police detective, because she would bet her pitiful bank account that Ray would make a very successful serial killer.

"Go on," urged Maria. "Why the railroad schedule and the alphabetical thing? How were they supposed to mislead the police?"

Rosemary interrupted. "He can't tell you anymore. You'll have to read the book."

"I will. I'll buy it tonight."

Megan punched Ryan in the side to wake him up. "That was the cleverest use of a red herring I ever saw," said Megan, unwillingly admiring Maria's guile, and wondering how much of her groupie's claims of having no sense of humor was a lie. "I couldn't have distracted the twins better myself. A fourth grader could figure out that an Unreliable Narrator means a liar."

"What does a fish have to do with anything?" Ryan asked, blinking the sleep from his eyes.

4

There are always so many stupid little details to take one's mind off a larger problem.

Nicolas Freeling's
A Dressing of Diamond, 1974

AMARILLO, TEXAS — SEVEN DAYS LATER

Another six days passed with hot, dry winds and a relentless sun unshaded by clouds, and Wild Horse Lake shrank close to its center. Then on the seventh day the lake gave up its secret. Two young boys skipping school to scavenge among the junk on its sloping banks were the first to see it. An old car, rusted, dented, with a broken window, and its parts held together with bailing wire, reared its truck end and rear wheels above the water's surface. Waterlogged and nearly completely rotted into tiny shreds to feed the murk clouding the water, was a mattress that had been wired to the roof of the old

68

car. The model year marked it as a Depression-era car, one of those barely functional, on the verge of breaking down, automobiles that carried a river of migrants along Route 66 to California in the thirties . . .

THE WILLOWS RETIREMENT AND CONVALESCENCE HOME

"I see you brought my newspaper with my breakfast, Manuela. Now if you'd help me find my glasses. Can't see my hand before my face without those glasses. That's what happens when you start getting old. The eyes are the first thing to go. And while you're looking, find my magnifying glass, too. Between the two of them I can see fine to read. Oh, you found them. You're a good woman, Manuela, looking after us old folks like you do with never a cross word. You can tell the supervisor I said so. And while you're at it, tell the cook to give me something besides oatmeal for breakfast. There's nothing wrong with my insides, and I've still got my teeth, or most of them anyway. Tell her to give me eggs and bacon tomorrow, and tell her I want that bacon crisp. And a slice or two of wheat bread toast would be nice, too."

Oatmeal! That cook thinks just because

I'm old I have to eat that mush. Well, I had to eat enough oatmeal during the Depression to dam up the Mississippi River if you packed it in sandbags. That and beans. But at least my two children and me were eating even if it was oatmeal and beans. And corn bread. Can't forget the corn bread. And once a week Mr. Albercrombie who owned the grocery down on the corner would let me and the rest of the folks around Sixth Street have the vegetables too wilted to sell to customers. We looked out for each other in those days. Not like today. Nobody would just watch out their windows while a woman was being killed. That happened in New York City once, but you wouldn't know about that, since it was before you were born. No, sir, we would run out of our houses with butcher knives or a rolling pin or a gun. Everybody had a gun those days, with nobody telling them guns caused crime. It's the person who's holding the gun that's responsible for crime. I don't know how those people can get things so backward.

I put my glasses on, picked up my magnifying glass, and opened the paper to the front page, and there it was. "So that old car turned up like a bad penny. It's the drought that's responsible. Wild Horse Lake must have dried up. Things always turn up when you don't want them found. Not that it matters much now. I've outlived everybody that knew about that old car except maybe for two, but I don't figure that they will hear about it. And if they do, there's no reason for them to say anything. None at all. Little as they were they might not remember. No, I figure if there's any danger it will come from another direction. That's the way it always is. Trouble comes from any direction but the one you're expecting it to. That's just life, and I'm old enough to know about unexpected trouble. No, I made a choice, and if I had it to do over again, I don't reckon I'd change anything, and if it comes down to it, the bad part was just an unexpected consequence. Nobody meant for it to happen, but thinking on it all these years I don't think there was any other way to stop her. No, I think if what happened hadn't of happened, I would have had to make a choice to do it deliberately, and I don't know if I could have. At least I don't feel guilty anymore. Not that I felt very guilty at the time. Do-gooders always rubbed me the wrong way. Still do for that matter. I was mad and I had to save that poor family. Then mostly I was worried about what would happen to my kids if I was caught. I don't have to worry about them anymore. They're grown and have kids and grandkids of their own. No, I'm not sorry it happened, just sorry at the way it happened. I'm not worried much for the time being. Likely the police won't pay much attention. Too much meanness going on these days for them to worry about how a car came to be at the bottom of Wild Horse Lake. If nothing else turns up, I don't have any cause to worry yet."

"Yes, Manuela, you come to take my tray? You can have it. I'm not eating that oatmeal, and you tell the cook I'm gonna fast until I get my bacon and eggs. It'll look real bad in the newspapers if I die of starvation. What's that? Who was I talking to? Myself, of course. I'm the best company I know. Most of the rest of the folks in here are too deaf or too feeble to carry on much of a conversation, and the ones who aren't always want to talk about the soap operas on TV and how filthy they are with everybody sleeping with everybody else. If they don't approve of that, then why do they watch them? They ought to read the newspaper instead. Filth and meanness is all they write about. What? Did I read about the car? Of course I did. It's all over the front page. What do I think happened? How would I know? I'm just an old woman who'll be one hundred next week. You be sure and tell the cook I want a chocolate cake for my birthday. Now, go away. I want to sit in this chair and look out the window at the pansies in the flower beds before the frost kills them and think about my life and the choices I've made. And, Manuela, don't forget to tell the cook about my cake."

TIME AND AGAIN BOOKSTORE, SIXTH STREET

Megan walked into the bookstore followed by Ryan to find most of the reading circle clustered around the card table that held the coffee and cookies. Ryan headed directly for the couch to claim his usual corner where he could prop his elbow on the arm, rest his chin on his hand with his notebook on his lap, and doze through the meeting. Megan headed for the refreshment table where Maria Constantine was scrubbing frantically at the front of her blouse with a paper napkin.

"I've ruined it," she cried. "I just bought it today at Dillard's, and now this coffee will leave a huge stain. You know how coffee stains. Damian will have a fit. He thinks I paid too much for it anyway."

"Soak it in a weak solution of bleach when you get home, Maria, then wash it in cold, soapy water, and it should be fine," said Agnes.

"She should try rinsing it out while it's still wet, Agnes," said Lorene. "That's what I do."

"Yes, I'll do that, but I'll skip the bleach. I'm afraid the red will fade. I'll slip back to the bathroom and do it now," she said, bending down to pick up her tote bag/purse. "Do you have a blouse I could borrow, Agnes? I can't wait until I get home. Damian works the day shift this week, so he'll be home before me, and he'll be all over me for buying the blouse in the first place, then being so clumsy and ruining it. Besides, I take so much sugar in my coffee that I feel sticky underneath where the blouse is wet."

Agnes put her arm around Maria and led her toward the door in the back wall of the bookstore that led to the public bathroom, the storage room, and Agnes's apartment. "I'll bring you a washcloth and towel and a blouse that I think will fit you. It's too big for me, and I've been thinking I should donate it to Goodwill or The Salvation Army. And tell that man of yours to get off his high horse. I imagine there have been times that he's spent too much on something he wants, too."

Maria stopped and looked back over her shoulder. "Megan, would you come with me, too?" Her blue eyes held a beseeching expression that Megan had no trouble ignoring.

"You'll be fine by yourself, Maria, or Agnes will stay if you want her to. I have to talk to Herb about something."

"Can't you wait to talk to Herb?" Maria asked, the beseeching expression shifting to that of a petulant child.

"No! It can't wait. Run along with Agnes before that coffee stains your blouse." Megan waited until Maria stomped through the door, then turned to Herb. "Having a groupie isn't all it's cracked up to be."

"I think rock stars hire bodyguards to keep their groupies away," said Herb with a sympathetic smile.

"How did it happen?" Megan asked Herb. Tonight he wore a brown pinstripe with matching vest. There was a wet spot on the front of the vest.

Call Me Herb looked worried. "She tripped over my briefcase that was sitting on the floor next to my feet. I feel responsible for her accident. I wonder if I shouldn't offer to pay for her blouse."

Megan poured a cup of coffee and watched Maria and Agnes disappear through the door. "I'm sure she would appreciate it, but I don't think it's necessary. It was an accident after all."

"But if I had left my briefcase by my chair it wouldn't have happened."

Megan wrinkled her brow as she thought about it. "I don't see how it happened anyway if your briefcase was sitting beside you. She must have been practically leaning on you when she tripped."

Call Me Herb flushed and Megan smiled. Herb was so proper and uptight that any mention of sex or any intimacy always made him blush. "I was standing here," he said pointing to the floor, "and she was standing just on the other side of the briefcase with that big purse of hers hanging on her arm, and we were talking about the railway guide and notes being red herrings to mislead the police and Poirot. I was blocking the plate of Lorene's chocolate macadamia nut cookies, and Maria wanted one, so she stepped in front of me to reach the cookies and caught her foot on the briefcase. She grabbed it for me and tipped her cup and spilled coffee on that beautiful red blouse. I caught her before she fell, but that purse of hers caught in my jacket and in trying free it, she tipped her cup, and I'm afraid my vest soaked up the rest of the coffee."

"I'm sure your cleaners will able to get the stain out," she said, thinking that Herb spent too much of his life sweating the small stuff. She wandered over to Candi, who was standing by herself. Usually Randel was standing by her with his arm resting on top her shoulders or around her waist, or they were holding hands. Megan supposed it was sweet that they were so affectionate, but they were both so awkward that they looked a little ridiculous. Still, they were good for one another. Candi had managed to improve both Randel's appearance and his social graces. He had trimmed his goatee and now wore socks with his Birkenstocks, so his hairy toes and yellow toenails were covered. He even showed signs of developing an adult sense of humor instead of spouting grade school potty jokes. Randel had encouraged Candi to trade in her ugly glasses for contacts, and she was styling her hair and even wearing makeup. She had lost weight, so she was no longer plump but nicely rounded. Megan thought that looking more attractive was important to Candi; it improved her self-esteem. She was still too obsessed with details, like knowing the copyright date of all of the numerous editions of Christie's novels, but she wasn't so intense about it.

"Where's Randel, Candi?" Megan asked.

"Over there with our Gypsy witch," she replied, pointing to the seating area where Randel was sitting on the arm of Pearl's easy chair with his arm resting on its back, and leaning so close to the fortune teller that Megan wondered how he kept from toppling into Pearl's lap.

"Last week he acted as if he didn't like fortune tellers," Megan said.

"I thought he didn't, and I was nervous about going for my reading and having to listen to him lecture me about how stupid it was, but he not only insisted I go, but he went with me, and the Gypsy witch told his fortune with tarot cards." She stopped and bit her lower lip. "And they sat at her little table and quoted Shakespeare to each other. I hate Shakespeare!" A tear rolled down her cheek. She swiped at it with her napkin.

Ray Roberts walked over and put his arm around her shoulders. "Not so loud, Candi, he'll hear you, and you don't want that. You don't need to be standing over here by yourself either. He's your man, you go get him."

Candi looked at him helplessly. "I don't know how."

Ray glanced at Megan, but she shrugged. "If it were Ryan, I would just go over and jerk him off the arm of that chair, but I'm not good at subtle."

Ray grasped Candi's shoulders and turned her around. "Go over there and put your arms around him, kiss his cheek, and tell him it's time to find his own chair. Rosemary looks like she's raring to go. Now, get over there, girl," he said, giving her a gentle shove. "And don't creep. Walk like you're in charge."

"Do you think it'll work?" asked Megan, watching Candi square her shoulders and start toward Randel and the Gypsy witch.

Ray shrugged his shoulders. "A bird in the hand is worth two in the bush. Randel sure has all his fingers around Candi, and Pearl's not only in the bush, she's old enough to be his mother. Candi ought to point out to him how ridiculous he looks flirting with an old woman."

"She doesn't look that old. She doesn't have many lines on her face, and her throat isn't wrinkled. The only thing old looking about her is the grey hair."

"It's dyed," said Ray. "I noticed last week. She must have been between dye jobs, 'cause I saw her roots. Now why would a woman dye her hair grey, do you suppose?"

Megan studied the fortune teller, a little miffed that she had missed that detail.

"That's a good question."

"I think it is, but short of asking her, I don't know how we'd find out." He stretched his arms over his head, then lowered them and rubbed his back. "There's Rosemary and Lorene heading for their chairs, so we're fixin' to start the meeting. Those damn chairs are killing my back. I got some padded folding chairs my wife bought when she was alive and belonged to three different bridge clubs. I think I'll donate them to the bookstore so Agnes will get rid of those metal ones before I have to start walking hunched over like an old man." He strolled toward the reading area, and Megan followed.

They were a few steps behind Candi and watched as she walked around the easy chair and threw her arms around Randel's shoulders. She didn't kiss him, though, since he reacted like anyone would when grabbed from behind: he jerked forward in surprise, fell into Pearl's lap, and rolled off onto the floor. He hit the small coffee table in front of the couch and knocked off the bowl of dried rose leaves onto his head. He sat up, rose leaves caught in his hair, his goatee, and resting on his shoulders like floral epaulets. The look of utter shock on his face sent Ryan into a coughing fit that Megan knew he was using to cover up his laughter. The twins and Call Me Herb rushed over and fussed about while Candi helped Randel up and led him to a chair as far from Pearl's as possible in the small seating area.

"I didn't anticipate how Randel would react if Candi surprised him. Did you, Ray?"

Ray winked at her. "I didn't anticipate him covered in roses."

Megan grinned at him. "You're a dangerous man, Ray Roberts. I want to stay on your good side."

He looked suddenly grim. "Randel deserved it for acting like a first-class jerk. Candi's a nice girl, and I don't like to see nice girls treated like that."

Megan nodded to him as if she agreed that Randel needed a comeuppance, then sat on the couch next to Ryan, scooting as close as she could without sitting in his lap.

He wrapped his arm around her shoulders. "Are you suddenly putting the moves on me, or are you cold in that tee shirt?"

"I just needed a little reassurance. Everybody is acting so strange tonight except you. Can't you feel the tension in the room?"

"Have you suddenly turned psychic? Trying to steal the fortune teller's thunder? I don't sense any tension emanating from anyone but Candi. Randel had better watch himself or she'll punch him out in bed tonight. That girl has a real mad going. Not that I blame her."

"Ray set Randel up. He knew what would happen when Candi suddenly grabbed Randel from behind." Megan remembered the grim look on Ray's face. "He said Randel deserved it."

Ryan stretched his legs out and crossed his ankles. "You disagree? Is that what's bothering you?"

Megan mulled over her answer, suddenly realizing that what upset her wasn't that she disagreed that Randel deserved being embarrassed — she would have set him up herself if she had thought of it in time — but that Ray had acted out of character, or what she thought of as his character. Before tonight she would have bet that Ray Roberts would never deliberately embarrass anyone. She was wrong about Ray. She wondered who else she was wrong about.

Before she could answer, Maria scurried into the reading area, her purse dangling from one arm, and wearing a ladylike white blouse that stretched over her generous bosom in an unladylike manner. She walked toward the couch, but Megan waved her away. "There's not enough room for three, Maria."

Maria looked hurt, but obediently changed directions and sat down by Call Me Herb and hunched her shoulders in an attempt to make more room where she needed it. Megan thought it was impossible. There was more of Maria than there was of the blouse.

Agnes clapped her hands for attention. "Candi, if you have fussed over Randel sufficiently enough, it's time for Rosemary to lead our second discussion on Dame Agatha."

Megan scrambled off the couch. "Agnes, Rosemary, if I could say something first."

Agnes gave her a curious glance. "If Rosemary doesn't mind waiting, go ahead."

Megan didn't wait for Rosemary to agree. "I'm sure everyone has read this morning's paper, or at least saw the photo on the front page of the old Depression-era car in Wild Horse Lake. According to the paper, it was a 1927 Ford sedan that had been in the lake since 1938. At least, it had a 1938 Oklahoma licence plate, and since there was what remained of an old mattress tied on its roof, we can conclude that it belonged to a family of Okies on their way to California."

"How can we conclude that?" asked Lorene.

"Because that's what the poorest of the

migrant families did," answered Agnes before Megan could reply. "I was just a child in 1938, but I worked in this bookstore even so. My mother was a widow, so it was just the two of us, and the bookstore was the only thing standing between us and the breadline. During the slow times I would sit in a chair and look out that window and watch the parade of Okies driving their old cars that were held together with spit and bailing wire. They always had a water jug tied to the front bumper, because driving across the dry Southwest they would need water. And many, many of them had mattresses and whatever household goods there was room for tied to the roofs of their cars."

"I always felt so sorry for those people. We were poor, but we had a place to live and food to eat, even if my mother did serve beans for supper almost every day. Those women were so gaunt faced they looked years older than I'm sure they actually were. The poor children, many of whom were my age or not much older, were so malnourished that their eyes seemed too big for their thin, pinched little faces. They were pitiful, but so were their fathers. Most of them were farmers who had lost their land to the banks through foreclosure because they couldn't pay their mortgages. In those days farmers wore blue denim overalls, and that was what most of the men I saw wore: faded, ragged overalls and equally ragged shirts. I always noticed how ragged they were, because my mother never let me wear ragged clothes, not even underwear. I felt rich compared to them even though I knew we weren't."

There was no sound in the store. Even the usual street noises were absent. Megan felt the hairs on the back of her neck stiffen. It felt as if they were wrapped in a cocoon, insulated where everyone held their breaths for fear of breaking the silence. For a moment Megan felt that if she looked out the window the Sixth Street she knew would have disappeared, replaced by the Sixth Street of 1938.

Agnes resumed, her voice low and sad. "If that car has rested in Wild Horse Lake all these years, what happened to the family who owned it?"

Megan glanced at the others, but everyone still seemed caught up in Agnes's memory, unable to speak. Now was the perfect time to tell the reading circle of her idea. "I think we should try to find out. It will be such a challenge to our mystery-solving skills. We've never faced anything this difficult before. Think how exciting it will be trying to trace the owner of that car, and what an accomplishment it will be to succeed. None of us will be in danger like we have been in our other cases. That ought to make Ryan happy. He's always so sure that one of us will be murdered, mainly me, but he won't have to worry this time. Is everybody with me on this?"

"I don't believe I am, Megan," said Rosemary in a firm voice. "Whatever reason the car's owner had for abandoning his vehicle in Wild Horse Lake isn't important after all this time and isn't any of our business anyway. Besides, it would be such a time-intensive research job to find the answer, if it was possible at all. Lorene and I have made such progress on our book about the influence of Dame Agatha and Miss Sayers on modern women mystery writers that we don't want to interrupt our work. At our age we can't be sure how much time we have remaining, and personally I don't want to waste any of it on such an ephemeral case. Isn't that right, Lorene?"

Lorene looked undecided. "I don't know, Rosemary, it would be such an interesting puzzle, and I so love doing research."

"Lorene, if we continue putting off our work, we'll never finish this side of Gabriel blowing his horn. We interrupted our work to help Megan with the last four investigations, but this isn't the same thing at all. We wouldn't be trying to bring a murderer to justice, but just satisfying our own curiosity."

"I guess you're right, Rosemary," agreed Lorene with what Megan thought was reluctance.

"I hope you're not upset with us, Megan dear," said Rosemary with a nervous smile. "If circumstances were different we would help, but we want to finish our book, and we are enjoying working on it so much."

"I think I'll save my psychic energy for a murder," said Pearl, her grey eyes focused on Megan with an intensity that made her feel like squirming. "This sounds too much like Nancy Drew to me."

"I am *not* Nancy Drew! And I don't need any hocus-pocus screwing up my murder investigations."

"Whoa, girl," said Ray, putting his hands on his knees and leaning toward Megan. "Calm down a minute. I don't think Pearl meant she would be conjuring up any visions the next time we go hunting for a murderer. She just isn't interested in a wild-goose chase. And that's what you're talking about. After nearly seventy years, it'll be impossible to trace that car. No state I know of keeps archives of licence plates, so how do you intend to even start looking? Besides, like Rosemary said, nobody's life is at stake here. So, I'll pass on this one and wait for the next hand that's dealt."

Disappointed and a little hurt, Megan nodded at Ray. "I'll let you know when it's time to ante." She looked at Randel. "What about you and Candi? Are you interested in old cars?"

A much-subdued Randel with a large swelling over his right eyebrow nodded his head. "My great-grandfather owned a filling station here on Sixth Street during the Depression, so I guess you could say I have a connection to cars of that era. He was still alive when I was a little kid, and he used to tell me stories about the Depression and the Okies who drove through Amarillo on Route 66. The old man was a terrific story-teller. He said sometimes the Okies would roll down Sixth Street in caravans, like wagon trains on the Oregon Trail, and he knew that he was watching history made. You would have liked him, Ryan, because he was a history buff. He took pictures of every person, every building, every event he thought might turn out to be important to history. He left a trunk full of Kodaks when he died, the ones with the ragged edges and the ones with the narrow black braid-like design around the margins. I'll do what I can to help, Megan, in the memory of that old man. As the Bard says, 'One for all, or all for one we gage.' *The Rape of Lucrece, act 1.*"

"Do you think he took pictures of any of the Okies that stopped at his filling station?"

"Megan, I'm the one who hit his head on the coffee table and am having trouble following a conversation, not you. Didn't I just say that Grandpa Elmer took pictures of everything — vegetable, animal, and mineral — that he thought might one day be important historically? And that included the Okies."

"Tell me you have that trunk of pictures, Randel. Tell me it's sitting in the back of your closet. Please tell me that."

Randel touched the knot on his forehead and avoided her eyes. "I, uh, haven't looked at those pictures in years. I know I saw that trunk a couple of years ago, but I don't remember where. But I'll find it, don't worry. Just as soon as I'm feeling better. I should stay in bed a few days and let Candi take care of me before I start searching for that trunk. Head injuries are serious. I don't want to chance any permanent brain damage."

His voice took on that poor-little-me tone

he used when he wanted Candi to feel sorry for him, and Megan stared at the ceiling and counted to ten. Sometimes she thought Randel was born with permanent brain damage. Swallowing her disappointment, she waited for another volunteer, but Call Me Herb was busy studying his wing tips, and Agnes remained silent. She wondered if it was Shakespeare who said that beggars can't be choosers. "Welcome to the Mystery of 1938 Detective Club, Randel. Since nobody else is interested or is too busy to join, Ryan and I will have to skip the rest of the meeting, so we can work out a plan. By the way, an anonymous source at Special Crimes told me that one of the cops found a toy car under that Ford's backseat cushion, so there was once a child in that car, a little boy. It was probably the only toy he had, so why do you suppose he left it — or if he had a choice. Somebody has to learn what happened to that little boy and his family. For all we know they might be buried under a mesquite bush somewhere." She picked up her notebook. "Come on, Ryan. I want to go home."

"Don't you think you were a little hard on them?" asked Ryan as they cut across Agnes's parking lot. They had parked

Megan's black behemoth GMC pickup behind the bookstore because once again the parking lot was full of SUVs with out-of-state licence plates.

"What's wrong with them, Ryan? Suddenly no one is interested in mysteries — real ones, I mean. Usually Rosemary and Lorene and Ray would be all over this case. Even Call Me Herb would jump in with both wing-tipped feet. And Agnes abstained," said Megan, flicking on her flashlight. Either the city hadn't replaced the bulb in the street light in back of the store, or some vandal broke it again.

"What do you mean Agnes abstained? I never heard Agnes say anything other than describing her childhood memories."

"Exactly! She stood mute when it counted, so we're stuck with Randel and Candi, and Randel drives you crazy."

He grabbed the back of her tee shirt to slow her down. "Whoa, Sherlock! Watson never volunteered for this gig."

Megan tugged her shirt out of his hands, and started down the alley, shining the power flashlight toward the ground in front of them. "Don't tease me, Ryan. Between Maria hanging around me like a bad smell, and nobody wanting to investigate the old car, I'm not in the mood to be teased.

Besides, I thought you'd be glad to help me if there were no dead bodies involved." Suddenly she stopped and Ryan bumped into her.

"What the devil's wrong now, Megan?" he demanded, peering over her shoulder.

She swung her flashlight from side to side. "There's a broken whisky bottle with glass everywhere."

"So? I smelled whisky when we parked back here. Some drunk must have dropped his bottle. Megan, where are you going? Here's the truck."

Megan walked farther down the alley, stopped, and pointed her flashlight at a bundle of rags on the ground. "Stay back, Ryan. It's Old Ben lying here."

"Passed out, I suppose. Let's haul him into the bookstore and pour some of Agnes's coffee down him, sober him up enough that the homeless shelter down the street will let him stay for the night." Ryan walked up behind her and looked over her shoulder at Old Ben. "Looks like he scratched his forehead pretty badly. We probably should call the paramedics. What's that puddle he's lying in? Shine your flashlight at it, Megan, so I can get a better look."

"It's blood. I think he's bled out." She heard him stumble backward, mutter something that sounded like "statistically impossible," then the sound of his body meeting the asphalt. Megan sighed. "I'm sorry, Ryan, but I've found another body."

She flipped open her cell phone and pushed 9-1-1.

5

Either therefore we all of us deserve the vengeance of the law, or the law is not the proper instrument for correcting the misdeeds of mankind.

Mr. Raymond in William Godwin's
Caleb Williams, 1794

I came to with Megan's words echoing through my head: *"It's blood. I think he's bled out. It's blood. I think he's bled out."* I opened my eyes to find a masked man leaning over me.

"How you doing, buddy? You bounced your head on the asphalt when you fell. Got a heck of a knot on the back of your head. Can you see me all right? Don't see two of me, do you? Don't try to talk yet. Give yourself some time to get your wits back."

"How can I answer your questions if I can't talk?" I asked, struggling to sit up. The alley seemed to be swaying, so I took the paramedic's advice and lay back down.

"Follow my finger, buddy. I have to check to see if your eyes are tracking." A large hand in a surgical glove swam into my field of vision.

"What happened?" I asked, my eyes following his finger side to side, up and down.

"Don't tell him, Chuck," said another masked man. "He's that professor that faints at the sight of hemoglobin, so don't say 'blood' whatever you do."

I thought of the dark, liquid puddle with Old Ben's body lying in the middle of it and sank into the welcoming blackness again.

When I came to the second time I heard the two paramedics talking.

"What did the guys back at the firehouse say his record was?" asked one.

"Forty-five minutes, twenty seconds — longest continuous faint in Amarillo history without being in a coma," said the other.

"You owe me five bucks. I bet he'd beat his old record, and he has: forty-six minutes, twenty-seven seconds," said the first medic. "That's from the time the 911 call came in and adding his two faints together."

"You two are real comedians. Ever think about trying to get on *Saturday Night Live?*" I said, sitting up despite my dizziness.

"Thanks, Doc, you think we're that good?" asked the second medic, the one I dubbed "Dumber."

"Hey, Sergeant Schroder! The professor is awake. Where should we take him?" asked the first medic, whom I christened "Dumb."

A voice that sounded like it was filtered through gravel answered. "He the one I heard about?"

"He's the one," said Dumber.

"Add him to that bunch in the bookstore, and tell the cop keepin' them company that I'll be in there in a minute."

"Why don't I go with them and start the interviews, Schroder? That way we might get home in time to catch a couple hours' sleep before we have to go back to work again." This voice was a baritone with a Texas twang.

"You're always trying to get away from the victim, Jenner. You just stick to me like a cocklebur to a pair of ladies' nylons, and you'll learn something about murder."

"I don't want to learn anything about murder, Schroder! I already know everything a traffic cop needs to know, which is what I am, a traffic cop! You're the one that's got it in his head that I need to be in Special Crimes! I don't like Special Crimes! I don't like murder! You got that?"

Dumb shook his head. "It's the same every time we get called out: Schroder and Jenner go head to head 'cause Jenner is really a sergeant in the traffic division, and that's where he's happy. Sergeant Schroder is in Special Crimes. Been there forever, and every time the department tries to rotate him out, he goes to the chief and convinces him that Sergeant Ed Schroder is the best homicide detective since Mel Gibson and Danny Glover, and bang, the chief lets him stay."

"Mel Gibson and Danny Glover are actors," I pointed out to my two mentally challenged guardians.

"I know that! You think I'm dumb?"

I remained silent.

"Anyhow, I can't think of their characters' names in those movies. But to get back to my story, Sergeant Schroder goes back to Special Crimes and requests a temporary transfer for Jenner, and boom, there he is: back knee deep in bl—, in murder victims."

There was a sudden outburst of loud voices from farther down the alley. "What's that outcry of voices?" I asked Dumber.

"What's that, Doc?"

"You know, flock of sheep, gaggle of geese, outcry of voices."

"I get you, Doc. You mean who's yelling

over the victim. Outcry of voices, that's pretty good. I'll have to remember to tell that to the guys back at the firehouse. Anyhow, that's Schroder trying to throw some girl off the crime scene."

I groaned. Why did I have to ask the obvious? In Megan's opinion any dead body she stumbles over is her exclusive property. Megan doesn't *aid* in an investigation as much as she tries to *direct* it. I could hear her voice arguing with the hoarse-voiced sergeant.

"Sergeant Schroder, I have a PhD in physical anthropology and archaeology. My specialty is paleopathology, and I can do an autopsy as well as the next man, and I can do it tomorrow morning. Not that there's any doubt of the cause and means of death. Unless Old Ben managed to stab himself thirteen times in the back, then roll himself over and fold his hands over his chest like he's laid out in a casket, he was murdered by means of a knife."

"Lady, the Justice of the Peace here just pronounced him dead and ordered him sent to Dallas for an autopsy. That's his job. And the autopsy will be done by an MD in forensic pathology. That's his job. Then the Special Crimes evidence techs — that's them in the white moon suits — will comb the crime scene for what you wanna-be detectives in that book club call clues. That's their job. Then Sergeant Jenner and me — Sergeant Ed Schroder — will investigate this case. And that's our job. You ain't got a job except to escort your professor into the bookstore and stay there with some smelling salts handy in case somebody mentions the B-word where he can hear it."

"Where's Lieutenant Carr?" demanded Megan. "He'll tell you that I've solved the last four murders in Amarillo, including the one in Palo Duro Canyon last month."

"The lieutenant is out with a lady friend since it's his night off, and I didn't see any reason to call him out over what's likely to be a fight between two drunks over a bottle of booze. Soon as I see where we're at with this case, I'll call him. And I've heard how you interfered in the last four murder cases. I don't know why the lieutenant didn't lock you in a cell and throw away the key for interfering with a public official in the pursuance of his duty, except the lieutenant's got a soft heart. I ain't got a soft heart, and another thing: it's awful funny how you keep finding dead bodies. This is body number five, and a sharp cop might start wondering how come you're always in the right place at the right time."

"Actually, it's body number seven — plus two suicides and an assault with a deadly weapon," said Megan. I could hear the pride in her voice and groaned again.

There was a long silence, and I waited to hear the click of handcuffs around Megan's wrists. I heard Sergeant Jenner's voice instead. He sounded awed and nervous at the same time.

"Good golly, Miss Molly. No wonder the lieutenant took another woman to dinner. He might find himself body number eight if he hung around with you."

"It's all coincidence!" cried Megan. "And I don't appreciate you calling me a murderer!"

"Lady, I don't believe in coincidence. Jenner, get her OFF MY CRIME SCENE!" roared Schroder.

"Don't get your bowels in an uproar, Schroder. Come on, miss, before the sergeant starts blowing steam out of his nose like an overheated Brahma bull."

"I'm leaving, Sergeant Schroder, but let me give you my professional opinion first. Old Ben wasn't the victim of a drunken argument. This was deliberate murder. And you might give some thought to why there are exactly thirteen stab wounds, and what the symbols scratched on his forehead might

mean. And why the body was POSED."
Megan marched by me in high dudgeon.
"Come on, Ryan. You'll catch a cold sitting
on the ground in this weather."

Sergeant Jenner cleared out the people
whose cars had out-of-state licence plates,
taking names, addresses, phone numbers,
and alibis. I guess he thought it unlikely any
of them had anything to do with Old Ben's
murder. I didn't think so either. The murderer was local, had to be to know Old
Ben's habits. Logically, that meant somebody who lived on Sixth Street or the sur-
rounding San Jacinto area. None of the
members of the reading circle lived in San
Jacinto or on Sixth Street either except
Agnes, and she had lived in the apartment
at the back of the bookstore all her life. I
deduced the sergeant was keeping us because Megan found the body and the reading circle members were guilty by association — with Megan, not the body.

After Jenner cleared out the last out-of-
staters, a couple of California vegetarians
— that was their defense against suspicion
of murder, that they didn't eat meat — I
took their place on the couch and pulled
Megan down with me. I told her what I had
concluded about the murderer being local.

She frowned, her complexion still flushed

from her argument with Schroder. "I think so, too. The chance that a stranger — someone from out of state or across town — should happen to stumble across Old Ben in his favorite spot in his favorite alley is astronomical, statistically speaking."

"His favorite spot was by the Dempster Dumpster?"

"That big tree by Agnes's parking space provided shade in the summer. The Dumpster protected him from cold winds in the winter, plus Agnes fed him whenever he knocked on her back door. She let him sleep in her storage room if the Shelter of Life was already closed for the night."

I went cold all over. "My God, Megan! I thought Agnes had better sense than to let a derelict wino inside her apartment. You never know what a drunk will do."

She nudged my arm. "Quiet. She's coming over here."

But Agnes walked past the couch to Sergeant Jenner. Her face was as solemn as a saint's. The sergeant was standing by the wall only a few feet away, so Megan and I could hear her even though her voice was low.

"Sergeant, how does one claim a body for burial when he is a murder victim?"

Jenner looked a lot like a young Mel Gibson, but his face had an innocent, Boy Scout look I don't think Gibson's ever had. I wouldn't have picked him out of a crowd as a cop.

"Well, ma'am, we contact his nearest relative and inform him that the victim has been murdered and release the body to him after the autopsy."

"Old Ben didn't have any relatives."

"Then the county buries him."

Agnes squared her shoulders. "I will bury him, Sergeant, if you will notify me when the body's released."

Jenner's blue eyes widened in surprise. "That's generous of you, ma'am. I'll call you myself."

"Thank you, Sergeant. I appreciate it. If you would do me another favor, please. Question those of us who are left, so everyone can go home. It's been a" — she hesitated a moment as if searching for the right word — "difficult night."

"I have to wait for Sergeant Schroder, ma'am. He likes to question likely witnesses himself, and you folks that are left are the closest witnesses to the victim." Jenner looked around the room, and I thought he looked uncomfortable at the idea of grilling the elderly. And five out of the eleven in the bookstore were elderly. I didn't believe

Schroder would be bothered by the age of the witnesses.

Agnes started toward her checkout desk, but Megan blocked her way. "Sit with us, Agnes. I want to ask some questions about Old Ben. Please," she added when Agnes seemed hesitant.

"You told me that the couch was too small for three people," said Maria in a flat voice as she stared at Megan with accusatory eyes.

"Agnes is smaller than you, and besides Old Ben was an old friend of hers, so she needs a little TLC," replied Megan, directing Agnes to the couch.

"She's not any smaller than me, or not much anyway."

"Please, Maria, not now!" said Megan, snapping off her words in an impatient voice.

"What the devil was that all about?" I asked as Megan practically pushed Agnes down on the couch.

"Nothing important. The woman is a leech. I think she would suck my blood if she could."

Agnes nodded. "She's a little immature but harmless. She'll get over her crush on you if you don't encourage her, and choose someone else in the group to worship in her puppy-dog way."

Agnes sat down between us, her feet not reaching the floor. It always surprised me that she was so short when her presence, I guess you would say, was so tall.

"This is a more immediate investigation than tracing an old car, isn't it?" she asked.

"Have you known Old Ben a long time, Agnes?" asked Megan.

"I met him after the war — that's World War Two, my generation's war. Ben moved to Amarillo to find a job. And he did. He was a jeweler, and he took a job working for Mr. Hilliard, who owned the jewelry store where Larry Spencer's Route 66 Gift Shop is now. Mr. Hilliard was childless and was planning to let Ben buy him out at a very good price. But Ben was already drinking, and of course it only got worse. Alcoholism had him in its grip, and Ben never fought his terrible craving. Soon he was going to work hungover, then he was coming in late or not at all, and when he did, he was drunk. Mr. Hilliard tried to help him. The minister at that time of the San Jacinto Baptist Church tried to help. I tried to help. None of us knew much about alcoholism at that time, so we failed. Telling an alcoholic to pull himself together, or that drinking to excess was a sin, were not helpful. He had that horrible disease and it was terminal.

He lost his job; he lost the home he was buying; he lost his fiancée. Then he felt he had nothing left but the bottle. He never left Sixth Street, just did odd jobs, enough to pay the rent on a horrible little apartment near Western Street, and to buy his daily bottle — that turned into two. Alcoholics develop a tolerance, and it takes more and more to make them drunk enough to bear their pain. The years passed, and he degenerated into what you saw when you visited Sixth Street: rail thin, dirty, ragged, a beggar with no pride left at all."

"Agnes, was Ben a danger to anyone?"

The elderly woman stared toward the window, but I knew she didn't see it. She was looking down the years to the beginning when a young veteran had a future within his reach and traded it for the oblivion whisky brings.

Agnes closed her eyes and drew a breath, then turned her head to look at Megan. "Ben was a danger only to himself. He never harmed a living soul — except those who loved him. Well, he's at peace now even if it came to him so cruelly." She reached out and clasped Megan's hands. "I want us to find who did this, Megan. I want *you* to find him because he betrayed Ben. It was someone Ben knew and trusted, because

Ben had lived on the streets for decades. He would never turn his back to someone he didn't trust."

Megan hugged the elderly woman who seemed so much older than when the evening began. "I'll catch him, Agnes, I promise you."

"Wait a minute! What's this about catching a murderer? Damn it, Megan, you're pushing the envelope. If you keep chasing murderers, you're going be a victim yourself. You barely escaped being murdered last month in Palo Duro Canyon. Have you forgotten that already? And Agnes, what's wrong with you? Do want us all walking by Megan's casket and saying how natural she looks?"

Agnes was saved from having to defend herself by Sergeant Schroder's arrival. He was a big man, built like a barrel, and wearing slacks and a sports coat that looked like he had slept in them. The collar and cuffs of his shirt were frayed, his tie had stains from last night's dinner or maybe breakfast from the day before, his shoes needed polishing, and an unlit cigarette hung from the corner of his mouth. He was the most disreputable-looking representative of public officialdom I had ever encountered. He had gall for dismissing Old Ben as just another drunk when he looked like he'd been living in dumpsters himself.

Then I looked at his eyes. Hunter's eyes, the kind that looked at faint footsteps in the sand; a cigarette butt that shouldn't be there; a bent blade of grass; a broken twig; animal hair caught on the bark of a tree. In short, he was a hunter who tracked his game to the kill; not a weekend sportsman who sat in a deer blind and waiting for game to walk by. I felt sweat break out on my forehead, and I wasn't even a suspect.

He walked toward the couch, and I felt Megan stiffen. "You the professor with the weak stomach?"

I felt the blood rush to my face. "A lot of men have sensitive stomachs."

He rolled the unlit cigarette to the other side of his mouth and regarded me silently. "That's true, but I ain't interested in other men. But you got a long-standing reputation as a man who spends his time at a crime scene unconscious. The paramedics are used to dragging your carcass out of the way, and you don't look underhanded enough to put on an act, so I just have one question for you. Did you hear any noises when you were walking down that alley, either before or after your conflab here in the bookstore?"

"It wasn't a conflab; it was a discussion group," Megan corrected him. I wished she wouldn't put her two cents in. Schroder was already suspicious about her talent for finding bodies.

"I didn't hear anything, no, nada, zilch."

"What about you, miss?" he asked Megan.

"The name is Dr. Megan Clark. You may call me Dr. Clark." I cringed. Megan never backed away from a confrontation even when her opponent was a cop and she could find herself wearing a white jumpsuit with Potter County stenciled on the back.

"All right, *Dr. Clark,* did you hear or see anybody?"

"If I had, I would tell you," Megan snapped back.

Schroder took the cigarette out of his mouth and stuffed it in his coat pocket as he continued to stare at Megan. "Now why do I have my doubts about that?"

"Come on, Sergeant Schroder, you know Old Ben was dead before our discussion group ever started," Megan burst out. "*Rigor mortis* was already beginning. I know, because I checked his carotid artery for a pulse to see if he was still alive and we could render aid. *Rigor* begins in the small muscles of the neck and face and progresses downward to the toes. His neck and face were already stiff, so time of death was at least two-plus hours before I found him."

I clenched my mouth shut to prevent any unacceptable expletives from escaping. When would Megan ever learn to either keep her hands off corpses or keep her mouth shut about it?

"So you were interfering with a corpse?"

"I checked for a pulse. I couldn't assume he was dead. All those stab wounds could have missed his vital organs. There could have been a flicker of life."

"How did you know he'd been stabbed? How did you know he'd been stabbed thirteen times?" asked Schroder, watching her like a cat watches a mouse hole.

"How do you suppose? I counted them!"

"Had to have rolled his body to do that," said Schroder. "That means you did a little more than check for a pulse."

Too late Megan saw the trap. She sat with her mouth open for a few seconds, and I knew that fertile, devious mind of hers was devising a lie that sounded reasonable, or one that couldn't be proved one way or the other. She licked her lips, a sign that whatever came out of her mouth next would have about as much relationship to the truth as I had to Napoleon.

"I saw that Old Ben had no wounds on

the front of his body, which meant they were on his back. I sort of tilted him up on one side to check. I was thinking that maybe I could stop the bleeding and he might survive."

I may have been wrong. Megan's eyes were not avoiding Schroder's. A liar's eyes always skidded away from meeting a questioner's. Thinking back to all the other bodies Megan had found, she had always left them *in situ,* examining without touching. She knew not to disturb a crime scene. She may have been telling the truth about her reasons for disturbing Old Ben. Or she had been so obsessed with learning the truth that she ignored what she knew was proper procedure.

Apparently Schroder was as uncertain as I was, or he was giving her a bye, because he didn't jump on her inconsistency. If she felt *rigor mortis,* why did she think if she stopped the bleeding on his back, she could save him? I mean, *rigor mortis* equals you're dead. Did Megan panic? Or did she want to deny a murderer his victim so badly that she ignored the evidence of *rigor mortis*? It would be consistent with her character.

"Take the professor and get out of here. Leave your name and address with Sergeant Jenner. Oh, before I forget, you'll have to

111

find another way home. No way to get that black pickup out without backing over the crime scene. When the evidence techs finish — which may be a couple of days with all the junk in that alley — then you can take it."

"How did you know it was my pickup?" demanded Megan. "You can't search it without a warrant."

Schroder grinned, and I wished he hadn't. He reminded me of a bulldog baring his teeth. "You match your truck, Dr. Clark. Oh, yeah, something else. Don't leave town without telling me." He ambled off to talk to Maria Constantine.

"What did he mean, I match my truck?" asked Megan, sounding both puzzled and suspicious.

Outside of working hours at the public library where she is an assistant reference librarian, Megan dresses for her profession. I believe that down deep she dresses that way to remind herself of what she is, or rather what she hopes to be: a working archaeologist. She wears lace-up hiking boots — no flip-flops on a dig — jeans in the winter, cut-offs in the summer, and a variety of University of Texas tee shirts. Schroder was very perceptive. Megan did match her monster GMC crew cab pickup.

"Didn't you tell him we were in the alley because we parked behind the bookstore?"

"Maybe I did; I don't remember. I didn't have it together, Ryan. This is the first body I've ever found that I knew and liked. I mean, that I knew before he was a body. When I worked at the bookstore in high school, Old Ben would drop by almost every day. Agnes would give him used books she didn't want to add to the inventory. He wasn't so bad then, or maybe he only came in after he recovered from his hangover and before he started drinking again. When I saw him in that alley, I lost it. I knew he was dead, there was too much blood, and his eyes were open and fixed. But I had to be sure. I've worked with corpses before, lots of them, when I was at the University of Tennessee. That's where the body farm is, you know. But those dead were subjects for study; I never gave enough thought to who they were before. Tonight, for the first time, I found a body who wasn't a victim or a subject or a cadaver to me. I found a friend. The only thing I did right was copy down those marks on Old Ben's forehead. They look random at first glance, but there's a pattern to them, I just don't know what it is."

6

Murder builds you a paper house and you must keep adding to the foundation.
Captain Duncan Maclain in Baynard H. Kendrick's *Blind Man's Bluff,* 1943

THE WILLOWS RETIREMENT AND CONVALESCENCE HOME

I read the newspaper cover to cover after those two boys playing hooky found the old Ford in Wild Horse Lake. I don't know what parents are thinking of these days. When I was raising my children, I'd have taken a belt to their backsides for skipping school, not allow their pictures in the paper like they were heroes. But I'm getting away from the subject — I do that more now that I've gotten old. I had a premonition that trouble was coming, and I wanted to be ready for it. Not that I intended to tell anything but the truth, or as much of the truth as I could tell without hurting somebody who didn't

114

need any hurt. Likely the one I was protecting was already buried nice and peaceful in some cemetery. I was looking at the same destination in the near future, and I wanted to rest in peace when I reached it. So maybe it was best if all the secrets were uncovered so I could clean my soul of them before I meet my maker. If that's necessary. If God is real like the preachers tell us, and I have no real doubt that He is, then He already knows all the intentions that we carried in our hearts that night. He knows we did what we could to make things right. But if there's fault, it's mine to claim. Maybe I was wrong as far as the law would be concerned, but I was right in what was good for that family.

I found the article about Old Ben being killed in cold blood on a back page next to the want ads. It made me sad to read about his death. I remember when he first moved to Sixth Street — 1947 or '48, it was. He was a handsome man, tall and lean and clean-cut and never a hard word for anybody. We all thought he was a fine young man, and when he got that job at Mr. Hilliard's jewelry store and started courting that young lady, we knew Sixth Street would have itself another upstanding family. We were all happy for him and his girl. Then the drink took him, and it was like he was riding a runaway horse that he couldn't stop. I guess his ride finally came to an end. I'd like to go to his funeral and see Sixth Street one more time before I turn up my toes, but I figure my children would pitch a fit. They would think it would be too hard on me, attending services for somebody I knew. They don't realize folks that live as long as I have are closer to the dead than the living. It's like the dead are just on the other side of the door, and I'll be opening it soon and closing it behind me.

The paper said that redheaded Megan Clark found Old Ben. Oh, I know about Megan Clark. What I haven't read in the newspapers about her, another source told me. She sounds like quite a girl. Sounds a lot like me that night near seventy years ago. Bullheaded is what she is; goes beyond the law to bring justice. I like to think she would do what I did.

Special Crimes Unit — Seven Days Later

Jenner missed Special Crimes's old offices in the Potter County Annex. They were in a ramshackle building, one of a block of equally ramshackle buildings, but they had character if you didn't mind wondering how long that whole block would stand before one of the Panhandle's 100-mile-an-hour winds blew it down. Not that there were many days like that — maybe one every five or six years — but Jenner never set foot in Special Crimes when one was blowing through.

Jenner supposed the offices were more efficient over in the new building that housed the police, Special Crimes, the municipal courts, the city attorney, and the city judges. There was plenty of space for the evidence techs to process all the physical evidence like weapons, cigarette butts, other flotsam and jetsam found at a crime scene, blood, and fingerprints. Most forensics like DNA, drug testing, hair and fiber analysis, and tool markings, for example, Special Crimes sent to the FBI or the Texas Department of Public Safety labs.

Which was why he and Schroder were walking down the long hall that led to Lieutenant Jerry Carr's office: forensics, as in "where the hell are the test results on Herbert Jackson the Third's vest and Maria Constantine's blouse."

"Where the hell are the test results on Herbert Jackson the Third's vest and Maria Constantine's blouse?" demanded Jerry Carr when Schroder and Jenner crowded into the lieutenant's office. There was barely enough room for a government-issue desk and office chair, a couple of government-issue, five-drawer filing cabinets, and two government-issue, barely padded visitor's chairs guaranteed to numb your butt in three seconds flat. Schroder had enough natural padding on his backside not to mind sitting in a visitor's chair, but Jenner chose to lean against the wall. His feet might get tired, but at least he would be able to feel his butt when he left.

Schroder lit one of his unfiltered Camels and received a glare from Carr. The building was nonsmoking, but Schroder never let a technicality like that get between him and his cigarettes. The lieutenant had tried to forbid Schroder from smoking, but the sergeant predated Carr at Special Crimes by several lifetimes and claimed he had been grandfathered in when the smoking ban went into effect on city property. Jenner never was sure if the lieutenant believed Schroder, or older employees warned him that his life would be a lot easier if he just ignored the cigarette that was perpetually hanging out one side or the other of the sergeant's mouth. Jenner thought the lieutenant chose to ignore it.

"I'm waiting, Sergeant," said Carr, tapping his fingers on the desktop.

Schroder expelled smoke from the corner of his mouth opposite the cigarette. "You know how the labs are, Lieutenant. We might get the test results back about the time the defendant dies of old age."

"We don't *have* a defendant." Carr slammed his fist down on the desk, his face flushed and a vein throbbing in his temple. A pencil holder tipped over and spilled pencils, pens, and paper clips across the top of the desk. Observing his red face and throbbing vein Jenner wondered if the lieutenant suffered from high blood pressure. If he did, he was courting a stroke getting upset over a few late lab results.

"I don't know about that, Lieutenant," said Jenner earnestly. Jackson and Constantine haven't been cleared yet. It's not likely they did it, but that spilled coffee story sounded weak to me. They were snuggled up together close enough that Jackson was able to catch the woman when she tripped. Maybe they got something going, and Old Ben saw them together, and they was afraid he might mention something to Damian Constantine, and then the fat would be in the fire. I know no blood showed when we used luminol on their clothes, but if the judge had signed the search warrant sooner, maybe we would've gotten a positive result.

As it was, it took two days, and by that time Jackson had his vest cleaned, and Constantine washed her blouse in bleach and water, and blood won't show up under luminol if clothes are washed with bleach."

"Shut up, Jenner," said Jerry Carr, still looking at Schroder. "I'll say it again: we don't have a defendant." He closed his eyes, and Jenner heard him counting under his breath. "Sergeant Schroder, Sergeant Jenner, my distinguished colleagues in Special Crimes —"

"I'm not in Special Crimes," said Jenner quickly. "I'm a traffic cop."

"Shut up, Jenner," growled Schroder.

Carr took a deep breath. "Let me start again. My distinguished colleagues in Special Crimes. Let me tell you what we do have." He held up one finger. "We have Herbert Jackson III, one of the most distinguished attorneys in town, and being a distinguished attorney, he knew better than to say a damn word other than his name and address and to refuse to allow you to take his clothes without a search warrant. And in case you think he's as much of a nerd as he acts sometimes, he's bright enough not to defend himself. He's bright enough to hire an attorney who called to remind me that the Constitution guarantees

120

no illegal search and seizure."

The lieutenant held up a second finger. "We have Maria Constantine, who is the wife of a distinguished cop."

"If she's a cop's wife, then she ought to have cooperated. If she's innocent, then she doesn't have anything to worry about," said Jenner.

"Shut up, Jenner," said Carr, staring hard enough at Jenner to burn a hole in his skull. He waited a moment to be sure the sergeant didn't have anymore to say, then continued. "Has it occurred to either one of you that she may not have known what Jackson already had on his vest that might have rubbed off on her blouse? She knew she spilled coffee on him, but what else may there have been? So when she heard Jackson refuse to turn over his clothes, she thought she'd follow his lead. You know as well as I do that cops are not your friends, if said cops are thinking even a little bit that you might be a murder suspect. Now, I suspect Maria heard enough talk around the dinner table from Damian to know that any smart person under police scrutiny doesn't co-operate."

"She's kind of a weird one, anyway," observed Jenner. "Cool as a cucumber when she told us she wouldn't turn over her blouse without a search warrant, then up and runs over to the couch and grabs Megan Clark around the legs and starts to boo-hoo about how she's afraid Damian will get mad at her for getting involved in a murder case, and will Megan take her home and explain to her husband that it's not her fault. All the time she's clutching and putting on a show, the lady doc is trying to peel her off like a tight girdle. Then the other women run over and try to calm down Mrs. Constantine until finally Ms. Caldwell, the lady who owns the store, tosses somebody's leftover coffee in Mrs. Constantine's face. She screeched like a cat with its tail caught in a screen door and let go of the lady doc, who crawls into the other doc's lap and wraps her legs around his back, I guess to keep Mrs. Constantine from grabbing her again. Anyway, the lawyer says he'll take her — Mrs. Constantine — home and explain to her husband. The only one of the bunch who looked like he was enjoying himself was Doc Stevens, and I would, too, in his place if that redhead was hanging on to me tighter than a tick on a dog's ear."

"Why do you suppose Mrs. Constantine acted like that? I know Damian, and he's soft as a marshmallow, almost too soft hearted to be a cop. He can't hardly bring himself to arrest anybody unless they're standing over a body with a gun." Jenner's voice trailed off when he noticed the lieutenant glaring at him with eyes so hot they would melt candle wax.

"Thank you for sharing your impressions with us, Sergeant Jenner," said the lieutenant in a soft voice. "Now SHUT UP!" The lieutenant wiped his face on his shirt sleeve, then held up a third finger. "Schroder, I know it took you two days to get a search warrant because none of the judges wanted to sign it. When one finally did, he called me up afterwards and I got an earful about how come Special Crimes was skating on thin ice when it came to probable cause. If those two tests don't come back positive for blood traces, that judge is going to be mighty unhappy. He's going to feel like he was conned."

Schroder blew out more smoke. "I didn't con him, Lieutenant. You see a guy wearing a vest with some kind of a stain on it, and that same guy is sitting in a bookstore with a bunch of other people who are the only ones close enough to hear anything from the murder scene, and I think maybe I got the only witnesses around. I sent men around to question everybody, except the nearest witnesses to the alley around the bookstore were two blocks away. That's a retail section of Sixth Street, and everybody closes up at five o'clock except the bookstore and the restaurants. I might have stretched a little on the size of the stain, but I think I had probable cause."

"For your sake I hope so, Sergeant. You don't want judges on the bench who are suspicious that the cops are being less than truthful on probable cause. To continue with my story." He held up a fourth finger. "Damian Constantine called me up, and from his position as Maria's husband, chewed me out for you and Jenner sending his wife into hysterics. You're right, Sergeant Schroder, I don't think either one of them did it."

Schroder tamped out his cigarette in a little ashtray with a lid on it and stuck it in his pocket. "Well, Lieutenant, the closest witness to the victim was the one who found the body, and her actions were suspicious, but I'm withholding judgment about her. The guy she was with fainted on the spot when she found the corpse, so I figure Old Ben was dead before they walked down that alley."

The lieutenant put his head in his hands. "How can one white, middle-class woman discover so many corpses and all of them murder victims, and not be involved?" He lifted his head to look at Schroder. "Did you tell her to keep that attractive nose out of this case, Sergeant?" he asked, a pleading sound to his voice. "Tell me you did. Tell me I don't have to worry about her setting herself up as bait."

"I thought you weren't dating her anymore," said Jenner, trying to figure out if he missed something. "She was with the professor last night."

"Shut up, Jenner," said Schroder, scooting his chair farther away from him.

The lieutenant's face darkened, and Jenner winced as he was on the receiving end of another of those death-ray glares.

Satisfied that he had cowed the sergeant sufficiently enough to silence him for the duration, Carr turned back to Schroder. "Tell me you told her and that whole group of weirdos you hoped they enjoyed reading their mysteries, but to stay out of the real thing."

"I did mention that I wouldn't mind throwing her into jail. I think I scared her into behaving herself," said Schroder.

The lieutenant held up a fifth finger. "I'm glad you think so, Sergeant Schroder, because last, but certainly not least, I had a visit from Dr. Megan Clark demanding to know what, if anything, we had concluded about the marks on Old Ben's forehead. She claims that the murder was ritualistic because of the marks, the thirteen stab wounds, and the fact that the body was posed. Anything to say about her claims?"

Schroder stubbed out his second cigarette into his portable ashtray and rubbed his chin. Jenner had seen the burly sergeant execute those same two motions when he was deliberating how he would answer a question. And this was a question loaded with bear traps and roofing nails. If he agreed with Megan Clark, then he validated her deductions, and that might encourage her to meddle. On the other hand, if he disagreed with her, then he would be lying.

"I'm waiting, Sergeant."

"Yeah, Lieutenant, she's got it right. That body was posed. No way is somebody gonna be stabbed thirteen times, then roll over and fold his hands across his chest with his legs more or less together. In the first place, he would've landed on his face, and I don't think he was going to move after that. In the second place, his arms and legs would've splayed out, like a rag doll when you drop it. I think she's right about it being ritualistic. You don't find a body posed unless it's ritualistic, or not that I ever heard of. That

Gypsy fortune teller thought it was, too. She pointed out that thirteen is an occult number — like I didn't know that. She believes the marks are some kind of incantation or spell or something, but she doesn't know what kind. Said she didn't recognize the language. I'd have hauled her butt into jail as a likely suspect, since she knew so much, but I couldn't find probable cause. No stains on her clothes, and she gave a list of her appointments from four o'clock on until nearly seven. I ain't no forensic pathologist, but I figure he was killed between six and seven o'clock. It's nearly dark at six this time of year, and he was beginning *rigor mortis.* Face and neck was already stiff when I got there. He wasn't somebody's fresh kill. So, yeah, Megan Clark nailed it on the head."

The lieutenant ran his fingers through his hair. "I wish you didn't agree with her. Maybe if she was wrong for a change, really wrong, she'd find another hobby."

"Don't tell her!" Jenner pressed back against the wall. He didn't mean to say that, but it was so obvious a solution that he couldn't figure out why Schroder and the lieutenant hadn't already thought of it. He flinched when Schroder and Jerry Carr both looked at him.

"You're right for a change, Jenner," said the lieutenant. "You hear that, Schroder. Not a word to the press and especially not a word to Megan Clark." He glanced at his watch. "It's seven o'clock. Let's call it quits. I want to go home, order in a pizza, and watch a movie to take my mind off the murder for a while. I figure watching *Cinderella* will be as far from murder as I can get. It won't remind me of Megan, either. Can you imagine Megan Clark putting up with a wicked stepmother? She'd throw the dirty dishwater in her face and walk out."

Schroder chuckled, which sounded like someone slowly beating a hollow drum. "If she'd had some dirty dishwater last week, she would've thrown it at me."

Jenner heard the first few bars of "Jailhouse Rock" and watched the lieutenant pull his cell phone off his belt. "Lieutenant Carr, Special Crimes." He picked up one of the pencils on his desk and found a notepad. "Where is it? Is someone there yet?" He listened for a few seconds, then his face went blank, and he snapped the pencil in two between his fingers. He closed his cell phone and cleared his throat several times. "There's another body on Sixth Street."

7

Killing two men in cold blood like that! The calculation in it — it's horrible. Most murders you can understand, even if you don't altogether agree with the outcome. Jealous husbands, neglected wives, sons and daughters wanting to inherit — murder's a family thing, as often as not. But killing strangers as a way to pass the time on a river trip isn't nice, not nice at all.
Constable Thackeray in Peter Lovesey's
Swing, Swing Together, 1976

ONG STREET IN AMARILLO — THAT EVENING
Megan slid the loop at the end of Horatio's leash over her hand so she wouldn't drop it while she readjusted the sling she wore around her chest and tied over the left shoulder. If Horatio could jerk his leash free, he would take off like a streak of lightning to explore the neighborhood. Calling him was a waste of breath since he im-

mediately lost his hearing, or so he always tried to persuade her when she finally cornered him. Anyone who thought dogs didn't have facial expressions had never owned one. Wide brown eyes, ears perked up, head tilted to one side said plainly how surprised Horatio was when she grabbed his trailing leash. "I didn't know you wanted me, human person. I didn't hear you call me," said his expression. No getting loose tonight; she didn't have time to chase him. She had to talk to Ryan before it was time to leave for the bookstore.

She crossed her lawn to Ryan's back door, gave her usual perfunctory knock, and walked into his kitchen. "Ryan, we've got to talk," she called, walking through the living room toward the back hall and his study.

Ryan stood behind his desk hurriedly pulling a sweater over his head. "Don't you know better than to walk in a man's house without being invited?"

His voice was muffled by the sweater, but Megan wasn't paying attention to his words. She was staring at his bare chest. She swallowed. What was the expression, abs of steel? My God, he had them. And he wasn't one of these wussy, hairless men, either. He had black, curly chest hair in a pyramid shape from his broad shoulders to a narrow strip that disappeared into his Levi's. She struggled to draw a breath as she felt her body flush from her nose to her toes. "Oh, my," she whispered.

"What did you say?" he asked as his head popped through his sweater's neck.

She felt him staring at her, but she couldn't seem to quit looking at his torso. She had always known he was a hunk, had even told him so, but until you see a man without his shirt on, you never really appreciate what the word means. She swallowed again and realized she was salivating. Over Ryan? But that would ruin their friendship. A man and woman couldn't be friends if one was always drooling. And he was her best friend's father! He would be so embarrassed if he knew she had a sudden attack of lust. She licked her lips and tried for a friendly, but platonic, smile. He must never know what she had felt — momentarily. She raised her eyes to meet his and stopped breathing. His turquoise eyes were burning. He knew! Immediately her glance went skittering off to a stack of books in the corner, while his skittered off in the opposite direction.

"We need to talk," she repeated and cleared her throat. Her voice sounded hoarse.

"What about?" His voice sounded hoarse, too. Maybe they were both catching a cold.

"Herb hired a lawyer today."

"Are the cops still questioning him? What about Maria? Has she hired a lawyer, too?"

"No, and I don't know." Suddenly, she broke out of her trance and began pacing the room, automatically avoiding the stacks of books on the floor. "Ryan, we have to do something! Herb didn't kill Old Ben. It's stupid for Sergeant Schroder to even be suspicious of him. Why would Herb murder a helpless drunk? Or anyone else, for that matter. All this business about a blood stain. Maria spilled her coffee on him. I just don't understand why Schroder picked on him. He's the most innocuous man in the reading circle. I'd sooner suspect Ray Roberts. At least he would probably know how to kill somebody. Herb would be afraid of getting blood on his three-piece suit and ruining it. And don't you dare faint! I need you."

"I'm not going to faint at the word, Megan, just the sight." His voice sounded like he was peeved.

"All right, I believe you. But what are we going to do, Ryan?"

"What about Maria? Aren't you worried about her, too?"

"No! Maria and her red blouse will be

fine. Her husband is a cop. I'm surprised they even questioned her, but I guess they had to after Herb finally told them what happened. The cops take care of their own, so Maria would slip through the cracks even if she was dripping with blood." Megan stopped pacing and looked at him. "I wish Schroder would catch her with a blood-stained knife in her hands. I wish he would lock her up and throw away the key. The woman is driving me crazy. She follows me all over the store, asking advice on every subject in the world. She even shows up at the library where I work. She's stalking me, Ryan! And that scene last week after I found Old Ben's body, when the police were there . . . My God! She's the groupie from Hell!"

"You'll have to get a restraining order, Megan . . ." His voice trailed off into silence as he stared at her chest. "What are you carrying in that sling around your neck? Is that a dog?" He sounded flabbergasted.

She finally looked at him, then down at the sling. A small black nose, white muzzle, and white streak between two short, floppy ears emerged from the sling, followed by a black leg with a white paw. The dog stretched his paw and patted Megan's cheek.

Megan loosened the sling and lifted out a

small black and white puppy. "This is Henry the Eighth, Henry for short. He's a border collie, I think. At least, the vet said she thought he was a border collie. That's what she put on his ID chip anyway." She sat the puppy on the floor. "He pats my cheek when he wants down."

Ryan stared thunderstruck at the puppy who was busily sniffing a stack of books. "Why are you wearing him around your neck?"

"We're bonding. I got him at the pound, so since he doesn't know me, we're bonding. That's what you have to do with puppies and babies. You have to bond with them. I had to get another dog, Ryan. Horatio has been so lonely since Rembrandt died. He needed a friend. Beagles are pack animals, and they're happier if they aren't the only dogs." There was a tinkling sound, and Megan gasped. "Oh, no, Henry! Bad dog!"

"Holy Hell, Megan, he just peed on my anniversary collection of Louis L'Amour!" He rounded the desk and grabbed for Henry but tripped over Horatio's leash that was pulled taut while the beagle was checking out interesting smells by Ryan's desk. Ryan landed on his hands and knees and skidded across the slick, hardwood floor into a tall stack of thick reference books on General George Armstrong Custer. Horatio began baying, and Henry disappeared into the hall.

Megan dropped the leash, and Horatio escaped into the kitchen where he had smelled something very interesting when he and his human person walked through. "Ryan, are you all right?" she asked as she crouched by his side and began excavating his head and shoulders.

"My God, Megan, he peed on my anniversary collection of Louis L'Amour." Freed from the avalanche of books, he crawled over to his precious Louis L'Amours. "Damn it, he didn't miss a single one. I can't even dry them out, because they'll smell like dog urine. I'll have to throw them away and buy a whole new set."

"I'll replace them, Ryan, I promise, but you really ought to buy more bookcases instead of stacking your books on the floor."

Ryan gave her a pained look just as there was a crash from the kitchen. "What the devil was that?" he exclaimed as he got to his feet and rushed for the kitchen.

Megan started to follow, but a series of profanities erupted from the other room, so she thought staying put was a better idea, especially when Horatio rushed by her with a sandwich in his mouth. He scooted under Ryan's desk and gobbled down the sandwich in two bites. "Ryan, what are you doing? Can I help?"

Ryan walked back in the study holding two halves of a plate. He contemplated her for a moment. "Megan, the one thing I don't want you to do is help. God only knows what kind of further catastrophe you would cause." There was a clatter from farther down the hall.

"I forgot about Henry," said Megan, climbing to her feet. "I'll find him."

"No!" shouted Ryan. "You stay there. I'll go get him. It sounds like he's in the bathroom. He can't do much damage in there. Everything's porcelain and tile."

Megan flinched when she heard a soft but high-pitched growl coming from a tiny throat, followed by Ryan's desperate voice. "All right, you little devil, you can keep it! I've got more." She squeezed her eyes shut.

"Take your dog, Megan, before he tears my house down to the foundations."

Megan opened one eye and squinted at Ryan holding Henry in front of him with both hands. Henry had the toilet paper roller in his mouth, paper and all. A trail of toilet paper led from the puppy's mouth, down the hall, and around the corner into the bathroom. Henry was still growling deep in his throat.

Megan sank to the floor and started laughing. Henry wagged his tail. Horatio stuck his head out from under the desk and bayed. Ryan's face wore a martyred expression.

"Are you mad at me?" asked Megan, adjusting her seat belt so Henry wouldn't be squeezed. Horatio sat in the middle of the bench seat with his seat belt fastened tightly around his middle so he couldn't sit in Ryan's lap. Ryan was driving her pickup since she couldn't drive with Henry belted across her chest in his sling, and Ryan refused to take his Ford Ranger for fear Henry might have another call of nature.

Ryan sighed and Megan wished he didn't sound so resigned. "Megan, it doesn't do any good to be mad at you. You're a force of nature like a tsunami. I've finally accepted that and found peace in my acceptance."

"In that case, what are we going to do about Herb?"

He glanced at her, then turned back to stare through the windshield. "Nothing. Herb didn't kill anybody, and the police will have to admit it when they finish playing chemistry lab with his vest."

"You hear all the time about innocent men going to prison for crimes they didn't commit —"

"Hardly ever," interjected Ryan.

"And I don't intend for Herb to be one of them," she finished. "We're going to have to find the murderer ourselves, because it's obvious the police are floundering."

"Don't even think about it."

She ignored him. "I called Jerry Carr today. He and Schroder won't even admit that this was a ritualistic murder. And you know what kind of men commit ritualistic murders."

"How do you know it was a man? Why are men always accused of every foul crime ever committed?"

"Because serial killers are usually white males in their late twenties and early thirties."

"How do you know it's a serial killer? There's only been one body."

"I just told you: Old Ben's murder was ritualistic. There are the thirteen stab wounds. The number might be coincidental, but I'm like Sergeant Schroder: I don't like coincidences. But the most important element, Ryan, the element that satisfies me that this is a ritualistic killing committed by a serial killer, are the symbols on the forehead. That is the killer's primary signature. A signature is an act that has nothing to do with taking a life. Those marks were not fatal; they were not part of the mechanics of death. In fact, they were postmortem. The killer added them to satisfy some psychological need. It may be as simple as an artist signing his work, murder as art, or the signature may have some other significance. I don't know. Oh, yes, the posed body? That's also the signature of a serial killer."

"But it's only one body, Megan. You can't conclude it's a serial killer with only one body," said Ryan with a note of desperation in his voice.

Megan sighed in exasperation. "A serial killer starts with one body, Ryan, then a second and a third and a fourth and so on until he's caught or self-destructs and commits suicide. I know that I'm a target of everyone's amusement. I autopsy mummies, ha-ha, but I spent my time at the body farm; I went out on consults as a doctoral candidate, and I actually performed autopsies on mummified remains of what turned out to be victims of a serial killer. I know death, Ryan, and I've studied serial killers. No forensic anthropologist, which I technically am although I specialize in paleopathology, would fail to study serial killers. If I'm right, and this is someone local, then there will be more bodies."

Ryan slammed on the brakes and turned in his seat to look at her. "You will not mess in this investigation. It's too dangerous, especially if it's a serial killer. If it's any kind of a killer. You're not a cop, Megan. Can't you understand that? You don't have several hundred men with badges and guns to back you up. A lone amateur doesn't have a chance against a killer like this."

Horns began blaring behind them. "Ryan, you've stopped in the middle of the street. You're in as much danger of being a victim of road rage as I am of this serial killer. I'm not his type."

"That's the most idiotic thing you've ever said. What do you mean, you're not his type?"

"I won't tell you anything else until you take your foot off the brake and start driving."

Ryan took his foot off the brake and shifted the pickup's manual transmission into first gear. There was a grinding sound underneath the hood. "Now, tell me."

"Listen. Can you hear the transmission grinding? It's been doing that the last few days. I'll have to spend the weekend working on it."

"Megan!" Ryan shouted. "Never mind the transmission. Tell me what you mean by not his type."

Megan put her hands over her ears, and Henry peered out of his sling and growled. "Ryan, quit shouting. You've been shouting all evening, and you're scaring Henry."

Megan heard his teeth grinding along with the transmission. "Tell me, Megan, my love. Pretty please."

"Sarcasm doesn't suit your personality, Ryan. You're too nice a man. Anyway, I'm not the murderer's type, if he's a serial killer like we think, because I'm not a man. Since his victim is a man, statistics say that men are his chosen victims. I wonder if Jerry has checked VICAP to see if he's killed before. This was a polished kill for a first-timer."

"You know what I think, Megan? I think this killer would make an exception in his pattern for you if you stick your pretty little nose in his business." He slammed on his brakes again and turned into the bookstore parking lot. "At least we have a parking place. In fact, the only cars I see parked on Sixth Street belong to the reading circle. That's strange. Between the restaurants and the clubs there are usually cars parked

141

bumper to bumper the whole length of Sixth Street. Is this a holiday? I don't see any business open besides the bookstore."

Megan unfastened Horatio's seat belt and grabbed his leash. She checked Henry's sling to make sure it was secure and slid out of the pickup.

Horatio jumped out after her and raised his head in the air and started sniffing. He let out his signatory bay and started to run across the parking lot toward the alley. Megan jerked on his leash. "Not that way, Horatio. We're going to see Agnes. Don't you want to see Agnes?" asked Megan, tugging on the leash while clamping an arm over the sling to hold in a suddenly wiggling puppy.

"You're not taking the dogs in, are you? Agnes may not want Henry targeting her books." said Ryan, walking around the pickup to take Horatio's leash.

"Of course, I'm taking them. Horatio, you can't go down the alley. He probably can still smell the blood. Beagles have really sensitive noses."

Ryan turned pale and swayed against the pickup's door. He leaned over and took several deep breaths. "Do me a favor, Megan. Don't mention that word again, not when the murder site is less than forty feet away."

"I'm sorry, Ryan, but if you faint, don't you dare let go of that leash."

They walked into the bookstore to find a somber group. When they saw the dogs they starting smiling. Except two. Herb sat hunched on his usual chair looking friendless and miserable. Maria circled around Megan, then backed away as Horatio trotted toward her. Puzzled, Megan watched her step behind Agnes and the twins.

Ryan tugged on Horatio's leash and led him over to the couch. He sank into his favorite corner, and Horatio jumped up to sit beside him. Megan sat down and leaned over the beagle to whisper to Ryan. "What do you suppose Maria's problem is? She's treating Horatio like he has fleas."

Ryan shrugged. "Maybe she's allergic to dogs. Maybe we should take them back to the pickup."

"Horatio and I have to bond with Henry these first few days so he'll grow into a happy, well-adjusted dog. I'm not locking him in the pickup. He would think I was abandoning him like his previous owners abandoned him at the pound." She patted Henry's head, and he stretched up and licked her nose. "If Maria is allergic to dogs,

I plan to take Henry and Horatio everywhere I go."

"Maria, are you allergic to dogs?" Ryan asked.

"No, I just don't like dogs or cats, either. They're nasty animals that carry fleas and ringworm. You don't let them in your house, do you, Megan? They're just good for anatomical studies and drug experiments. And cats will steal a baby's breath, did you know that?" Her face expressed disgust as she waved her hand toward Horatio. "Would you leave the big one on his leash, please, Ryan?" she asked. "I'll sit over here behind Rosemary and Lorene, and I'll be fine." She didn't look fine to Megan; she looked like a person who would put out poisoned meat for her neighbor's dogs.

"I've definitely decided. I'll skip the restraining order and just take the dogs everywhere with me," Megan whispered to Ryan, then stood up and gave Maria "The Look." The groupie shrank back into a chair, but there was no fear in her eyes.

Ryan, on the other hand, looked worried. "Don't kid about that, Megan."

"About what?" she asked, still studying Maria.

"Taking the dogs everywhere."

"Who says I'm kidding?" she asked. She

144

leaned over Horatio again to whisper in Ryan's ear. "Look at Maria. She's not scared or nervous."

"Yeah, what about it? You know, I think I'll take your suggestion and buy more bookcases before I have to play host to Henry again."

"Forget about the bookcases. What about Maria? If she thinks dogs are nasty, why doesn't she look nervous or frightened? In fact, she looks more like a cat who swallowed the cream. I wonder how she would like that analogy?"

"She does look pleased with herself," said Ryan. "Maybe it's because she thinks she's controlling your actions, which doesn't say much for her judgment. I've never known anybody to control your actions short of a blunt instrument."

"There's something out of kilter in her brain, Ryan. Her reactions don't correspond to the stimuli."

"Worry about it tomorrow. I want to take a short nap."

She looked at Ryan with resignation. "Hold on to Horatio; I'm going to talk to Herb."

Megan got up and walked over to Herb. She sat down beside him and patted his shoulder. "Hang in there, Herb. None of us think you had anything to do with the murder."

Herb looked up at her, such a look of gratitude in his eyes that Megan wanted to cry. "Thank you. You don't know how much I appreciate your faith in me. This is the most wretched experience of my life. I feel so ashamed, but I don't have anything to feel ashamed about. It has been all I can do to get out of bed these last few mornings and go to work. I'm becoming paranoid, Megan; I feel like everyone is whispering about me behind my back. I couldn't even write this week, so I don't have a chapter to give to everyone tonight. You know Jerry Carr. How long will the police be suspicious of me?"

"Until they get the test results back on your vest. Then they had better apologize to you. But we're not going to leave it at that, Herb. I'm going to track down this killer, and I want the reading circle to help me. Will you help me, Herb? Fighting this vile suspicion is the best way to regain your self-respect." She held out her hand, and after a moment's hesitation, Herb clasped it.

"Megan, I need to talk to you in private," whispered Randel, motioning her to follow him.

Megan patted Herb's knee and told him

she would talk to him later, then followed Randel and sat next to him. Candi sat on the other side, twisting her hands together. "What is it, Randel? Did you find a photograph of the car among your great-grandfather's Kodaks? Were there any people in the photo?"

Randel looked around the circle, then whispered to her behind his hand. "Somebody has broken into my house. I know because things are out of place. Just little things, like the clothes in my drawers were rumpled, and the toaster was sitting too far from the wall. It's happened twice, Megan. The first time on Wednesday morning and again on Wednesday afternoon. I think somebody's after those photographs."

"But why, Randel? They're just old photographs, nothing that threatens anyone."

"It's the old car, Megan," said Candi. "Someone's afraid that we'll find a picture of that old car and the people who owned it. I'm scared to death. What if someone breaks in while we're in the house?"

"How did they get in, Randel? Was a door forced or a window broken?" asked Megan, chills running up and down her spine.

Randel kept wiping sweat off his forehead or rubbing his hands together. His eyes kept jerking from face to face in the reading circle. "I don't know for sure, but I think whoever it is must have a key, or maybe a set of burglary tools. I had the locks changed today — deadbolts this time. And I'm thinking about buying a gun."

Megan shuddered at the thought of Randel Anderson with a gun. He would probably shoot himself or Candi before he shot the burglar. "I think you'll be safe now that you have new locks. Or if they've found the photographs, if that's what they're after. Have they found them, Randel?"

Randel rubbed his hands up and down his thighs. "No, because I didn't know where they were myself until this morning when I remembered where I put them." His voice dropped until Megan could hardly hear his whisper. "They were at my office at the college. I have a little storage room behind my desk, and they're filed by subject in an old filing cabinet. I'm having someone cover my classes, and Candi and I are going to spend tomorrow looking at every one of them."

"Who did you tell that you were looking for a photo of that car?" asked Megan, trying to look more concerned than scared — which she was.

He looked blank for a moment, then fearful. "I didn't tell anybody but the reading circle."

Megan felt as though her back was pierced by a thousand stares. "Find that photo if there is one, Randel. It's the only way you'll be safe."

She told Ryan what she had learned from Randel. Never had she seen his face look so grim, but not more so than she felt. Her world — work at the library, quiet life in the white frame house with wraparound porch, her dogs, Murder by the Yard Reading Circle, evenings and weekends with Ryan — while lacking excitement and sometimes colored blue by thoughts of her unfulfilled ambition to be a working paleopathologist on a major dig instead of an assistant reference librarian — was comfortable and secure. Now that world had turned into the black and white and grey of a 1930s prison movie, and she a prisoner betrayed by her friends.

"It's someone in the reading circle, Ryan," she whispered. "They're the only people who knew Randel had a trunk of old pictures. They're the only ones who knew I was interested in that old car. It has to be either Maria or Pearl. They are the only newcomers. I refuse to believe that it's any of our friends. We're a band, a pack, a brotherhood, a circle of friends."

"What could either Maria or Pearl have to do with that car?" asked Ryan softly. "Maria is too young. Even if Pearl is a lot older than she looks, she still would have been a very young child in 1938. That's the hang-up for me. Everyone who had anything to do with that car has to be dead, or so old that whatever their motive is for ditching that car in Wild Horse Lake doesn't matter anymore."

"It matters to someone very much, Ryan. We have to know why. Once the story is told, then Randel and Candi will be safe."

Megan listened to the discussion, this one on *The ABC Murders,* but hardly remembered a word except how Christie used the obvious red herrings of taunting notes to Poriot and the railway guide to misdirect attention from the more important red herring of the apparent random selection of victims to fit the alphabetical nature of the murders. If real murderers were as clever as Christie at misdirection, the police would never catch anyone.

When the meeting was over, Megan was ready to bolt, but Ryan had to satisfy his curiosity. "Agnes, what's the deal? No cars parked on Sixth Street; no businesses open; even the bars are closed."

"It's the murder and those marks and thirteen stab wounds," said Agnes. "We're too frightened to go outside at night. Everyone is sure it's Satanism, and the Satan worshipers could make sacrifices out of any one of us."

"But how do they know, Agnes? There was nothing in the paper about the number of stab wounds, or about the marks on the forehead."

Agnes smiled. "We on Sixth Street and the San Jacinto neighborhood have our own system of communication, and it's more efficient than Southwestern Bell. Everybody knew everything about the murder by four o'clock in the afternoon the next day. One neighbor would tell another, and so forth, until no one remembers who first mentioned the murder. Once everyone knew, Sixth Street and San Jacinto went into overdrive. The locksmiths in town will be vacationing in Cancún on all the money they're making changing everybody's locks. And anyone who didn't have a gun already has bought one. I bought one myself, but I didn't buy any little lady's revolver or automatic. I'm not taking any chances on missing with a handgun; I bought a double-barreled shotgun. If I have to defend myself in the middle of the night when I'm not wearing my glasses, I'll at least be able to hit something. All I have to do is point it in the general direction."

"Can't you ask for more patrols by the police? Or have more bicycle cops in the neighborhood?" asked Megan.

"Megan, I love this neighborhood. I've lived here all my life, but I'm aware that many of my neighbors, while good people in some ways, are self-destructive in others. They have frequent encounters with the police, so they don't necessarily see them as protectors. We'll do what we've always done: rely on ourselves and our neighbors, and keep the police out of the loop."

Megan put her arm around Agnes. She felt so frail, as if energy was slowly seeping out of the old woman's body, an osteoporosis of the spirit. "Agnes, you and your neighbors can't act like some kind of vigilante organization. Self-reliance is one thing, but walking around packing heat isn't safe. I like all your neighbors on Sixth Street and San Jacinto, but some of them are a little excitable at the best of times. Like Larry Spencer for instance. His edges aren't glued down tight. Sometimes, when I go into the Route 66 Gift Shop, he's whizzing around the room like a punctured balloon. Give him a gun and he's liable to — well, I don't know what he's liable to do, and that's the problem. And there are others I could list, but you understand what I'm saying."

Agnes pulled away and dabbed at her eyes with a handkerchief she carried tucked under one sleeve of her sweater. "Tell me what you would do, Megan. You wouldn't sit waiting for this maniac to break into your home, then defend yourself with a rolling pin."

"My mother doesn't own a rolling pin. She wouldn't recognize one if she saw it," said Megan. "She's not domestic. Her idea of baking is Sara Lee."

Agnes laughed. "Your mother is an admirable woman, but she's not a warm and fuzzy homemaker. If it weren't for Ryan and his late wife watching after you when you were growing up, I'm not certain you would have turned out as well as you have. Neglected children often don't."

Megan felt as if someone had squeezed her heart. It was true — she had always known it — but she didn't intend to invite pity by admitting it. "I wasn't neglected!"

Agnes nodded. "No, you weren't. You had Ryan. You still have him."

"I don't need a father anymore."

"And Ryan doesn't want to be a father to a grown-up Megan, but caring for you as a child has complicated your relationship." She kissed Megan's cheek. "I'm confident you and he will work through your difficulties and your story will have a happy ending."

Megan felt her heart pounding as if she was racing in a marathon. She knew she was rushing toward an emotional abyss. If she fell in, what would Ryan do? "What's happening, Agnes? Everyone's changing, and I don't know anyone like I thought I did. It all started with that old car. It's a catalyst that's stirring up everyone's life, but I don't know why."

"I'll admit there were some strange reactions from some of the members when you asked for help to learn the original owners and what happened to them, but you became awfully upset when the Twins and Ray and Herb, and Pearl, for that matter, opted out. Are you sure the changes started with the old car, or is there a more personal explanation and you're obsessing over the car to distract yourself?"

"I don't know what you're talking about, Agnes. If I've personally changed, it started with that car — and I'm not saying I've changed," she added defensively at Agnes's skeptical expression. "I have to find out about that old Ford. Randel has to find a photo of that car and the family that owned it. Then life will return to normal. He and Candi will be safe and my curiosity will be satisfied."

Agnes frowned. "Why won't Randel and Candi be safe unless he finds the photograph?"

"Because Randel says his house has been broken into twice, but nothing's been taken. He thinks someone is after the photographs, but nobody knows about them except the reading circle."

Agnes suddenly looked concerned and gazed over Megan's shoulder, one of those long-distance stares the old bookseller sometimes engaged in when she was mulling over a problem. "I don't like this at all, Megan. Not at all." Her focus returned to Megan. "Why don't you forget about the old car. You've frightened one of our friends, and I don't think you have a really good reason."

"How do I know what kind of reason there is behind that car being dumped if I don't investigate? If I leave it alone, will everybody return to their old selves?"

"I don't think so, dear. Once change happens, there's no turning back. *You'll* learn that if you let yourself."

Megan thought of Ryan's bare chest and

her moment of lust. What if she could never be with him without breaking out in lust like a bad case of hives? What would she do then? What did she *want* to do?

Megan hastily stepped away from that thought. "Agnes, I'm going home. I can't think anymore tonight."

"Tomorrow is another day, as Scarlett O'Hara was fond of saying."

Megan smiled. "That philosophy didn't work out very well for her in the end, did it?"

"That's why *Gone with the Wind* is such a wonderful book. We don't really know."

Megan walked away feeling depressed. She didn't like enigmatic endings.

"What were you and Agnes talking about so seriously?" asked Ryan, holding Horatio's leash in one hand and pushing open the bookstore door for her with the other.

"Life," she said, adjusting the sling where Henry lay with his head resting over her heart.

The moment the door closed behind them, Horatio began circling, pulling his leash tight around Ryan's legs and sniffing the air until he decided from which direction came the ripest scent. Baying like the hunting dog he was bred to be, Horatio bolted, pulling Ryan off his feet. Instinctively, Ryan dropped the leash to brake his fall to the asphalt surface of the parking lot, while the leash whipped around his legs in reverse to free Horatio from his human anchor. Immediately, the dog darted down the alley by the bookstore.

"I told you to hang on to his leash!" yelled Megan as she clamped both arms over the sling, so Henry couldn't escape to join his partner in crime. "Get the flashlight out of the pickup and follow me." She heard Ryan cursing Horatio's parentage as she ran after the beagle.

She ran down the alley screaming the dog's name. She stopped by Agnes's parking space behind the bookstore to listen to Horatio's signature bark. She heard him down the alley that ran perpendicular to where she stood and bisected the block on which Agnes's and other business establishments stood. Suddenly, Horatio's bark turned into an eager keening that announced he had caught his prey.

Panting, Ryan caught up with her and handed her the flashlight. "Let's catch that four-legged imp of Satan and haul his fuzzy little butt back to the car. Next time you rescue an abandoned dog, find one small enough to zip up in your purse."

Megan ignored Ryan's commentary and his advice and shined the flashlight down the narrow alley. She could hear Horatio's keening and the sound of his frantic scratching. The flashlight beam caught him digging in a pile of leaves a few feet from the mouth of the alley. A few feet farther away she saw a bicycle lying on its side. Without thinking, Megan dropped the flashlight, lunged at Horatio, and grabbed his leash. "Horatio, I swear the next time you run away, I'm going to skin you alive and make a vest out of your spotted hide!"

The flashlight rolled on the asphalt by the pile of leaves where she had dropped it. The blood-splattered leaves and human leg lay exposed in its beam. Megan gasped with horror, then sighed in resignation. She hauled a protesting Horatio back to Ryan and handed him the leash. "It's not my fault! Horatio found the body."

8

The reason for murder often lies as much in the murderee as in the dispatcher.
Inspector Borges in John and Emery Bonett's *The Sound of Murder,* 1970

TIME AND AGAIN BOOKSTORE —
A FEW MINUTES LATER

I tied Horatio's leash to the leg of the couch. "I'd like to see you haul that anchor through the door, you furry little devil." He woofed at me. Horatio didn't always bay; sometimes he woofed, but not enough to ruin his reputation as a macho dog. I gave him a drink of water out of a coffee cup, then eased the sling enough that Henry could slip his head out and take a drink of water, too. Megan had stayed behind to guard the body and doubtless snoop until the police got there. I was proud of myself for not fainting, but then again, I hadn't seen any blood. Megan had handed me

Horatio's leash, then transferred Henry's sling from her neck to mine. Handling two dogs, both of whom were barking and trying to escape, didn't give me a lot of time to check out the body. In fact, all I saw of it was that one leg and foot sticking forlornly out of the pile of leaves. I stayed in the mouth of the alley that runs behind the business buildings and ends at Agnes's parking place, while Megan borrowed my pen and an out-of-date credit card receipt.

"I want to copy down the marks on the victim's forehead before the cops arrive," said Megan. "They're different from the first set of marks, like the murderer is leaving us a message in installments, but I can't read it. There's something familiar about it, but I can't figure out what. I will, though; it's just that I haven't had time to think about it yet."

"Do you recognize the victim?" I yelled over Horatio's barking while periodically hauling back on his leash and patting Henry as he emitted short puppy yips.

Megan nodded, wrinkling her forehead as she always did when she was stressed. "It's Damian Constantine, and he's been stabbed thirteen times in the back."

"My God, Maria's back at the bookstore. What do I tell her? How do I tell her?"

"Let the police do it, Ryan. They'll come get her to identify the body. I could always be wrong about it being Damian. I didn't know him that well. Personally, I wouldn't want someone telling me that you were dead if there was the smallest chance it was a mistake. It would be cruel. I don't much like Maria, in fact, I don't like her at all, but she is a member of the reading circle, so I owe her loyalty — this one time."

"Megan, we're not King Arthur and the Knights of the Round Table. We didn't take a blood oath to always be faithful and loyal."

"Call the police from the bookstore, Ryan," she said as she turned and walked back to the body.

After watering the dogs, I turned my back to the other members clustered around the checkout stand waiting for Agnes to ring up their evening's purchases, and called 911 on my cell phone. I had hardly given the dispatcher the information she'd wanted before she transferred my call.

"Lieutenant Carr, Special Crimes."

Let me be clear about this. I don't like Lieutenant Carr. He and Megan were an item until he more or less accused Megan of murder in the Lisa Heredia case on the basis of very weak circumstantial evidence. I rejoiced at his misstep, and Megan hasn't forgiven him yet. That's fine with me. Jerry Carr is tall, good looking, and worst of all, a scant six years older than she, so he was a serious rival for a time. Jerry Carr doesn't like me much either, since he sees *me* as a rival for Megan's affection. Fine with me. If that expression in Megan's eyes when she caught me without my sweater on means what I think it does, then I'm up to bat, and he's already struck out. I informed Jerry about the latest body and hung up.

I heard the sirens a few minutes later, so I called for attention. With curious faces and tense bodies, members of the reading circle drifted back to their chairs. I told them about the latest body and how they all had to wait for the police. Fear replaced curiosity as the expression of choice on their faces. Even Agnes looked frightened, but she had cause to be; she lived on Sixth Street, which this maniac had apparently picked as his private hunting preserve. Pearl Smith, too, showed some reaction to my news, but she looked more apprehensive than scared, like she knew there was a monster loose, but was more confident she could handle it. Rosemary and Lorene huddled together, and Rosemary pulled her car keys out of her purse. She and Lorene looked ready to flee back to their part of town where killers didn't roam up and down Ong Street. Maria sat scrunched down on a chair behind the twins. I wasn't sure if she was more scared that the monster might burst through the front door with his knife, or that Horatio would break loose and devour her. Randel and Candi clung together like two overage children watching a horror movie — only this wasn't a movie, it was real life, and they were scared.

If they were scared, Herb was terrified, but not of the monster. He already had been questioned by the police and had his vest seized under a search warrant. The thought of having to go through that again demolished his usual pleasant, calm exterior and left him shaking. Ray was the only person who didn't look as if he was on the verge of losing his wits to fear. He was the first to speak.

"I better go out there and wait for the cops with Megan. I don't think the street is safe enough for a woman to be out there alone."

I felt like a sniveling coward not to think of that myself.

"But, Ray, the police told us to stay here," said Lorene. "Won't they be angry?" Lorene had a crush on Ray and probably worried that he might run into the monster.

Ray patted her shoulder as he walked toward the door. "I was a cop with the Amarillo PD for thirty-five years, Lorene. I was there when Jerry Carr was a snot-nosed rookie and Sergeant Schroder had just been promoted to homicide as a detective before the Special Crimes Unit had been formed. I don't think either one of them will take offense at my sticking my nose in far enough to guard a corpse. Megan's the one who will draw their fire, and I want to deflect some of it if I can."

I stood up, adjusted Henry's sling, and walked toward him. "I'll go stay with her, Ray. It's my place." I wasn't sure what I meant by that last statement, but Ray apparently was because he smiled in sympathy.

"I know you want to be out there with her, Ryan, but I don't think your stomach's up to standing by a bloody corpse. I don't believe Megan will think so, either."

I flinched at his announcing my weakness in front of my friends. I'd never hear the last of it from Randel. "I'll stand at the mouth of the alley with my back turned."

"You wouldn't be much help if the killer was sneaking up on Megan from the other end of the alley, would you?" asked Ray. "And if you stood close enough to the corpse to offer her any real protection, then you'd faint, and the killer would step on you to get to Megan. You stay here and watch over the women with Randel and Herb." He turned and walked through the door, leaving me feeling like a babysitter.

As the door closed behind Ray, there was a large thunderclap and sizzling flash of lightning that lit up Sixth Street. The women all screamed, and Randel jumped from his seat and ran toward the door. He slammed the steel bars across the door top and bottom and flipped the knobs down to secure them. Agnes hurried over with keys and locked the dead bolt in the center of the door. The temperature began its slide down to the freezing mark as a cold north wind lashed at the building. There was another crack of thunder, and another lightning flash that once more turned the dark outside to daylight. The sound of sirens drew nearer. Horatio howled and Henry growled. I felt like howling and growling myself.

We waited.

The sirens cut off as car doors slammed. The sound of voices was muted by the bookstore's thick walls — background sounds against the continuous thunder and lightning flashes, the smell of ozone, the wind whistling around the building. Then the rain came. It hammered on the roof, against the outside walls and the door, against the window. The heat inside the store leaked out around the door and window and through the unseen pores of the building. The cold seeped in, a damp cold that everyone knew was worse than dry cold. The heat and the cold skirmished until a monster clap of thunder and a bolt of lightning that seemed to strike the earth next to the bookstore. In the quiet afterwards somebody or something jiggled the door knob. Then it hammered on the door. We waited. No one wanted to open that door.

Then another peal of thunder so loud the door and window shook, followed by another bolt of lightning that sizzled from sky to earth and ended in a burst of light like a Roman candle outside the window. We all heard something crack and a dull crash as whatever it was hit the ground.

And the lights went out.

The women screamed again and so did I. It was the moment in the movie when the mad killer with the butcher knife suddenly appears behind the teenager in her nightie who is looking through her CDs while waiting for mom and dad to come home from the Carsons' dinner party. Stereotypical scene in a stereotypical slasher movie, but there's a reason for that: nothing scares the hell out of the average person like the unexpected. It doesn't matter if you know that the electricity often fails in a thunderstorm. This is a *bookstore,* a business establishment. You don't expect the lights to go off in a business establishment. I couldn't ever remember it happening to me at the shoe store or the grocery store. Horatio howled, and Henry's head popped out of his sling. He tucked his head under my chin and growled that little puppy growl.

In the flashes of lightning I saw Agnes go behind her desk. She started setting candles on the checkout desk and lighting them. Soon there were candles on the coffee table and along the wall behind the chairs. Flickering candles may be romantic on the dining room table when you're having dinner with a woman, or in the bedroom when you have a beautiful, naked woman in bed waiting for you, but not in a bookstore in the middle of the mother of all thunderstorms and somebody is hammering on the front door.

I saw Agnes go behind her desk again, and then I heard a sound like someone ratcheting a shotgun — I know that sound because I hunt pheasant during the season. Then

Agnes, tiny, elderly Agnes, turned the corner of the checkout counter with a shiny, lethal-looking shotgun that was nearly as long as she was tall. She walked toward the door, stopped, threw her keys to Randel, and raised the shotgun. "Open it," she told Randel. Whoever was behind that door better come in with his hands up, or he was liable to find a part of his anatomy blown across to the opposite side of the street.

Randel unlocked the door, threw the bars back, and ducked behind the door as it opened and a soaking wet Megan burst in followed by Sergeant Jenner in a plastic raincoat. They shouted in unison, "Don't shoot!"

Agnes ejected the shells from her shotgun and cradled it in her arms barrel down. "You should have identified yourselves. Shut the door; you're letting in the rain. Megan, go back to my bathroom, dry off, and find some of my clothes that might fit. Sergeant Jenner, please take off your raincoat and drop it on the welcome mat. Do you want a cup of coffee to take the chill off? It should still be hot."

"Ma'am, please put the shotgun down on the floor and move away from it," said Jenner. I couldn't tell if he was sweating because he could have been missing part of his anatomy, or if it was rain dripping down his face. From his pallor, I would guess the first of the two alternatives.

"Sergeant Jenner, don't be absurd. This is my gun, and I'm standing in a building I own, so don't quote me lines from the police handbook or a TV cop show. Serve yourself a cup of coffee and sit down on the couch next to Professor Stevens — if you're not afraid of dogs — and I'll put away my shotgun behind the desk. With a madman running loose on Sixth Street, an old lady like me needs an equalizer. Nothing equals like a double-barrel shotgun with double-aught buckshot."

Jenner's eyes widened, and I reconsidered my scenario. Jenner wouldn't have been looking for a piece of his anatomy across the street; he would have been looking for scraps of his anatomy. Double-aught buckshot will blow a man into little pieces. If a madman with a knife broke into her bedroom at night, of course Agnes would want real stopping power. I don't blame her.

"But, ma'am, that gun is dangerous — and double-aught buckshot — my God!"

"The gun's not dangerous, Sergeant, I am." She gestured toward the refreshment table. "The coffee is over there. And have some Toll House cookies. Mrs. Pittman and

Mrs. Getz baked them, and they are delicious."

Jenner poured himself some coffee and picked up a handful of Toll House cookies. He sat down next to me. "What's that in the sling, Doc?"

I despise being called Doc like I'm the old family practitioner. "Call me Ryan or Professor Stevens, but not Doc."

"Sure, Doc — I mean Ryan."

"And this is Henry. He's a puppy border collie, we think."

"And you always carry him around in a sling around your neck?"

The question sounded respectful and not sarcastic, so I answered. "No, but you have to bond with puppies as soon as you bring them home, so they will grow up people-friendly." I thought I heard a snicker from Randel's direction.

He nodded his head. "That's what the doctor told us about our oldest son, but we were young, ignorant parents and didn't know how you bonded with a newborn, so we took turns holding him all the time. By the time he was six weeks old, he was the damnedest spoiled rotten kid you ever saw. Even my mother thought he was rotten, and grandmothers are supposed to think their first grandkid is perfect. Took us two years

170

to break the bond, and by that time he was into the Terrible Twos. If my wife and I hadn't slipped up a couple of times, he would've been an only child." All the women laughed except Candi. She didn't have any kids, so she didn't understand what we were talking about.

"It's easy to spoil kids. My wife and I were lucky. We were young and stupid and ended up with stairsteps: two kids a year apart and a set of twins two years after that. And Megan spent a lot of time at our house, too. My oldest daughter was her best friend."

"I arrested her mother a couple of times when I was a rookie, disturbing the peace, leading a march without a permit, things like that. I can see why she would rather be at your house. So you must feel like her father, huh?" he asked, his mouth full of Toll House cookies.

If I could've growled at him, I would have, then I would've bitten Randel. I definitely heard him snickering. "No! I do not feel like her father!"

"So that's how it is between you and Megan Clark. I told the lieutenant he was jealous for nothing."

I bared my teeth — really. "What's that supposed to mean — so that's how it is between Megan and me?" Out of the corner of my eye I saw Agnes and the twins smiling.

He choked on his Toll House cookie, and I took great pleasure in pounding his back. He took a swallow of coffee and scooted away from me to the other end of the couch. "Nothing! I didn't mean anything disrespectful, just commenting on how close you must be with her nearly growing up in your house. You must feel like you got to protect her even if she is grown up. But you don't have to worry about the lieutenant. He's got a lot of respect for her. Talks all the time about how smart she is."

As far as I was concerned as long as Jerry Carr wasn't neutered, he was a threat. "Didn't you have something you had to do, Sergeant? Someone you had to talk to?"

Suddenly the humor vanished from his face, and he looked older and more like a responsible cop than a kid. "Yeah, but I wish you hadn't reminded me. I've done this a couple of times, but to tell the truth, I'd rather attend an autopsy."

I had to tell my kids that their mother died while holding my hand, and I thought attending an autopsy sounded like a better choice than telling Maria Constantine that she was a widow.

He put down his coffee cup, got up and

brushed crumbs off his jacket, then took forever to walk the few steps across the reading area to Maria Constantine. He knelt down by her chair and whispered to her. He might not like to carry this kind of message to a soon-to-be grieving woman, but he was good at it. Sympathy oozed from his pores, and so did sincerity. I couldn't imagine that Schroder or Jerry Carr would do as well.

"No! No! You're lying to me! Damian told me cops sometimes lied like you when they suspect someone of murder. And you must suspect me. You served a search warrant on me and took my beautiful new blouse because you thought I was lying to you. You're scum for doing this and I'm going to tell Damian! I'm going to tell the chief." She started beating Jenner's head and shoulders with her fists. "Liar! Liar!"

She was working herself into a hysterical fit, or maybe she was already in the middle of one. I didn't know because I had never seen a woman act like this. Megan slammed open the bookstore's back door and ran down an aisle of books to Maria and Jenner. She grabbed Maria's hands and held them with that surprising strength that no one credited such a small woman as having. She leaned over and whispered rapidly into

Maria's ear, then released the woman's hands. Dazed, Maria looked from Megan to Jenner and back again. They both nodded, Megan with her face so sad that I wanted to cry myself.

Then Maria spoke, her voice clear of any sound of tears. What was stranger, so were her eyes. She might have been asking what the weather was like outside. "I want to see Damian."

That was it. She still didn't believe them and wanted to see for herself. That explained the normal voice and dry eyes. Jenner was already shaking his head. "You don't have to identify him, ma'am. Sergeant Schroder and Lieutenant Carr already did. You stay here with Dr. Clark, and I'll get you a cup of coffee."

He had barely taken a step toward the refreshment table when she screamed, "I want to see him. It's my right!" She pushed Megan away and started for the door with that same kind of determination it took to climb Mount Everest or lead men behind enemy lines.

It took more than a shove to stop Megan Clark. She took a couple of fast steps and wrapped her arms around Maria's waist from behind, enfolding the taller woman in a death grip. Five years of rowing for various universities here and abroad had endowed Megan with tremendous strength in her arms and shoulders that wasn't apparent when you looked at her. She turned Maria around and forced her back toward a chair where the other women were waiting.

When Maria was sitting down five women surrounded her, holding her hands and shoulders, brushing the hair back from her face, lifting the coffee cup to her lips. Sergeant Jenner stood shifting his feet, but not interfering.

Megan knelt at Maria's feet again. "Do you believe me now, Maria, that Damian is dead?" When Maria nodded, Megan continued. "Don't look at him now. He wouldn't want you seeing him dirty and helpless looking. Wait until the funeral director calls you — when Damian is wearing the uniform he was so proud of, when he looks at peace. But remember what you're looking at is just a shell. The real Damian kissed you goodbye this morning and left for work. Can you remember him as he was this morning?"

Maria nodded, and Megan got to her feet and walked toward me. Her hair was still damp and curled in dozens of ringlets around her face. She looked exhausted and vulnerable, and I wanted to pick her up and carry her to the pickup and take her home with me, where I would tuck her into bed with a cup of hot chocolate. Megan always loved hot chocolate.

Behind her there was silence except for the sympathetic murmurs of the women. Megan was almost to the couch where I knew she would curl up next to me and rest her head on her chest. I don't know what she would be looking for when she came to me for comfort, whether she sought a father or a friend or a lover. At the moment it didn't matter.

That's when the keening started, followed by the sobs that rose to a crescendo, broke, and repeated. Maria Constantine reminded me of a hired mourner at a funeral in the Middle East, except she didn't rip her garments or pour ashes on her head.

Megan hesitated, then circled the coffee table. "Ryan, hold me."

"Always, sweetheart," I said as I raised my arm so she could snuggle against my left side where my heart is.

She curled against me and lifted her head. If we hadn't been in public, I would have kissed her, and not one of those quickies that are by nature and intent ambiguous. I would linger until she pushed me away. Maybe my eyes revealed my thoughts, but she caught her breath and her face expressed a yearning I never saw before. Alas, that kiss was not to be, to be poetic about it. Henry popped his head out of the sling, freed his front legs, and with a tiny white paw on each of Megan's cheeks to hold her still, he began a thorough licking of her face that said as clearly as if he had spoken: "I love you, Human Person, and I want to make you feel better."

It was that very instant that the door opened and Jerry Carr entered, followed by Sergeant Schroder and Ray Roberts. Standing dripping in the doorway, all three focused on the scene on the couch.

9

Just as no man was a hero to his valet, so no member of a Profession was sea-green incorruptible to a policeman.

Catherine Aird's *Passing Strange,* 1980

TIME AND AGAIN BOOKSTORE — SAME TIME

Jenner felt sorry for the professor. He looked — not ridiculous exactly, but like a man caught unaware while picking his nose or chewing his toenails. He looked foolish, Jenner decided finally. This good-looking man with wavy black hair barely greying at the temples, broad shoulders, turquoise eyes, and a lean, muscular build that most men fifteen years younger would envy, is sitting on a couch carrying a puppy in a sling around his neck. He would look effeminate if he hadn't been holding Megan Clark. If Jenner ever saw a man who wanted to jump a woman's bones more than Ryan Stevens wanted to jump Megan Clark's, he couldn't remember it. There must be more going on than Jerry Carr knew, and the lieutenant had good reason to be jealous. He had probable cause, as a cop would say.

Stevens knew he looked foolish, Jenner decided, since the professor's face was turning red and his whole body tensed like a man on the defensive.

"Heh, heh, heh." Schroder's laugh sounded like it came from a cartoon soundtrack.

"What the devil are you doing, Stevens? Carrying a dog around like that. You got some kind of maternal instinct you been hiding?"

If possible, Jenner thought the professor's face turned even redder. "We're bonding," he told Schroder in a snappish way.

"It's my puppy," said Megan. "I asked Ryan to hold Henry while I waited for the police."

"Henry being the dog," said Schroder over the sounds of the beagle tied to the couch.

"Yes, and the other one is Horatio."

"And you brought them to the bookstore?"

"Yes, so the three of us could bond. It's very important to bond with a puppy as soon as possible."

Schroder rubbed his chin. "I know your

mother. I arrested her a few times before I went to Special Crimes. I don't remember what cause she was supporting, but she damn near caused a riot at City Hall. I guess fruit doesn't fall far from the tree."

"If you're inferring I'm as eccentric as my mother, I'm not. I'm a librarian, I pay my taxes, and I occasionally help the police. You may remember the mummy case last month."

"You're not eccentric, but you just happen to stumble over bodies every time you turn around. What's your excuse for finding this one?"

"I didn't find it! It was Horatio who found the body this time, not me. As a matter of fact, it was Horatio who found the skeleton last month."

"He ever been trained as a cadaver dog?"

"No! It's just all coincidence. I didn't get up one morning and decide I'll find a body today. I can't explain it, Sergeant, it just happens."

Lieutenant Jerry Carr spoke for the first time. Jenner felt sorry for him, too. Must be hard to act professional when you want to wring somebody's neck, specifically Ryan Stevens's neck.

"Megan, I want to warn you to stay out of this investigation. I'll charge you with interfering with a public official if you do. I mean it this time. I don't care if my mother won't speak to me again if I do. My mother may think acting like Nancy Drew is just wonderful, but I don't."

She sprang from the couch and stood with clenched fists. "But I can help, Jerry. Those marks on the victims' foreheads for example. I think they are examples of a real language. If I can study them, maybe I'll be able to translate. I speak six languages besides English, including three Middle Eastern languages. Well, I don't actually speak a couple of them because they are dead languages, but I can translate them."

"No, Megan. If we decide we need help, we'll check with the language department at West Texas A&M University. Besides, we've pretty well decided that they are satanic symbols of some kind, which would make sense when you combine the marks with the thirteen stab wounds."

"I don't know, Lieutenant," blurted Jenner before he could stop the words. "I haven't seen any marks like those used by any of the nuts we arrest who claim they're Satanists." He caught the stares directed at him by Schroder and the lieutenant, but he continued anyway. "I don't think it would hurt anything if she looked into those marks. She's just as educated as those professors at WT."

"Thank you for your contribution to this discussion, Sergeant Jenner. We'll talk further back at my office," said Jerry Carr. Jenner knew what kind of talk that would be. He was going to get a royal butt-chewing from the lieutenant for contradicting him in front of civilians.

"Excuse me, Lieutenant," said Pearl Smith, smiling at Jerry Carr as one professional speaking to another. "Sergeant Jenner is correct. Those symbols are not satanic symbols unless those nuts, as the sergeant calls them, have invented new ones. As you know, I earn my living dabbling in the occult arts — reading palms and telling fortunes with tarot cards — so I am familiar with satanic symbols. I'm not a Satanist in any way shape or form. I find the real ones misguided and possibly emotionally disturbed with their standing inside circles and reading spells out of old books to try to raise demons from Hell. Who in their right mind would want loose demons, anyway? They're pathetic overgrown children, the ones I know, and I know most, if not all, of the Satanists in Amarillo. They come to me to have their fortunes read and spout their nonsense. Many of them play at it because people love secret societies with passwords and handshakes and so forth. They love the idea of being in a witch's coven because it's naughty and most people disapprove. It's a belated rebellion they should have experienced as teenagers. But the one thing I can tell you with certainty: none of the Satanists are dangerous. None of them would commit these horrible murders. They certainly wouldn't attack a young, strong man like Damian Constantine."

"How come you're a fortune teller, Ms. Smith? You sound like an educated woman," said Schroder.

"I am. Berkeley, class of 1954. But I can make more money as a fortune teller than I can teaching biology, and I don't have to put up with teenagers. It's a sad commentary on American society, isn't it?"

There was silence as everyone thought about a graduate of Berkeley telling fortunes for a living. And she even graduated before that university started turning out nuts in the late sixties. Jenner still wasn't sure she was telling the truth. There was something phony about her story, or maybe some of Schroder's skepticism was rubbing off.

Schroder stuck an unlit cigarette in the corner of his mouth and turned back to Megan Clark, who was looking appreciative of Pearl Smith's support.

"So, Ms. Clark, you just happened to be in the general vicinity of the victim when your dog found him?" asked Schroder.

"That's right. And it's Dr. Clark."

"Well, then, Dr. Clark, how come dead bodies just show up when you happen to be on Sixth Street at the bookstore? Do you think the murderer happens to have your schedule?"

Megan's face registered surprise, then what Jenner would swear was speculation. Megan Clark and speculation seemed a lethal combination to him. "I wouldn't know, Sergeant Schroder, since I don't know who the murderer is." Then she mumbled something under her breath that made the professor look at her with something like horror.

"Where were you from about five o'clock on, Miss Clark?" asked Schroder.

"I left my job at the library at five o'clock and drove to the vet's to pick up Henry. When you buy a dog at the pound, they're neutered and given their shots at a local vet's. I drove home, changed clothes, fashioned my sling and walked over to Ryan's. He was going to have to drive to the bookstore, because I was carrying Henry. It's very —"

"— important to start bonding immediately with a dog. I know, I already heard it from the professor. And Dr. Stevens, you can corroborate Dr. Clark's alibi?"

"Yes, but I think it's ridiculous for you to even question Megan, much less suspect her of murder." Jenner thought the professor was working himself into a real mad.

Schroder rolled his cigarette to the other side of his mouth. "You'd be surprised how many people who find bodies are also the people who killed them. If I were you," he said to Megan, "I'd try to avoid finding any more dead bodies. Another body just might be the straw that broke the camel's back, meaning me."

"There'll be more bodies, Sergeant. This is a serial killer, a ritualistic serial killer, and he won't stop short of getting caught or dying himself. You know that as well as I do. I don't know why you won't admit it instead of standing around here questioning all of us."

"Now, I don't have the benefit of your schooling, but I learned to rule out the obvious first, and the obvious suspects are the people who knew the deceased."

"I didn't kill my husband!" screamed Maria Constantine who wasn't too lost in her grief not to be listening. He hoped

Schroder wouldn't set her off again.

"I'm not accusing you, Mrs. Constantine. I need to know where you were from five until seven o'clock just so I can eliminate you. You know I have to ask you, ma'am." For Schroder, he sounded sympathetic.

She drew a sobbing breath, and Jenner braced himself, but she sounded in control of herself when she answered, if you discount the tears rolling down her cheeks. "I know you do, Sergeant, and I'm sorry I'm such a mess. But I never expected to be a widow at my age." She paused and wiped her eyes. "I fixed an early dinner, so Damian could go to work, did a few things around the house, and I drove to the bookstore. I arrived a little before seven. You can ask Agnes." She paused again, stifled another sob, then let loose on Schroder. "Why don't you get out like Megan says, and find the real killer?"

"Fair enough, Mrs. Constantine. Did your husband have any enemies?"

"He was a cop, of course he had enemies. But that wouldn't explain Old Ben, would it? I don't think a cop and an old drunk would have the same enemies."

"That's true, Mrs. Constantine," admitted Schroder. "I'll be over tomorrow with a search warrant for your house."

"What! You've already been in my house. Why do you want to come back? You and your partner will be searching my husband's underwear drawer while I'm in the middle of calling relatives and making funeral arrangements. How callous can you be, Sergeant? Megan, you talk to these people." She covered her face with her hands and started keening again.

Megan Clark looked up when Mrs. Constantine called to her, but to Jenner the lady doc seemed more uncertain than sympathetic, like something about the new widow bothered her. She remained silent.

Lieutenant Carr looked like he had just been caught stealing candy from a baby. "Sergeant Schroder, do you really think it's necessary?"

"S-O-P, Lieutenant. We always search a victim's residence."

"I know, Sergeant. I'm sorry I said anything." Jenner thought the lieutenant was awfully soft-hearted to be in his position.

Schroder turned to Mrs. Pittman and Mrs. Getz and asked about their alibis. Jenner thought Schroder was wasting his time. Those two old ladies looked old enough to have one foot in the grave, and too frail to be murdering anybody, except maybe for swatting a fly.

"Sergeant Schroder," said one of the ladies. He thought it was Mrs. Getz, but they both looked so much alike, it was hard to tell. "Rosemary and I were together from two o'clock up to this very minute. We were baking Toll House cookies for the meeting, then I took a shower and prepared dinner for the two of us. I fixed linguini with clam sauce and we had a glass of white wine with it. Then we arranged the cookies on a plate and drove here in Rosemary's car."

"And I suppose you corroborate Mrs. Getz's alibi?" he asked Mrs. Pittman.

The old lady didn't stand up, but somehow you felt she did, thought Jenner. Mrs. Pittman had a presence about her that demanded attention and respect. "Sergeant Schroder, I hope by that question that you're not indirectly accusing Lorene of lying? I'm outraged that you would even think it."

"Just covering the bases, ma'am," Schroder mumbled, looking embarrassed. Jenner didn't recall him looking embarrassed as long as he'd known him.

"Then go find another baseball field, Sergeant, because you're about to be ejected from this one," said Mrs. Pittman with a commanding air that Jenner concluded she was born with. Must be old money.

Maria Constantine's keening had tapered off into quiet sobs as Schroder turned to the nerdy-looking guy with the goatee. "What about you?"

"My name is Professor Randel Anderson, and Candi and I were together all afternoon. We live together." Jenner thought he said it like he was still surprised at his good luck. His Candi wasn't much of a looker, but she had nice skin and was on the buxom side. Anderson wouldn't have to toss the sheets to find her.

Schroder finally looked at Agnes Caldwell. Jenner didn't envy him. This old lady was as tough as a marine drill sergeant. He still remembered that shotgun.

"Sergeant, I own this bookstore, and at present I don't have an assistant. In between waiting on customers, unpacking books and bar-coding them, and straightening the shelves, I just happened to find the time to go stab Officer Constantine thirteen times. If you would like copies of my sales receipts for the afternoon, you are welcome to them. In addition to a cash register receipt, which automatically records the date and time as well as price, tax, and total due, I also hand out an old-fashioned, hand-written one with my customer's name at the top and titles of the books she purchases. You can question

189

each and every one of the customers if you like, but please don't leave the impression that I'm a suspect. I wouldn't like that all. In fact, I would like it so little that I would consult with Herb about a possible slander suit. But I'm sure I won't have to."

She smiled at Schroder, and a chill went up my spine. I once arrested a man on a routine traffic stop who had his wife in the back seat. She was beaten half to death. That man smiled at me just like Agnes Caldwell smiled at Schroder.

"I'll be sure and remember that, ma'am," said Schroder, and walked over to Herbert Jackson III.

Lieutenant Carr said something to Schroder too quietly for Jenner to hear, but he'd bet next week's paycheck that Carr was telling him to be careful and not take a wrong step with the lawyer. Jenner agreed with the lieutenant. Jackson looked like a mild-mannered mouse, but so did Clark Kent right before he disappeared into a phone booth.

"Mr. Jackson, sir, you've heard what I asked the others. Would you tell me where you were between the times we have reason to believe the murder was committed?"

Herbert Jackson III cleared his throat. "I had appointments at the office until six o'clock. I stay open late on Tuesdays and Wednesdays to see certain clients who can't come in until after work. You may ask them; I'll give you their names. Then I went out for a quick dinner at Amarillo Country Club, then drove here. I did not murder Mr. Constantine. I don't know Mr. Constantine except by sight. I have personally never met him. My only connection with him is knowing his wife. That will be all I have to say, gentlemen. If you have further questions, you will have to call my attorney and set up an appointment that will be convenient."

Lieutenant Carr motioned Schroder and Jenner over to a corner for a conference. "What do you think, Schroder? Did you hear any false notes in anybody's statements?"

Schroder rolled his cigarette to the other side of this mouth, finally took it out, and dropped it in his pocket. "I'll check out the alibis for Jackson, Caldwell, and the fortune teller to see if they hold up, and if the other people weren't lying, then we struck out, Lieutenant. But I still don't trust Megan Clark. How can one woman run across so many dead bodies and not be guilty of murder? It's against nature."

"I don't understand it, either, Schroder. I don't think even Stevens understands. It's like she's some kind of a magnet for murder victims. I know for sure that she's a magnet for trouble."

The three police officers turned to stare at Megan as she was gently transferring Henry and his sling from Ryan's neck to her own.

"Did trouble ever come in such a cute package, Schroder?" asked Carr as the three men left the bookstore.

10

What did it matter where you lay once you were dead? . . . You were dead, you were sleeping the big sleep, you were not bothered by things like that.

Philip Marlowe in Raymond Chandler's
The Big Sleep, 1939

THE WILLOWS RETIREMENT AND
CONVALESCENCE HOME —
THE NEXT MORNING

Manuela, tell the cook I appreciate the bacon and eggs. It was real kind of her to accommodate an old woman. The chocolate cake was fine, too. My family enjoyed it. What did you say? You're sorry my family is so small? Manuela, you got to remember that my children are old. Lord, I can't believe how old. My grandkids are all grown and scattered. They don't live in Amarillo anymore. But one of my granddaughters did come to visit before my birthday. You remember her, the one with the sour face. She looked like she'd been eating green persimmons. I can't say that she's pleasant company, though. She's one of these know-it-alls. Knows better than you what's good for you. I just let her talk and nod every once in awhile. She's happy and that way we don't get in an argument. Oh, you think I shouldn't talk like that about my own granddaughter. Let me tell you something, Manuela. Once you pass the one hundred-year-old mark, you ought to be able to say anything about anybody and not be chastised for it.

"How do you like my new word? Chastised. I read it in one of my books and thought I'd use it if the opportunity arose. Person shouldn't ever stop learning even if they're older than Methuselah. Here, take this tray back, but bring me my glasses off the bureau over there. I can't figure it out about my glasses. They must wander around at night, because they are never where I think I left them. Must be losing my short-term memory. Hand me my newspaper before you leave. Thank you, I appreciate it. Oh, Manuela, close that door, will you? Can't have folks listening to me talk to myself. It's none of their business."

Now that she's gone, I'll read the front

page again. A cop murdered. That's a shame. It just burns me up when I hear people complaining about the police not doing the job. Sure they're doing the job, but my Lord, there is so much job for them to do. Take this latest murder for example. Nasty business that was, but it's a lot nastier than what newspaper readers in Amarillo know. But I do. Got my own unimpeachable source. This one is just like the last one: nasty marks on his head and thirteen stab wounds on his back. That redheaded Megan Clark found this one, too, though the paper says that a resident's dog found it. Of course, that dog happened to belong to Megan Clark. I wonder what it is about that girl that she finds bodies so often. Here I am, one hundred years old, and I haven't found but one body my whole life. You might say I was on the scene for that one, so I don't suppose it counts. Still, that Megan Clark has a nose for the dead. That's a heavy burden for a young woman to carry.

AMARILLO PUBLIC LIBRARY, MAIN BRANCH — SAME DAY

"Jared Johnson! Is that you?"

The towheaded little boy grinned. His hair was neatly combed, his face and hands clean, and his clothes, while not new, at least fit him. He was a changed little boy from the first time Megan saw him a year ago when he wanted to know if tooth fairies could get sick. He was the only witness in her first case, and his story had helped break the case.

"It's me all right, Miss Megan."

He hadn't called her that last year, but Megan decided she liked it. It was informal, but not disrespectful.

"Don't you look spiffy, and taller." In fact, another few inches and Jared would match her five feet, two inches in very thick-soled shoes.

"I've grown three inches since we caught the witch," he said proudly.

"I can tell, Jared. You're nearly as tall as I am."

He tilted his head, his bright blue eyes serious as he studied her. "But you're kind of short, aren't you?"

If he were an adult, she would skewer him with a sharp-tongued response. She sighed. "Yes, Jared, I'm short. But fairies are too, and look how powerful they are." She propped her elbows on the reference desk and leaned over. "So, Jared, what kind of help do you need today? Do you need to know how tall giants are, or if trolls really turn to stone in sunlight?"

He pursed his lips and shook his head. "I know about all that stuff. I saw *Lord of the Rings* three times."

She had seen the entire trilogy six times and bought the collector's edition DVD. She was glad that he was watching good movies instead of ones where the protagonist wore a mask and carried a sharp knife. "No giants or trolls today. What else do you need to know?"

"I need a book on sails. We're studying sails in science class."

His class must be studying wind velocity and the rest of weather's elements. "Okay, step behind the reference desk and I'll let you sit on my work stool, and we'll pull up the card catalog on my computer."

Jared grinned and walked inside the hollow, rectangular reference desk. His eyes darted around its interior, checking out all the shelves and cubby holes. "This is really cool, Miss Megan."

After a few keystrokes Megan accessed the card catalog and typed in sails on the subject line. The first screen came up, and she scrolled down to find an easy reading book on sails. "Here's one that sounds good: *The Wind in My Sails* by Roger G. Chandler."

Jared frowned and shook his head. "No,

that's the wrong book. I need one on sails."

"Sails?"

"Yes, sails."

Puzzled, Megan thought a minute. It was a good thing she didn't take that job in the children's department, because she was a total loss at understanding what kids were talking about most of the time. "Can you spell it for me, Jared?"

"Sure. I made an A in spelling last six weeks. C-e-l-l-s, sails."

She spent way too much time with the educated crowd. She needed to rub elbows with the common folk who still spoke with a Texas twang. "Cells, of course. I guess I wouldn't make an A in spelling."

"I don't figure you would — but it's okay. You know a lot of other stuff, bones and dead bodies and things."

Megan quickly found a suitable book on cells and wrote down the information for him. "So, Jared, what are you doing out of school today? This is a school day, isn't it?"

Jared looked guilty and avoided her eyes. "Well, there wasn't much going on today in school, and when I heard about the skeleton from Freddy Garcia, who goes home for lunch and walked by the old laundry, I figured I'd learn a lot more skipping the afternoon and going to check it out."

Megan felt her heart beat faster. "A skeleton? Someone found a skeleton in the old laundry?"

Jared squinted one eye and thought. "Not *in* the laundry exactly, more like in between the walls."

Megan picked up the phone and pushed a button, conscious that she couldn't tell a lie in front of Jared. A voice on the other end of the line answered. "Miss Crosby, would you cover the reference desk until the others get back from lunch — and put me down for a half day of vacation." She spoke rapidly so Miss Crosby wouldn't have a chance to speak, and if she couldn't speak, she couldn't say no. A skeleton was an unusual occurrence, and she didn't intend to miss out. "A skeleton has been discovered on Sixth Street, and the police will need my expertise to determine age, gender, and cause of death. I'm sorry I have to leave you short-handed like this, but the police don't have another anthropologist to turn to who has my training. I'll see you in the morning. 'Bye."

She hung up and grabbed her purse. "Jared, would you like to go look at a skeleton with me?"

His eyes grew as wide as if it was Christmas morning and he had just seen what

Santa left under the tree, and he nodded his head until Megan feared it would fly off his shoulders. Megan smiled at him. Kids were so easy to please.

There was a crowd standing around the back of the old laundry, including Special Crimes evidence techs, Sergeant Jenner, and the Justice of the Peace, she noticed. No sign of Sergeant Schroder or Jerry Carr, thank God. There would be nobody to interfere with her. She pushed through the crowd toward Jenner.

The old laundry was a narrow, rectangular building that dated from the twenties and had stood vacant since the late fifties or early sixties. It had been an eyesore and a target for vandals on Sixth Street as long as Megan could remember. Apparently it was also a dump site for bodies.

Megan touched Sergeant Jenner's sleeve. "Hello, Sergeant, I got here as soon as I could. As a physical anthropologist with the most training with bones in the Panhandle area, I wasn't surprised that you would be needing me." A clever use of words, she thought. She inferred that she had been called by Jerry Carr without actually lying. Ryan wouldn't approve, but she would be old and grey before Ryan approved of her involving herself with a murder victim, either fully intact or in the form of bones.

"I didn't know Schroder was calling you," said Jenner, visibly unsure of whether to welcome her or check with Schroder first.

"He's smart that he did," said the Justice of the Peace, an elderly African-American gentleman that Megan met during her first case. "Young lady, I'm happy to see you. I can pronounce the victim — any fool can do that seeing as how he's nothing but bones — but I'm not happy sending him downstate for an autopsy. He's not just any deceased; he's special. Been in an unconsecrated grave for the Lord only knows how long. I feel we owe him the respect of keeping him here at home to be tended to, so you just do what needs to be done."

Megan felt a growing elation. She was going to have her cake and eat it too. "Then you're officially ordering me to do the autopsy, sir?"

"Absolutely. Go to it, girl, and send your report to me. I have to be getting home now. That wet, cold weather yesterday aggravated my wife's arthritis something terrible, and I need to look after her. You get to work now, girl, and bless you." The JP hobbled away with the help of a cane.

Megan squatted down by the grave. "In

my opinion you ought to demand to be kept in the loop, Sergeant. It seems to me that your input in cases is not appreciated for the well-thought-out advice that it is. Last night, for instance, your suggestion that I attempt to translate the marks on the victims's foreheads is a valid one. But instead of considering your suggestion, Jerry and Sergeant Schroder just looked mad that you had said anything. I'm disappointed in Jerry."

Jenner blushed with pleasure. "I try to think up ways to help."

"Of course you do. But we had better get to work. Why don't you tell me what happened while my assistant runs back to my truck and brings me the big metal box that looks like a tool box."

Jenner looked around at the crowd. "Where is your assistant?"

She pointed to Jared darting through the crowd toward her truck. "There. His name is Jared Johnson."

"A kid!" Jenner said.

"I'm his mentor," she said as though her assistants were always seven-year-olds, and he shouldn't find anything odd about it. "You were about to tell me what happened here, Sergeant."

"Mr. Phillips over there in the business

suit talking to Mr. Ramsey, the contractor in the hard hat, bought the building about two weeks ago. He's going to remodel it as a gift store for his daughter. She's in a wheelchair and unmarried, and he thought this would be a good way for her to make a living for herself. He hired Mr. Ramsey to do the remodeling. So Ramsey shows up with his crew, and they start demolishing the back of the building. According to Ramsey the building had been added on to back in the thirties, and whoever did the job botched it. The concrete foundation was crumbling, and there were two walls, one in front of the other, like the other contractor poured the foundation too short, and to cover his butt, he threw up an inside wall and an outside wall three feet farther on. No foundation between the inner and outer walls, just plain dirt. I don't guess the owner noticed that the space inside was three feet shorter than the building on the outside. Somebody dug a six-foot-long hole between the two walls and just laid our victim in there and threw a few inches of dirt on top. Over the years the dirt must have settled, because when the outer wall came down, there he was with his skull plain as day. When Mr. Ramsey moved the old dryers out, he found where somebody had cut a four-foot doorway in the inner wall and patched it up when he was through. Did a good job of the patching, too. Ramsey said you couldn't hardly tell if you didn't look for it."

He stopped and ran his fingers through his hair. They stood looking down at the grave. "So, what are you going to do first, Doc?"

"Borrow a couple of white sheets and some gloves from the evidence techs and start excavating our friend," she said as Jared ran up with her dig kit.

It was nearly five o'clock before Schroder and Jerry Carr showed up, both of them with faces like thunderclouds. By that time Megan had uncovered the skeleton, which turned out to be a fairly easy job. There had been no disturbance to the grave by scavengers such as rats, and all of the bones were present and intact. She and two evidence techs had transferred the skeleton from its grave to one of the white sheets. Then she had taken several soil samples from the bottom of the grave, removed a pitted metal object and a tarnished penny. She polished the penny as well as she could, then examined it with her magnifying glass. She dropped it in a paper evidence bag and paused to think. After a minute or so she picked up the other artifact found in the grave. Megan rubbed the metal object to get as much of the dirt and grime of the decades off as possible. She noticed that the base of the figurine had been broken off another object. She sat back on her heels studying it. It was a figurine of a woman holding something in one hand above her head — a sword or spear as nearly as she could make out. Whatever it was, it was still sharp despite the years it had laid in that grave.

She handed it to Jenner. "Send someone over with this to that old car. See if it fits the spot where the radiator cap should be — and remind him, Sergeant, that in those days the radiators were outside at the front of the car."

"You think the skeleton has something to do with that old car?" asked Jenner.

"The penny was dated 1937, Sergeant. If you look at the change in your pocket, you will find that most of them are only one or two years old. At most, maybe five. Since the car's licence plate is for 1938, I am assuming the car and the skeleton are connected. It would be a coincidence if they weren't, don't you think?"

"Sounds reasonable to me."

"There's one way to prove it. There's a

tiny nick on this rib that would be approximately in front of her heart, with a narrow cut mark from the indentation to the edge of the rib. The tip of the cap fits the nick and the cut mark. My theory is that someone broke off this radiator cap — if it is a radiator cap — and holding the base between two fingers of his fist, someone stabbed her in the back. When she fell, her weight pulled downward on the metal tip, causing it to move in the opposite direction and leave the cut mark on her rib. She was a tall woman for her time. Without measuring her long bones and applying the correct equation, I estimate her height as between five feet eight and five feet ten, so she was no lightweight."

"And you're sure it's a she?" asked Jenner.

"Absolutely. The pelvic structure, the ridge above her brows, and her chin prove conclusively that our friend is female. As for who murdered her and buried her between the walls, I don't know, but it had to be someone who knew about the two walls, and that means someone on Sixth Street."

Jared, squatting on the ground in an identical pose as Megan, started clapping his hands. "You're so smart, Miss Megan, and this is so much fun! I want to be an anthropoglogist when I grow up."

She smoothed his hair down. "That's anthropologist, Jared, and I think you will be a brilliant one."

Jenner climbed to his feet, brushed off his trousers, and picked up the paper evidence bag. "I'll have someone run this radiator cap over to the impound area and see if we've got a match." Whistling, he strolled toward the Special Crimes van parked in front of the old building.

"What do we do next, Miss Megan?" asked Jared.

"Not a thing, kid," said Sergeant Schroder, pulling both up by their collars. He turned around, still holding them so that they faced a glowering Jerry Carr.

"Let them go, Sergeant. They won't run away if they know what's good for them. Damn it, Megan, I warned you about interfering in an investigation again, but you couldn't leave it alone. And who's this kid? Are you corrupting minors now? What's your name, son?"

"I'm not your son, and I take the Fifth," said Jared, his lower lip stuck out so far that Megan was afraid it would fall off.

"You can't take the Fifth, kid. You're not charged yet, but if you keep hanging around with Megan Clark, you're liable to end up in the Juvenile Detention Center."

"Leave him alone, Jerry! His name is Jared Johnson, and he's a friend of mine."

"Megan," called Jenner. "I sent someone over to check it out. He ought to be back in about thirty minutes. Uh-oh." The young sergeant skidded to a halt, looking like a man who desperately wished he was somewhere else.

"Sergeant Jenner!" yelled Jerry Carr. Jenner slunk up beside Megan like a puppy caught chewing a house shoe. "Jenner, didn't you hear me warn Megan last night about staying away?"

"Yes, sir, but that was a different case, and this one is all about bones, and I thought you called her." Jenner looked bewildered.

"Jerry, the Justice of the Peace ordered me to do an autopsy, so you have no authority to throw me off the case or throw me in jail. If you're polite, I'll tell you what I found so far."

Jerry stood in front her, his face turning red and his eyes practically bulging out. "The Justice of the Peace? Is this true, Jenner?"

"Absolutely!" said Jenner, looking relieved at dodging this particular bullet.

Jerry Carr walked around in a small circle in front of Megan, attempting several times to speak, but catching himself each time. Finally, he actually spoke. "So what have you found so far?"

"I think she was killed in 1938, and that old car is connected to her." Megan explained as Jared stood beside her nodding his head.

"Nineteen thirty-eight! There's not a prayer of finding who did it. Chances are they're dead anyway. Take dental impressions, and Jenner can check local dentists if there are any of them still alive."

"Didn't you hear me, Jerry? She's part of the mystery of the old car, and it has an Oklahoma licence plate, so she's probably from Oklahoma, too. Maybe we can still identify some suspects. It's got to be somebody from Sixth Street who's familiar with the laundry. We can find out who owned it, maybe who worked here."

"Megan, do you know how many open cases we have as of this moment? Did you forget the Back Stabber is still running loose on Sixth Street? Do you think I can devote manpower to identify this woman? My God, she's been dead nearly seventy years. Get real. She'll go in the files as a cold case."

"Then I'll investigate her case, Jerry. You can't say that I'll be interfering if she's a cold case anyway. I won't bother Special

Crimes unless I need them to run finger-prints or check VICAP or something like that. Please, Jerry."

He reached for her, ran his forefinger down her check. "I wish I knew what moti-vates you to pursue a case like this one. You'll find no conclusion, no solution, just frustration. Whatever happened, it happened a long time ago, before you or I were born; before your mother or Ryan were born."

"I don't know what kind of person she was. Maybe she was a saint; maybe she was evil, but she was murdered on Sixth Street. I think we owe it to her to at least investi-gate."

She watched the anger fade out of his eyes to be replaced by regret, but regret for what? "Would it do any good if I told you no? Would it, Megan? Do you respect me enough, like me enough, to go along with what I want?"

She swallowed back the tears. "Please, Jerry."

He dropped his hand and nodded his head slowly. "I guess I have your answer. Play with your bones, Megan. It doesn't really matter anyway."

11

I was surprised to find out how few strangers, when I watched their lives for a few days, turned out to be perfectly boring. Almost everyone, it seemed, led at least one secret life.

"Milo" Milodragovitch in James Crumley's
Dancing Bear, 1983

THE WILLOWS RETIREMENT AND CONVALESCENCE HOME — THE NEXT MORNING

I already knew the body — I couldn't think of it as a skeleton since it had flesh on it the last time I saw it — had turned up. I saw the story on the news on TV last night. I'd usually read instead of watching TV of an evening, but last night I had the heebie-jeebies for some reason and couldn't settle down with a book. Good thing, too. If I had opened up the newspaper not being prepared for the headline, I'm afraid I would have squealed or cursed, although I seldom take the Lord's name in vain, and Manuela would have wanted to know what was wrong. I guess she probably would have thought that a story about a skeleton upset an old lady like me, but you can't take chances like that. Nobody ever really knows what the next person is thinking, I don't care how well you think you know them. Manuela might have been suspicious. Anyhow, I was prepared for the headline. I wasn't prepared for the other foolishness that was going on.

Some damn fool was talking to CCN, claimed he lived just a block from Sixth Street, and used to walk by the old laundry every day and every evening for his daily constitutional — imagine the old geezer using that word, probably didn't even know what it meant. Then the old fool said he had to start walking down the other side of the street because ever since the car was found, he'd seen a fog shaped like a woman standing by the corner of the old laundry. You can bet CCN just ate that up.

Then some old woman ugly as a mud fence said she used to take a shortcut to Sixth Street by cutting behind the laundry, but she had to quit because there was a cold spot that reached all the way down the alley. Then some kid with tattoos everywhere you look and a ring through his nose and God knows where else, said he used to watch the mist whirling and dancing behind the laundry. I swear every fool in the universe comes crawling into the light when there's a TV camera around. And TV likes it that way. CCN, MNBC, Fox, and every cable news network didn't interview one person who owned a business or lived on Sixth Street, because they would all say those ghost stories were a bunch of lies made up by people who wanted attention. I never needed attention so bad as to make a fool out of myself to get it. The local news said all the networks, papers from Japan and Germany and England, and maybe even Larry King would be on Sixth Street today. And there's some ridiculous-looking fool, calls himself an independent producer that says he's telling the history of Sixth Street and the skeleton's discovery "ties together history and the present murders." I don't know how he figures that.

I hope all the people who own businesses on Sixth Street raise their prices and really stick it to them TV and press people, because you know they're going to make fun of us, so we need to get some of ours back.

The paper says that Megan Clark examined the skeleton and said it was a woman, about five feet, eight inches tall, between thirty and forty years old, and she had been murdered. As long as they don't put the car and the body — I still think of it as a body — together in the same package, I don't have to worry. But Megan Clark is real sharp, and I don't think it will be long before she makes the connections, and then I'll spend every day wondering when the knock on the door will come. My spy in the book club tells me that the police have washed their hands of the skeleton and the car, but it's not the police I worry about, it's Megan Clark. But if she comes to my door, she'll have to find her way without any help. From what my source tells me, everyone turned her down when she asked for help. Makes me wonder that they're hiding.

TIME AND AGAIN BOOKSTORE — THAT EVENING

"Agnes seems nervous tonight," I told Megan once we had our coffee and a selection of sugar cookies and chocolate peanut butter bars and were sitting in our usual spots on the couch.

"Why, do you suppose? And what are

Larry Spencer and Barney Benson doing here? It can't be to join the book club, since Barney always brags about not having read a book since high school. And there's Hazel Gilbert, the antique store owner. Did Agnes mention anything to you about having any kind of meeting besides the reading circle?"

"I don't imagine she told me anymore than she did you, just to come tonight because she needed us. But this might be interesting with Barney Benson here. He's as dumb as a post, but I enjoy listening to him. He reminds me a little of Red Skelton's comedy sketches, especially his hobo, Freddy the Freeloader."

"Who?" asked Megan, wrinkling up her forehead.

"You do know who Red Skelton was?"

"I've heard of him, some comic in the early days of television, wasn't he?"

"Never mind. It's not important," I said, feeling older than Jed Clampett. Megan probably doesn't know who he is, either. I've got to stop talking about TV stars whose shows went off the air before she was born.

Agnes clapped her hands to get everyone's attention. "I'm glad the reading circle members answered my plea for help, although I didn't expect you to come under the circumstances, Maria."

Maria Constantine looked nervous and worn around the edges, understandable if your husband was found under a pile of leaves just last night.

"I had to get out of the house, Agnes. It's so — so empty! And I keep thinking Damian is just in the next room. But I don't want anyone staying with me, either. I couldn't stand anyone sitting around watching me and feeling sorry for the poor widow. It's just harder than I thought it might be to learn to live on my own."

Agnes and the twins smiled at her in sympathy. I noticed Pearl and Megan didn't.

Agnes cleared her throat and continued. "Larry and Barney and Hazel have joined us on behalf of the Sixth Street Self-Protection Association. Hazel, why don't you tell us about the association."

Hazel Gilbert, owner of Hazel's Hidden Treasures — Antiques for the Discerning Buyer, which translates to really damn expensive, stood up, dressed for success in the antique business. She wore a muted blue suit and a silk blouse with lace at the collar and cuffs. She wore hose and what Megan says are called business pumps. How Megan would know is the question of the century, since hiking boots laced just above the

216

ankles are her shoes of choice, and I've never seen her with a fashion magazine in my life. Maybe fashion know-how floats in the air like pollen and women just breathe it in. I sat back in my corner of the couch, crossed my ankle over my knee, and waited to find out just what besides alliterative the Sixth Street Self-Protection Association was. I might even skip napping to satisfy my curiosity.

"With the morbid discovery of the skeleton between the walls of the old laundry, the business owners on Sixth Street decided it was time to band together for our mutual protection against the inevitable backlash from our customers." She had a prissy, Junior League voice becoming to someone who sells expensive used furniture, but it grated on my ears.

"Just say what you mean, Hazel," said Barney Benson, who looked like what you'd expect the owner of the B&B Blues Bar to look: white shirt unbuttoned at the neck, sleeves rolled up past his elbows, shiny black slacks, and a belly that hung over his belt. "We all got a problem, folks. If the Back Stabber, as Megan Clark calls him, wasn't bad enough, now we got a skeleton and the TV people spreading ghost stories faster than some of our nuts can make them up.

217

It's gonna hurt business. My customers will be seeing ghosts once they guzzle three or four beers. The women will be afraid to go to the john by themselves."

"When have you ever seen a woman go to the john by herself anyway?" asked Larry Spencer, owner of the Route 66 Gift Shop, where all kinds of Route 66 memorabilia are for sale, some of which are even authentic. "She's got to wait until her girlfriend can go with her. They march in two-by-two like they're boarding the Ark."

"That ain't the point," replied Barney, trying to pull his belt and slacks over his belly. "The point is I could have a bunch of hysterical women on my hands if one of them thinks she sees something — what do you call it?— supernatural. I could have a riot! The Alcohol Control Board would be on my back from now to next June. We gonna nip this ghost thing in the bud."

Pearl, amusement in her voice, spoke up next. "Barney, if you sold decent booze at your bar, maybe your customers wouldn't be seeing things."

"What are you saying? That my booze is cheap? Jezebel, it's four fifty for a shot of whisky, eight dollars for a margarita — that's the regular; the El Grande is more — and three fifty for a bottle of beer. I don't call that cheap!"

As I told Megan before the meeting started, Barney isn't the sharpest knife in the drawer. He's not the dullest, either, because he makes a good living keeping bar.

"Please, let's not waste time arguing," said Agnes. "I have a suggestion. Let's exploit the skeleton and the ghost. We won't even have to buy advertising. Cable is doing it for us for free with all the interviews and specials. Sales of books about the supernatural have already increased my bottom line for this month, and I intend to milk this ghost craze for every last cent I can get. Barney, you can do the same. Spray some of those artificial cobwebs around your bar; hang some paper skeletons from the ceiling; sit some carved pumpkins on the tables; and invent a new drink and call it the Halloween Horror."

"Agnes! I'm appalled at your behavior — and your advice. It's — it's repugnant!" screeched Hazel Gilbert.

"Hell, no, it ain't!" said Barney as though he knew what repugnant meant. Like rising bread dough his belly oozed over his belt again. "Agnes, you old sweetheart, you win the lottery with that advice."

"That won't solve your problem," said Megan, rising to her feet and circling the coffee table to stop in the middle of the reading area. The urgency in her voice turned my blood cold. She was up to something. "Don't you see? The TV people will be on Sixth Street only until there's another shooting in a school or a hostage situation in Iraq or the President makes another Supreme Court nomination."

"What's the Supreme Court got to do with Sixth Street?" asked Barney with bewilderment. It doesn't take much to bewilder Barney.

"Don't you understand what Megan's saying?" asked Larry Spencer.

"I wouldn't ask if I did," snapped Barney.

"The TV cameras will leave, Barney," said Megan. "The cable networks will cover another story. Halloween will be over, the skeleton will remain, and you'll still have a problem. It's fun now to shop and eat and drink on Sixth Street because the TV cameras are here and some famous anchorman you never thought you'd meet will interview you. And I'm convinced that TV and all the commotion will keep the Back Stabber at bay. Once they're gone, he will be back to hunt again. And people have created so many ghost stories because it's fun to be scared while there are people around. But when things are back to normal they will still be scared, and might not want to come around the source of their fear."

Agnes twisted her hands in her lap. "I had not considered that, but Megan is right."

"Dern right she is," said Larry Spencer, tapping his fingers, bouncing his legs, and twisting in his chair like a hyperactive ten-year-old. "We gotta do something and we gotta do it quick. Winter is coming on, and the tourist trade will shrink down to nothing. If the locals are too scared to come to Sixth Street, then we're looking at bankruptcy."

Silence came to the bookstore as the business owners contemplated a possible future scarier than any ghost.

"There are two solutions to your problem: catch the Back Stabber and uncover the identity of the skeleton." Megan's voice still epitomized earnestness, with persuasiveness added to the mix. I don't know why I was surprised. She's intended all along to solve these mysteries regardless of Jerry Carr's threat to throw her cute buns in jail. She cannot resist a puzzle.

The group was in an uproar with everyone talking at once. "Quiet!" shouted Megan, then continued her seduction as if there had been no interruption. "A serial killer is the most difficult criminal to catch because they murder strangers. There's usually a pattern to their choice of victims — brunettes who parted their hair in the middle were Ted Bundy's favorite victims, for example — but sometimes it's so subtle that no one discerns until after the killer is caught. Sometimes it's convenience that determines the victim. Someone in the wrong place at the wrong time. What I'm trying to tell you is that I don't know that we can identify the murderer and trap him. He does leave one clue, however: the marks on the forehead. If I can figure out what they mean, then maybe there's a chance we can discover his identity."

She paced in a semicircle so she was facing everyone at one time or another. I didn't move from the couch or say anything. What was the point? Megan had two motives for always sticking her nose in murder: a compulsion for solving any kind of mystery, including those defined as word games such as brainteasers and crossword puzzles, and an equally strong need to obtain justice for the dead. Even knowing what drives her, I've never succeeded in stopping her. The most I've been able to do is slow her down and watch her back.

"The skeleton is a different story. We can solve that mystery by identifying the victim.

She's only frightening because we don't know who she is, so there are all these silly stories about ghost sightings. If we know who she was, then we can humanize her and turn the mystery into a sad story of a woman we can identify with. We can erect a monument of some kind near the old laundry to commemorate her life and death, and suddenly we have a tourist attraction instead of a haunted building."

"So we have to try to identify some poor Okie who pissed off one of her fellow travelers and earned herself a cement overcoat?" asked Larry Spencer.

"I don't believe the woman was an Okie," said Megan. "For one thing, she wasn't poor. She had wonderful dental care, which the poor didn't have in the 1930s. Also, her bones show no evidence of malnutrition. The emigrants who traveled to California along Route 66 survived on what amounted to a starvation diet. They barely had enough to eat, so they would not have the thick, healthy bones of this woman. So we may be talking about a local person who disappeared in 1938. We are certainly talking about a local murderer, because a stranger wouldn't know about a false wall in the laundry. Another interesting twist to the mystery is her connection to the old Ford."

Megan explained about the radiator cap and why she believes it is the murder weapon. She had already told me her theory, described the woman's height, weight, and so forth. The one fact that Megan didn't know — and it was driving her nuts — was the motive for the murder. How did an apparently wealthy woman get involved with the family who drove that old Ford, and why did they abandon their car? Not only abandon it, but hide it so it wasn't found for seventy years. What was the point? To be truthful, I found the mystery intriguing myself. Since there was no danger that a murderer would come out of the woodwork to threaten Megan, I didn't have to worry about protecting her. The more I think about it, the more I'm considering getting involved myself. Why not help Megan?

Because it would set a bad precedent.

"Can any of you business owners think of stories about a woman disappearing in the 1930s?" asked Megan. "Agnes, you've been on Sixth Street longer than anyone. Can you remember anything about a missing person?"

"I've been thinking, but the only one I can think of is Margaret Dickey, but I heard later than she had run off to California with the church choir director. Los Angeles, I believe."

"No, Agnes, that's wrong. They went to Georgia, and it wasn't the choir director; it was a vice president at First National Bank. I believe some bank funds accompanied them." Hazel Gilbert, in addition to sounding prissy, is always convinced she's right.

"You're full of it, Hazel," said Larry Spencer, still bouncing, twisting, and generally acting antsy. "My grandfather told me the story, and it wasn't Margaret Dickey at all, it was Maude Hooper, and she ran off with the whisky salesman who used to sell to Barney Benson's granddad when he owned B&B Blues Bar. Ray, was it your father or your mom's second husband who ran off with the waitress who worked at that café?"

Megan whirled around to face the retired cop. "You never told me you lived on Sixth Street when you were growing up."

"I never thought to mention that when Ray joined the reading circle," said Agnes.

Ray looked angry like he didn't want anyone to know he'd ever lived on Sixth Street. "I lived in a house just off the Sixth," he admitted. "And Barney, it was my father who died. My mother never remarried."

Barney frowned in thought. "Then who

ran off with the waitress?"

Agnes snapped her fingers. "I believe you're right about Margaret Dickey, Hazel. The choir director ran off with the waitress. I can't remember her name, but she was a flashy girl. Always sewed rhinestones on her hairnet and chewed gum. Her absence improved the class of employees, though."

"She was always free and easy," said Larry Spencer with a reminiscent gleam in his eyes.

"That's one way of putting it," said Hazel with a sniff of disapproval.

"I don't think this is getting us anywhere," said Megan. "Why don't we meet again next week on our regular night, and you think about missing women."

"I don't mean any disrespect, Megan," said Barney. "I think your idea of making Miss Bones into a tourist attraction is a good idea, but I think we need to worry more about whoever is icing the locals and using their foreheads for a scratch pad. That guy is a danger to the living."

Maria Constantine burst into tears, those same kinds of sobs that rose to a crescendo, slid down the scales, then rose again. The women fussed over her with Pearl commenting on Barney's eventual destination after he shed his mortal coil, while the men looked uncomfortable.

"Was it something I said?" asked Barney, looking bewildered again.

"Shut up, Barney," said Ray, who I noticed looked jittery and exhausted.

"I can't stand it!" cried Maria between sobs. "I can't stand to sit here talking about that horrible man who killed Damian. Let the police try to find him because it's too dangerous for us to try to catch him. Now, please, let's talk about the skeleton. We can solve that mystery; I know we can."

"I agree with Maria," said Megan, "so let's tackle this scientifically. Rosemary and Lorene, will you check census records for Sixth Street and the San Jacinto area? Anyone listed on the 1930 and 1940 census who is still alive today we'll question. Candi, will you check old newspaper files for any mention of a missing person or an altercation in 1937 and 1938? Randel, keep looking through those photos. Ryan and I will do a title search on the property. Pearl, I don't have a specific task for you."

Pearl smiled. "I'll read the cards to forecast the future."

"Bah, humbug," said Larry.

"I'll look through my mother's sales slips," said Agnes. "I still have them boxed up in a storage unit. I thought some day I would do an article for some journal on the public's changing tastes in literature."

"That'll be great, Agnes," said Megan.

"Megan, I'm still more worried about this Back Stabber. I get an itchy feeling between my shoulder blades every time I go outside at night, and it ain't the skeleton that's causing it. I'm gonna start standing outside in the alley with my back against the brick wall, so I can see who's coming," said Barney. "Five o'clock came today, and I never saw as many business owners locking their businesses down and boogying off Sixth Street like their pants was on fire as I saw today. Hazel, I saw you lock your door right in front of one of your snooty customer's nose. I'm telling you, Megan, if Hazel Gilbert gives up an opportunity to make a buck, then she's scared, and if she's scared, tough as she is, then everybody on Sixth Street is scared."

"I resent your comments," said Hazel Gilbert. "I'm not afraid. I had some errands to run, so I decided to close a little early."

"I'm just telling you what I saw," said Barney. "And if you ain't scared, Hazel, then you got less sense than I think you do. You'd be a damn fool not to close up early and get off Sixth Street before dark."

"When were you in the alley, Barney?"

asked Maria.

"Every night. I gotta get away from the smell of spilt beer and sweat at least a couple times a night. A man's gotta have a little time to himself. So I go out back to the alley and have a cigarette and breathe some fresh air along with Lim Yee's Chinese next door. Look at the stars, listen to all the sounds of Sixth Street."

"Were you out there when Damian" — Maria paused — "when Damian was killed?"

"Yeah, but I was down at the other end of the alley, and I reckon I just missed the Back Stabber, because I didn't hear anything, but I did hear a pickup with a bad transmission speed away from the alley a little after six thirty. I usually grab a barbecue sandwich or some of Lim Yee's takeout about six before the night crowd hits and go out and have a cigarette, gather myself for the evening."

"Then you heard the murderer's vehicle," said Megan. "Do you know what it was?"

"Well, I didn't see nothing — that street light's out down by Agnes's back door — but I reckon it was a pickup of some kind. I don't know what make or color or anything, 'cause I didn't see it, just heard it."

"Did you tell the police?" asked Maria.

"They never asked me. All they wanted to know was if I heard any screams or saw anybody running down the alley. I didn't hear screams or see anybody, so I told them no."

"I swear to God, Barney, you're dumb as dirt," said Larry Spencer. "Why didn't you have sense enough to tell the cops you heard a pickup in the alley?"

"Hey, don't be insulting me! I didn't know that the pickup had anything to do with the killing. Besides, every third person in Amarillo drives a pickup."

"But not on Sixth Street," said Megan thoughtfully. "Most of the people on Sixth Street and San Jacinto are elderly and depend on the buses to get around. And a lot of the others are so wiped out on drugs or alcohol that they can't hold a job and can't afford a car or pickup. That means the killer isn't local."

"That's worse," said Barney, wiping his sweaty forehead on his shirt sleeve. "That means he's just killing whoever he finds. I felt better when I thought the Back Stabber was killing particular people 'cause he had something against them, and I don't know anybody who's got anything against me."

"Barney, will you and Larry and Hazel question everybody on Sixth Street to see if anyone else saw or heard a pickup with a bad transmission? Maybe you'll find out more than the police because the people know you, and you know what questions to ask." Megan looked at each of them until they nodded their heads in agreement. "Good. Bring your report to the reading circle's next meeting on Tuesday, six days from now. Now, let's go back to the skeleton possibly being a missing person. Ray, do you think the police have any records left from that period?"

"I imagine they have some, but I'm not going to help with this foolishness, Megan. It's a waste of time."

Megan looked shocked, and frankly, so was I. This was Ray Robertson, retired cop, who always before had been anxious to help. I was beginning to understand what she meant when she stressed over everyone changing. What the hell was going on?

12

Circumstantial evidence is a very tricky thing. It may seem to point very straight to one thing, but if you shift your own point of view a little, you may find it pointing in an equally uncompromising manner to something entirely different.

Sherlock Holmes to Dr. Watson in Sir Arthur Conan Doyle's "The Boscombe Valley Mystery," *The Adventures of Sherlock Holmes*, 1891

AMARILLO ABSTRACT COMPANY — SIX DAYS LATER

"Tell me again why we're checking the abstract of the property the laundry sits on," said Ryan, pushing open the carved wooden door of the abstract company. "You know I have a class in forty minutes."

"I'm hoping the abstract will give us a lead. Maybe the owner knew that skeleton was there. Maybe he didn't. But there has to be a reason that building has been empty since the late 1950s. I want to know what it is."

"It probably belongs to some realty company in southern California, and no one has been out here since the Depression."

"Realty companies turn their properties over regularly. My mother was a Realtor in between causes before she became ill with diabetes. She still works three days a week. No, Ryan, an individual owns this property; I'm sure of it."

The reception room was a stereotype: grey carpet, a love seat with small coffee table, a few occasional chairs, potted plants, desk with the ubiquitous computer and monitor, and several pictures of the receptionist's children. What was really different about the office as compared to others were the magazines: they were all business magazines, and they were all new instead of several months old.

Megan walked to the reception desk, identified herself, and asked for a copy of the abstract she had called about this morning. In return, the receptionist handed her a business-sized manilla envelope. Megan wrote her a check, received a receipt, and it was over. No explaining to some skeptical business type why they wanted an abstract;

no grubbing through filing cabinets; no straining one's eyes reading microfilm.

Megan couldn't believe it was so easy. It pays to have a mother who is a Realtor.

Nor could she believe it when she ripped open the envelope and she and Ryan perused the papers inside.

"I don't believe it!" Ryan exclaimed.

"I didn't expect this. Ray or Rosemary because they are so vehement about not investigating; Pearl because we don't know her, and she strikes a wrong note with me. But not this. Look, Ryan, the property was sold the day the Ford was pulled out of Wild Horse Lake. That has to be a coincidence. Some events really are coincidences."

"Do you believe that, Megan?"

"I don't know, but I'm going to ask. If it's true, I think I'm going to be sick"

"What next?" asked Ryan as they drove off.

Megan struggled with nausea. "To Rosemary's. I would rather walk across live coals than have to question Rosemary Pittman. But she's hiding something, Ryan. Otherwise, she would've been the first person to volunteer to help track down the family who owned that Ford. But what could she be hiding? I'm not certain how old Rosemary is, but she must have been a child in 1938.

She couldn't have killed our Miss Bones."

"And she never lived on Sixth Street," added Ryan. "Her daddy was involved in the oil and gas business, and it was booming in the twenties, thirties, and forties. She grew up with money, and she married more money. The monied class didn't live on Sixth Street."

"Drop me off at home so I can take my pickup. Then you'll have twenty minutes to make it to class."

"Don't you have to go back to work?"

Megan avoided his eyes. She always felt so guilty when he caught her lying. "I called in sick."

She could feel his disapproval and scooted as far away from him as the Ford Ranger's bench seat would allow. "Aren't you risking losing your job?" he asked.

"No. Yes. I don't know, I hope not."

"That was an unambiguous answer."

She thought her best option was not to say anything at all.

"I'm going with you. No way will I let you question Rosemary alone."

Megan didn't argue.

Rosemary lived in a three-story, Depression-era mansion, the kind with a gazebo in the backyard and the maid's apartment above the garage. Rosemary had some serious money.

Rosemary answered the door, and Megan felt disappointed. Whenever she visited Rosemary, she expected at least the downstairs maid to answer the door, if not a butler with a haughty English accent: "This way to the withdrawing room, Miss Clark, and I shall inform Madam of your presence." Instead it was Rosemary in slacks and a casual sweater.

Rosemary didn't look happy to see them, and Megan dreaded the coming conversation. Right up to the moment she rang the doorbell, she had hoped she was wrong. Apparently, she wasn't, or Rosemary would have welcomed them with a hug. Her elderly friend was hiding something, and Megan was here to find out what. Happy or not, Rosemary graciously invited them in and led the way to the sunroom at the back of the house. Or maybe she called it a conservatory. It was a pleasant room with rattan furniture upholstered in lime-green linen embossed with white willow branches. There was a palm tree tall enough to reach the ten-foot ceiling sitting in one corner. Baskets of flowers on long wrought-iron chains hung from the ceiling, and geraniums in pots stood in a line like squat soldiers in front of the tall windows that made up the south wall. The north wall was lined with black lacquered bamboo cabinets, and in the corner hung a rattan swing large enough for two.

Rosemary brought them coffee in fragile china cups, another sign they weren't really welcome; otherwise, she would have brought out tall rum drinks. Or maybe she didn't trust herself to stay in rigid control if she had a few drinks. Either way, there was no rum.

Rosemary took a seat in a chair opposite them, her back stiff and her hands locked together in a stranglehold. She cleared her throat before she spoke. "What brings you out here today?"

"I think you know, Rosemary," said Megan. "What is your connection with the old car? You completely changed once it appeared. You've never failed to join one of our investigations, but you refused to help find out why that car was abandoned. And your excuse was so flimsy." It was obvious from Rosemary's face that she was caught by surprise.

"I could say that I don't know what you're talking about."

"I would be very disappointed in you."

She leaned forward in her chair. "Would

you believe me if I told you that my story wouldn't tell you any more than you know already? That it wouldn't help you identify that woman, and that upon reflection, it has nothing to do with that old car?"

"I can't judge whether your story would help me or not until I hear it. You know that Ryan and I will carry your secret to the grave if it's not pertinent to learning the name of the murderer. Is it pertinent or not, Rosemary?"

"The name of the murderer? I thought you only wanted to ask me about the car and the woman's identity, and I can't help you there. But you're really serious about learning who the murderer is even after all these years?"

"Yes, I'm serious. I want to know the murderer's name even after all these years."

"You're just as merciless as your mother is about one of her causes," cried Rosemary.

Megan felt a pain jab her stomach and fought down a sudden attack of nausea. "Don't say that, please!"

"I'm sorry, dear, I didn't mean to say such an ugly thing." Suddenly Rosemary began crying. She pulled a tissue out of a box sitting on a low table next to her chair and dabbed at the tears running down her cheeks. "I don't know, Megan," she said in a voice thick with tears. "I truly don't know if the murderer is someone close to me or not, but I must tell you a shameful secret I've kept more than seventy years and let you judge if what I fear is true. Most of the time I haven't thought about my secret, but with the old car and its 1938 licence plate, then the skeleton, I haven't thought of anything else. Let me send the servants away for the afternoon. I don't want to risk any of them overhearing me."

She left the room, and Ryan leaned toward Megan. "You were right about her hiding something, but this is embarrassing and painful to watch. I would never have made it as a priest. I can't stand to listen to my friends bare their souls. Except you. I'd like to hear you bare your soul. Maybe then I'd know what you're thinking."

"About what, Ryan?"

He shrugged his shoulders. "About the weather, about life, about me."

Megan looked away. "I didn't grow up confiding in people. My mother never really wanted to know my feelings. I think she was afraid I might distract her from her latest cause."

"Whenever you're ready to practice confiding, I'll be waiting."

Megan swallowed repeatedly to keep from

crying. "Thank you."

"You're welcome."

They waited in silence until Rosemary returned.

She poured more coffee, then sat down. Her back was straight, but Megan saw her hands tremble before she clasped them together, and she knew Rosemary was desperately holding on to her composure. "I grew up in a house on Ong Street that was a mansion by anyone's standards. Ragged Okies in dented old cars didn't drive down streets in my neighborhood, so I know I never saw that old car in my life. I'm not being a snob, just setting the stage. That was simply the way it was. I remember the Depression even though I was isolated from it. Mother always insisted that my sister and I donate our clothes and toys that we had outgrown to the church, so that poor children would have something to wear and to play with. We would always take Thanksgiving and Christmas baskets to the poor members of our church. My mother said it was our duty to help those who weren't as fortunate as we. So I saw the hardships the Depression caused without actually experiencing it myself. There were many occasions when I envied those families and would have traded places with their daughters if it meant I would find happiness and see love between parents. At five years old I learned one of life's hardest lessons: wealth does not guarantee a happy life; it only guarantees a physically comfortable one."

"I understand, Rosemary," said Megan, thinking of her mother and her causes. Ryan reached out and clasped her hand, and she clutched it as if he had thrown her a lifeline.

Rosemary tilted her head and smiled. "I'm sure you do, Megan, but you're out of step with your generation." She unobtrusively blew her nose and continued her narration.

"I remember those few years before 1938 because my home was filled with the poison of those oh-so-polite arguments between my parents. 'Not in front of the children' was their mantra, but there are hardly ever any secrets in a family. My older sister and I would crouch at the top of the stairs and listen to them fight. At that age — I think I must have been around five — I didn't know what the words 'affair' and 'mistress' meant, but I knew the meaning of the word 'kill' even if I didn't totally understand what death meant.

"By 1938 the tension and anger between my parents was almost tangible. Then, on a night I have never forgotten, the tension between my parents had been growing like a malignant tumor all evening. My sister and I were sent to bed early, but hardly had my mother returned downstairs before we were crouched at the top of the stairs like always, and my parents were fighting. The words they exchanged were uglier: white trash whore, frigid bitch, and more that I don't remember — don't want to remember. Finally, my mother screamed out, 'I'll kill your diseased whore, that filth you sleep with!' The front door was at the bottom of the stairs, so we saw my mother stalk across the marble floor, fling open the door, and slam it afterward. I heard her little sports car start up and watched her from the window seat on the second floor landing as she drove off down the street. My sister and I were awake all night waiting for her, but she never came back until the sun was well up. When she finally returned, she and my father locked themselves in the study where a truce must have been negotiated, because they were polite to one another the rest of their lives and died within a year of each other."

Rosemary filled the coffee cups again and sipped hers for a moment. Her hands no longer trembled and seemed calmer as though telling her story released a lifelong tension. "So, you see, Megan, I have no connection with the car, and I truly can't see my wealthy, factitious, and slightly arrogant father having an affair with a woman who would drive a dilapidated wreck like the one pulled from Wild Horse Lake. The skeleton with her good teeth and healthy bones sounds more like his equal, and I can't deny with any certainty that mother didn't murder her if she was sleeping with my father."

Rosemary looked at Megan with a hopeless expression in her eyes. "Now you know: my mother may have been a murderer."

Megan leaned forward in her chair. "Did your mother know of the false wall in the laundry?"

Rosemary sat motionless for a few seconds, then started laughing. "I doubt that my mother ever stepped in a laundry in her life."

"Then I don't see how your mother could be involved," said Megan.

Rosemary dried her eyes and blew her nose. "I have thought of nothing else but our Depression-era mystery for so many days that I let my fear and shame get away from me. It is a coincidence that the murder happened in 1938, the same year that my parents' marriage imploded and my mother ran away for a night, but it is a happy coincidence for me. It's forced me to confront my unhappy childhood. I wish I had done it fifty years ago. Thank you so much, Megan and Ryan, for forcing me to share that night with you. As I listened to myself, I realized how foolish I was all those years for not confiding my secret to a friend."

She rose gracefully and gave each one a hug. Then she clapped her hands, a mischievous sparkle in her eyes. "How about I break out the rum and let's tie one on?"

"I have a better idea, Rosemary. How about you come with us to interrogate a witness?" asked Megan.

"What's this all about?" Megan laid the abstract in the center of his cluttered desk. "I think you know something about the skeleton and her connection to the old Ford, don't you, Herb?"

Herbert Jackson III abruptly sat down in his chair and stared at the abstract as if it was a coiled rattlesnake in the mood to bite. "I — I don't know what you're talking about."

"It amazes me that you can be an attorney and at the same time lie so poorly, Herb," said Rosemary, frowning at him.

"Come clean, Jackson, we caught ya with the goods," said Ryan in a bad imitation of the gangster. Megan wished he would update his slang. That's what comes from watching 1930s gangster movies.

"I didn't know about the skeleton," said Herb, blotting his forehead with his handkerchief.

"You're telling us that you just happened to sell that property the very afternoon the Ford made headlines in the morning paper? You're telling us the timing is just a coincidence? You're telling us you didn't sell that property because you didn't want to get caught with a skeleton on your hands — or in your laundry, to be precise? You're telling us your family owned that property for sixty-five years and you suddenly decided to sell it the same day you learn the Ford has emerged from its watery grave? Do I have that right, Herb?" asked Megan.

"Yes, that's what I'm telling you!" said Herb in a desperate-sounding voice.

"Herb, I'm disappointed in you. I expected better from my family lawyer. I at least expected a more imaginative lie," said Rosemary, shaking her finger at him.

"Do I get the rubber hose out and give him the business, Boss?" Ryan asked Megan out of the corner of his mouth.

"Ryan, do you know how ludicrous you sound talking like Edward G. Robinson? You're not even wearing a black shirt and fedora and a big gold ring on your pinkie," said Megan.

"I am too wearing a black shirt."

"Tee shirts don't count." Megan turned her attention back to Herb. "What's your answer? Do you expect us to believe you're entirely innocent?"

"Yes! You don't understand what happened," said Herb, blotting his forehead again.

"Why don't you tell us, Herb? We're your friends."

"Yeah, Herbie baby. We won't rat ya out to the coppers."

"You're enjoying this, aren't you, Ryan?" asked Megan, exasperated with him.

"Yes, I am. More than Herb is."

"Please, Ryan, this is serious," said Megan, ready to wrap a rubber hose around his neck.

"Herb, I don't believe Megan is as anxious to learn what you know as she is disappointed that you don't trust your friends. Who are you protecting? Your father? Your grandfather? I noticed that he is the one who originally bought the laundry. Why would he want to buy a laundry? I always heard he was a shrewd old coot, too shrewd to let that property sit for years without a tenant. And your dad let it sit for a couple more decades. That's as peculiar as your granddad buying it in the first place, especially since your dad had the reputation for being tight with a buck. I can't see him paying taxes on that property without a good reason — like a skeleton between the walls." Ryan picked up the abstract and studied it for a few seconds. "You on the other hand, inherit the property two months ago when your father died and put it on the market immediately. Know what that tells me, Herb?"

Herb watched him with eyes like a deer's caught in the headlights.

Ryan walked around the desk and put his arm around Herb's shoulders. "It tells me you're telling the truth. You really didn't know about the skeleton. But your grandfather and your father did. Unfortunately, they didn't pass the information along to you with their DNA. Let's take the story a little further, shall we. Why would your grandfather buy that laundry if he knew about the skeleton? Could it be because he killed her?"

"No," said Herb in a weak voice.

"I believe you — because why would he wait until 1940 to buy the property if he killed her in 1938? Unless" — Ryan straightened, patted Herb's shoulder, and perched one hip on the corner of the lawyer's desk — "unless he didn't know there was a body between the walls until someone told him in 1940, at which time he bought the property. Who told him? Why, the person who killed her. How am I doing so far, Herb?"

"Ryan, you're brilliant!" cried Megan, clapping her hands.

"You're wonderful, Ryan," said Rosemary, giving him a hug.

Ryan rose and bowed. "Ladies, please. Much as I love your accolades, let's allow the gentleman to speak. I repeat, how am I doing so far, Herb?"

Herb stared at Ryan, seemingly unable to talk.

"Struck dumb by my brilliance as so often happens," said Ryan, circling Herb's desk to sit by Megan. "But let me continue to expound on my theory. Let me see, where was I? Oh, yes, this mysterious person who persuaded your grandfather to buy a secret burial ground. Who might this person be? A client? Doubtful. A good friend? Also doubtful. Let's remember, owning a piece of land where a murder victim is buried is risky, because you are at the mercy of the person at whose behest you bought the property. That person, whoever it is, could tip off the cops, and Herbert Jackson the Original is suddenly in more trouble than one lawyer can handle. Likewise with your father. Neither one could safely either rent or sell. It must have galled them both to be in effect, blackmailed. It would have me. Who might your grandfather trust with his sacred honor and, more importantly, his personal liberty? For whom will a man always risk his all?"

Ryan paused and dropped to one knee in front of Megan. He lifted her hands to his mouth and kissed each one. "A man will risk his all for a woman. Would you care to fill in the blanks, Herb?" he asked as he continued to gaze at a stunned Megan.

"I don't suppose you'd let me plead the Fifth, would you?" Herb examined each face like a man searching for salvation. "No, I see that you are determined to wring the truth out of me. Wait one moment, please. I just want to jot that down . . . Wring the truth out of me," he murmured as he made a note in a small notebook he pulled from his inside coat pocket. "I always jot down colorful phrases made by my clients or myself, although I rarely say anything colorful myself. Later I'll insert them as dialogue in my book. According to what I've read on writing fiction, you should keep a record of pithy comments or lively incidents you can use to give your work verisimilitude, although there's a shortage of pithy comments in my practice. Contracts and wills are rather dull, I'm afraid. If it weren't for what I hear at the reading circle, my notebook would be blank."

He looked so discouraged that Megan felt sorry for him. "Don't give up, Herb. Personally, I noticed some real improvement in your last chapter, a liveliness in your narrative that's new. Haven't you noticed that, Rosemary?"

Rosemary was quick to pick up her cue. "Absolutely, Herb. I mentioned it to Lorene, and she agreed. We're looking forward to next week's chapter, aren't we, Ryan?"

Megan thought it was fortunate that Ryan's back was to Herb, because Ryan's expression plainly said that she and Rosemary had lost their literary judgment. Megan kicked Ryan's knee. "Oh, yeah, Herb, you may end up with a real page-turner on your hands. I even stayed up later than usual reading your last chapter." Megan translated that to mean that Ryan remained awake longer than the usual minute and a half it took to fall asleep reading one of Herb's offerings.

Herb's face lit up like a Christmas light.

"You really mean it? You're not just telling me that?"

"We're not kidding you, Herb," said Ryan. "If that's all settled, why don't you finish filling in those blanks."

"There's not much to say, really. You guessed most of it, or most of what I've been able to figure out since the skeleton was uncovered. You were right, Ryan. I never would have sold that property if I had known about it. I'm not so sure of certain other of your conclusions."

"Oh? Which conclusions?" Ryan pushed himself off the floor to rest one hip on the arm of Megan's chair.

"Why don't you start at the beginning, Herb, 1940, with your grandfather buying the building?" asked Megan, pinching Ryan's arm to warn him not to interrupt.

Herb leaned back in his chair and pulled his vest down. "That would be 1937 when my grandfather set up practice on Sixth Street in a narrow, two-story, red brick building with bars on the windows. It's still there today. Grandfather ran a storefront operation until he built up his practice enough to afford to move his office downtown to the Fisk building, and his family to a cottage near Amarillo College. That was in 1940. My grandmother died in 1937 so she never lived long enough to see the husband her family didn't want her to marry finally succeed."

Herb stopped to blot his forehead with a neatly pressed linen handkerchief. "While Grandfather's practice was on Sixth Street, he used to walk down to the filling station that was across the street from the laundry to have a Coke and talk to people who stopped in to buy gas. It was the same filling station Randel was talking about the other evening."

"And that's where he met the woman?" asked Megan, the hairs standing up on the back of her neck. She could visualize a man in an old-fashioned, three-piece suit with a gold pocket watch and chain strolling down busy Sixth Street, perhaps stopping halfway to remove his coat and roll up his sleeves.

"It must have been. I know he drove back to Sixth Street to that filling station to drink a Coke every weekday until it went of business. I don't know where he met her after that. I went with him a few times when I was just a small child, and I remember him always talking to a woman while I played around the filling station. And before you ask me, no, I don't remember her name even though he introduced her. Of course, at my tender age I thought she was ancient, but she must have been my grandfather's age or a little younger. That doesn't mean much, because I thought my grandfather was ancient, too. Even then I knew she wasn't an educated woman because her grammar wasn't the best. Children are cruel, aren't they? She wasn't as "good" as my family, so I didn't pay any attention to her. Now I know she was his mistress, and she must have spent time at the cottage when my father was growing up. I think my father must have been fond of her, that he saw her as his mother since his own died when he was three."

"You can't know that, Herb," protested Rosemary. "Children often resent stepmothers or anyone who stands in place of his own mother."

Herb shook his head. "Not in this case, Rosemary. And this is where one of your conclusions is wrong, Ryan. To his dying day my grandfather kept a picture of a family of Okies standing in front of a wreck of an old Ford, and by the trunk, just turning away from the camera but still in focus, is a woman holding a Coke bottle in one hand. When my grandfather died my father kept the picture in his office and displayed it with all the other family photos. He wouldn't do that if he hated that woman. You don't give a blackmailer a place of honor, Ryan. My father and grandfather were protecting her."

"Where's the picture now, Herb?" asked Megan urgently.

"When my father was diagnosed with liver cancer, the picture disappeared. I don't know where it is."

"Where might it be?" asked Rosemary. "When my husband developed congestive heart failure, he boxed all of his papers and financial records, and I stored them in a commercial storage unit for our children after I'm gone. Did your father store any of his papers, and might the picture be there?"

Herb nodded. "It could be. He stored several boxes and gave me the combination to the storage unit. He said that I could sort through his papers after he died if I was curious or thought records I needed were there. My father was very pragmatic when he discussed his own death. He even told me that he had paid all his debts and taken care of certain long-term obligations he and my grandfather had accepted for reasons of gratitude and lasting affection, so probate should go smoothly.

"But he never discussed the laundry or its morbid history. I knew nothing about the skeleton until it was discovered. What is that slang term that describes my state of mind?

I wrote it down in my notebook," Herb said as he rapidly flipped through the small spiral notebook. "Here it is: I hadn't a clue," he announced with triumph.

Megan smiled. Call Me Herb didn't have a clue about much of anything outside of contracts, wills, and his unfinished legal thriller.

"Your father said that he had taken care of certain long-term obligations on behalf of himself and your grandfather," said Ryan, pacing back and forth across Herb's office. "I can think of only one interpretation of that statement. Do you know what it means, Herb?"

"Well, I'm not sure," began Herb.

"Oh, my God!" cried Megan, standing up because she was too excited to sit down. "Oh, my God! She's still alive."

13

Feed: I heard on the radio this morning that the police are looking for a man with one eye. Comic: Typical inefficiency.
Vaudeville gag used as a chapter heading in Simon Brett's *A Comedian Dies,* 1979

A Restaurant and Randel's Home — That Night

"Do you know who you reminded me of this afternoon?" asked Megan as we scarfed down a couple of El Grandes at our favorite Mexican restaurant before going to Time and Again for a meeting with our assistant sleuths, aka the reading circle and the Sixth Street Self-Protection Association. Together, Megan referred to them as the Skeleton Task Force. I had just finished my tamale and started on my chicken enchiladas with sour cream when she asked her question. I looked up from my plate, swallowed my first bite of enchilada, and arched my eyebrow.

"I don't have a clue," I replied.

Her eyes shimmered like sunlight shining through a glass of fine Tennessee whisky, and the candlelight tipped the curls around her face with gold. I thought for an instant that I might actually melt like candle wax and drip all over my chicken enchiladas and beef tacos, or lunge across the table and crawl all over her panting like a dog. I felt light-headed for a few seconds. Another minute staring at her, and I'd start baying at the moon and growing hair on my palms. I hadn't suffered such an attack of lust since — well, since never. If I didn't get control of myself quickly, I'd be in a condition socially unacceptable in a family restaurant. I had to say something, anything to take my mind off the fantasies crowding out whatever self-control I had left — which lately wasn't much when it came to Megan. Even our bickering and my nagging at her about getting involved with murder again hadn't slowed down our advance toward crisis point.

Then I had to show off this afternoon like some macho idiot. Why didn't I just beat my chest and stomp around Herb's office grunting like a demented teenager with an overload of testosterone? Instead I had shown off my power of deductive reasoning to demonstrate my intellect. Then once I started, everything seemed to fall into place. All the scattered puzzle pieces came together. I couldn't have picked a better way of seducing Megan if I had done it deliberately. Good looks and a washboard belly don't impress her. Her vulnerability is a man's intelligence. She's always been a brain over brawn girl.

Her looking at me this afternoon like I was the greatest thing since sliced bread had activated my thermostat, and now I was in serious danger of overheating. I hadn't really done anything extraordinary, just applied what the abstract revealed to what I knew about Call Me Herb and his family. My deductions were just common sense, but to Megan I was brilliant. When a woman as intelligent and as beautiful and as feisty as Megan believes you're brilliant, and looks at you with those whisky-colored eyes with an expression just short of reverence, you would lie down and let her walk on you with spike heels; you would kiss her feet; you would carry her dog in a sling around your neck even though you knew Randel Anderson would laugh at you; you would even dust the furniture and scrub the toilet, because she made you feel like God's anointed prophet.

She made me burn.

If my eyes revealed even half what I was thinking, Megan would reach across the table and slap me six ways from Sunday. She had spent much of her young womanhood fending off men whose hard-ons overwhelmed their brains. She wouldn't appreciate adding me to the list. But it was too late to stop looking at her. The image of her was burned on my retinas. God, I had to say something to break her spell.

"You're the most beautiful woman I've ever met."

The words burst out of my mouth without conscious thought, and they weren't words that would cool down my rising temperature. She blushed, and I watched that tide of color wash down her face and disappear under the collar of her sweater. I wanted to disappear under her sweater, too. I grabbed my napkin and wiped my mouth in case I was drooling.

Her lashes, long, thick, and gold tipped, fluttered down to cover her eyes for a split second, and I felt bereft. What was wrong with me? She was just blinking. Everyone had to blink or their eyes dried out.

She lifted her lashes and looked at me with concern. Concern?

"Ryan, are you having another allergic attack? Your voice is so hoarse and you're breathing hard — and you're sweating. Are you okay?"

"I'm fine," I croaked. Did this woman have no idea what she did to me?

I grubbed through the mush that remained of my brain searching for some memory of our conversation prior to my meltdown. "You said I reminded you of someone?"

"Did I? Oh, yes, I did. You reminded me of what I always imagined Daniel Webster or John Marshall or John Adams must have been like in the courtroom: persuasive, logical, passionate. You totally mesmerized Herb, and he told us I'm sure more than he waned to. I don't think I could have done so well as you, Ryan."

"You determine behavior by studying the artifacts people used in everyday life. You look at a birthing chair and theorize how a woman giving birth to her eleventh child in fifteen years might feel about the new infant, especially when she knew that as likely as not that infant would not live to age five. You examine the known sites of Anglo-Saxon burial grounds and theorize why they were always in sight of their villages, and what their location said about Anglo-Saxon attitudes toward their dead. I read the abstract and theorized why the three Herbs behaved the way the abstract proved they did, when from what I knew of the family, Herb the First and the Second acted against their characters. Between the two of us we make an unbeatable team."

"Do you think Herb will find the picture?"

I checked the bill and tossed the money on the table to cover it and a tip. I have no idea if the waiter deserved as big a tip as I left, because I didn't see anyone in the restaurant except Megan. World War Three could have been fought three tables away from us and I wouldn't have known.

"If the picture still exists, Herb will find it, honey. One thing you can say about Herb is that he's detail oriented."

"But as long as the picture was in his family, you would think he could describe our suspect and be able to say if the car in the picture is our car in the lake."

"I said he was detail oriented; I didn't say what kind of detail. Give him a contract or a will or a deed of trust, and he can dissect it and find any detail that will be to the benefit of his client. Ask him whether that client has a moustache, and I don't think he can tell you with any certainty. I like Herb a lot. He's a good, solid guy who has come to your rescue when you needed a lawyer to keep your buns out of jail. I'd trust him with the family fortune or your life, but he's the kind of guy who overlooks personal details like what the lady in the picture looks like out of shyness, disinterest, or a terminal avoidance of someone else's privacy, and his definition of privacy is broad enough to include his client's moustache and that picture. The picture was his grandfather's and father's personal business, so he avoided it." I leaned across the table and touched the tip of her nose. "Not like a nosey redhead I know."

She grinned and slapped my hand away. I took a deep breath and relaxed. I had dodged the crisis again. Barely.

I parked the pickup in front of Randel's Depression-era cottage. It was one of the smaller of its style, built of dark tan and brown brick, with two roof lines: one narrow, peaked roof covered the entrance and small concrete porch that abutted it on the right. Another peaked roof covered the rest of the house. I doubted the cottage had more than two bedrooms and one bathroom, with most of its square footage set vertically rather than horizontally on the lot. Someone had planted marigolds and pansies in flower beds that bordered the front of the house. I'd bet that someone wasn't Randel.

"Look, Megan, I wasn't saying anything as long as the case was just about the skeleton, but someone doesn't want that picture found and Herb the Original's girlfriend identified. I don't know who, but they're dangerous."

"I know who," said Megan, sliding out of my pickup and waiting for me to join her. "It's a member of her family. Someone doesn't want Auntie or Mom or Grandma identified, because Auntie or Mom or Grandma is a murderer. There's no statute of limitations on murder."

"Burglarizing a home is serious business. What's to keep our thief from breaking into your house and killing you in your bed if you push too hard?"

"The dogs," she said as we walked up the sidewalk to Randel's front door. "Their barking would wake up the dead. Ask any cop. Burglary is a business of stealth. A barking dog takes away the stealth factor, and the burglar runs away to rob again another day."

Megan Clark has a ready explanation to justify ignoring any of my cautions. I wasn't impressed with this one, though. "We aren't talking about a just burglar; we're talking

263

about a murderer, and he would probably kill the dogs and your mother, too."

Megan smiled, but it wasn't a happy smile. "He might find my mother hard to kill. Besides, I don't think Ray or Pearl will go so far as to kill someone."

"Ray! What are you talking about? Have you completely lost it, Megan?"

"Ray is a retired cop. I bet he opened a few locked doors in his career; I bet he even has a set of burglary picks to open locks. And he knows how to conduct a search. Think about it, Ryan. Four people were vehemently against investigating the skeleton: Ray, Rosemary, Herb, and Pearl. We've eliminated Rosemary and Herb. Ray is what, in his late seventies? He grew up on Sixth Street at the time of the murder. What might his relationship with our mystery woman be? Sister? Doubtful. Remember, Herb said the woman was the same age as his grandfather, which should be thirty-plus. Mother? Much more likely. Remember he said his mother was a widow, so no husband to cheat on."

"That's all circumstantial evidence, and shaky circumstantial evidence at best."

"Circumstantial evidence convicts murderers all the time."

"What about Pearl? And Maria? You

haven't mentioned Maria?"

"Maria is too flighty and unstable to plan and carry out a successful burglary. And she's too young. If she has any relationship to the skeleton, you would have to go back three generations to her great-grandmother. I don't think she would care about who killed her great-grandmother. Sometimes I wonder if she cares who killed her husband. I don't buy her grieving widow act. She overdoes it sometimes, and sometimes she doesn't grieve enough. She's inconsistent, and I trust inconsistent like I do coincidence. Do you agree?"

"I think she's nuts, but I also think she might be smarter than you think."

"She may be, but she's too emotionally disturbed to access her intelligence. Pearl, however, is a very bright woman, bright enough to use a credit card on a locked door if the locks aren't deadbolts."

"But what relationship would someone from California have with a skeleton in Amarillo?"

"I don't know, Ryan, but I don't believe her story about being a fortune teller because she could make more money than she can earn teaching. And why come to Amarillo? Why not set up her business in California?"

"I don't know."

"I don't either, but I'll find out. Ring the doorbell, Ryan, and let's investigate Randel's story."

Candi, warmly dressed in a sweater and corduroy slacks, looked almost pretty as she answered the door. "Come in, Megan, Ryan. I have some coffee ready. I thought we'd have time for a cup before we have to leave for the bookstore."

Over her shoulder I saw Randel sitting in a recliner in the living room. "Are the lovebirds here finally? 'My bounty is as boundless as the sea, my love as deep; the more I give to thee, the more I have, for both are infinite.' That's from *Romeo and Juliet,* act 2, scene 2. I had a raunchier quotation that fit the situation of lovers coming late, but Candi threatened to make me get my own dinner for a week if I used it."

Megan turned a rosy pink and so did Candi. I just smiled as an idea suddenly occurred to me that would quiet our Bard-quoting annoyance for a week. To paraphrase Shakespeare: two can play this game. I grasped Candi's hand and knelt on one knee. "My troubled mind doth bid me ask thou, oh, maid, wise and wonderfully fair, why doth thy live with a fool?"

Candi's eyes widened, then she giggled. She was an English major, too, and she knew Shakespeare. She pulled her hand free and curtsied. "Oh, fair sir, thou are wicked to so question a poor maiden's heart."

Megan could say what she wanted about Candi being sweet but too serious and sometimes boring. There was a sense of humor buried beneath that seriousness.

"What play are you quoting from?" demanded Randel with a frown.

"I'll help you serve the coffee, Candi," said Megan in a voice strangled with laughter, and she rushed by Randel to the kitchen that was visible beyond an archway, with Candi following on her heels. I heard muffled sounds from the kitchen, muffled, I suspected, by the two decorative pillows I saw Candi snag off the couch as she passed it at a fast walk. I also suspected those sounds were made by two women trying desperately to disguise belly laughs. They almost succeeded.

Randel gave no indication he heard them, and I figured he hadn't. I had my suspicions about Randel's ability to hold two simultaneous thoughts in his mind at one time. Right now he was trying to figure from which play Candi and I had lifted our quotes. We didn't quote from a play.

"Come on, Ryan. Which play was it?" asked Randel again.

"Just because you identify your source doesn't mean I will. I'm going to let you guess. It'll be as good for your brain as a daily dose of codfish oil."

Candi and Megan came back with the coffee and pink faces. Megan poured and Candi passed around the tray with cream, sugar, and three different kinds of sweetener. I hardly had time to lift my cup and saucer off the tray before Megan started her questioning.

"Randel, why are you and Candi so sure that you had two break-ins?"

"We came home for lunch on that Wednesday after discussing the pictures the night before, and that's when I noticed the toaster too close to the edge of the cabinet —"

Candi cleared her throat. "No, I guess it was Candi who noticed the toaster and a dusting of flour on the lid of the flour canister. Then she checked all the cabinets —"

"I found my cookware disarranged," interrupted Candi. "And my spices were out of order."

"Out of order how?" asked Megan.

"I keep my spices in alphabetical order and my canned goods by food groups —

peas and green beans as pod vegetables; sweet potatoes and beets, parsnips, and carrots, and sweet potatoes as root vegetables, and so forth."

Megan's mouth had dropped open just slightly, and I was reconsidering my conclusion that Candi wasn't as serious and boring as Megan thought.

"My carrots were stacked with peas and green beans, and my spices were out of alphabetical order. I would *never* do that!" she finished on a note of triumph.

"When Candi found that someone must have been in the kitchen, we both rushed to the office in the second bedroom. Things were rearranged just a little according to Candi. I wouldn't have caught it. There are filers and there are pilers, and I'm a piler. As long as that scumbag put my books, papers, and so forth in the same pile, I wouldn't know if Napoleon's army had searched my office, but Candi found one thing that made her uneasy —"

"Our bookshelves. Someone had obviously pulled the books out to look behind them. I always shelve the books with their spines absolutely even with one another, and exactly one quarter of an inch from the edge of the shelf. I know I sound obsessive-compulsive. That's because I am. I'm under treatment, but even with the wonderful medication I take, I'm still a little bit obsessive about certain things. My kitchen, the bookshelves, and straightening pictures on the wall. My psychiatrist suggested it. If I obsess about certain parts of my environment, then I can keep the other parts tidy without being so compulsive. It works for me, and I don't drive Randel crazy. That's the important thing."

I would bet you a kiss from Megan that the marigolds and pansies in the front flower beds were planted exactly the same distance apart.

"I'm so sorry, Candi. That disorder must be like being in prison," said Megan, looking sympathetic and just a little guilty for criticizing Candi in private to me so often. The poor kid couldn't help being so serious and meticulous about every detail — Candi's knowing the copyright date for every edition for every book Agatha Christie ever wrote, for example. That drove Megan crazy.

Megan rose from the couch and walked over to Randel. She leaned over and kissed his cheek. "Randel, you are such a sweetheart for helping Candi manage her OCD. Most men wouldn't bother. No wonder she loves you."

Megan walked back to the couch and sat

down. The rest of us, and that includes Randel, sat with our mouths open. Randel's face was crimson, and if I'm not mistaken, he might have had a tear or two in his eyes. Anybody whose personality would have annoyed Mother Teresa must feel pathetically grateful for admiration from anyone, much less a woman like Megan.

"Did you find anything missing after the first break-in?" asked Megan. She was the only one in the room still capable of talking.

Randel gobbled a time or two before he had his tongue and brain working together and could answer her. "Nothing! That's why Candi and I decided he was after the Kodaks."

"How did you know there was a second break-in, Candi?"

"One of the same reasons as for the first time — my spice cabinet was out of alphabetical order."

"And this second break-in occurred when?" asked Megan.

"Wednesday afternoon. Candi noticed when she started dinner. I came home first like always — Candi always stays at WT until five to work on her dissertation — and I didn't see anything out of place. Of course, I wouldn't have noticed anything unless the burglar had left me a note. I'm basically a slob. If it weren't for Candi, I wouldn't be able to find my way to the front door for all the clutter."

"Anything else except your spice cabinet, Candi?"

"No, and that's what makes me think the second burglar was a woman."

Megan looked puzzled, and I imagined I looked the same. What the hell did Candi mean by that statement?

Candi picked up on our puzzlement and explained. "Another woman would notice how obsessive I am about the way I stack the cookware, and she would notice that my canisters are always clean and shiny. Even the books were shelved almost as carefully as I would do it. But not quite. A few were out of alignment, but not by much. A person without OCD probably wouldn't have seen anything wrong. But I did because I'm the one who does the shelving. A psychiatrist will tell you that anybody with OCD will repeat an action over and over again in exactly the same way. If there were any way to fix my brain, I would, because I waste so much time repeating an action. One of my medications treats my anxiety caused by my OCD, because I know I'm repeating actions, but I can't stop, and I used to have terrible anxiety attacks. Randel won't even try to return a book to the shelves, because he knows I would just do it over again. But I know those books were moved by someone looking for something. I know it! I'd swear to it in court! But it was the spice cabinet where she gave herself away. Spices being in alphabetical order is something you can overlook. The tall spice cans and the shorter ones, the different-sized bottles, are all filed together, but normal people will put the tall jars and cans at the back. She must have thought there was no apparent order. But there was! I can't help the way I am!"

"Calm down, Candi. I understand and I believe you," said Megan. "But nothing was taken?"

"No," answered Randel, casting worried looks at Candi. "I told you, that's how we knew that the burglars were looking for the Kodaks. Well, they didn't find them."

"Did you find the picture?" I asked.

"I found a picture of that car with a ragged-ass Okie family standing beside it. No, I take that back. The mother and father were standing beside it. There were a couple of kids looking out the back window. A boy and a girl, I think, judging by the haircuts. But it's the car, I'm sure of it — except this car has a radiator cap and ours doesn't. It's a fancy cap, too, the fanciest thing about the car or the family. I checked it with a magnifying glass. It was a Roman goddess of some kind holding a sword up in the air in one hand.

"Another thing, there was a woman standing by the car, a tall woman. There was nothing ragged-ass about her. She had on a hat and a suit and heels. Her outfit looked just like those you see actresses wearing in movies made in the 1930s. My great-grandfather would have said she was dressed fit to kill, but I guess we'd have to say she was dressed fit to *be* killed."

"Where is it?" asked Megan, squirming on the couch and leaning toward Randel like he'd found the Holy Grail. At that moment I think she shared Candi's propensity for anxiety attacks.

"Candi's got it. I was afraid I'd lay it down someplace and lose it. I don't have to worry about Candi misplacing anything."

Candi reached down her blouse and pulled out the Kodak. "My grandmother always tells me to put money in my bra if I go on a date and he misbehaves. That way I always have cab fare. I figured if that hiding place is good for cab fare, it's good for a Kodak."

Megan and I both reached for the Kodak, but Candi gave it to Megan. I think the two of them bonded while they laughed into the pillows. I looked at the picture Megan was holding, and there she was: our murder victim.

"I wonder what she's telling the parents?" asked Megan, that thoughtful frown on her face that always wrinkled her forehead. Her mother always told her that she would have permanent wrinkles before she was thirty. I didn't care; I'd pay for the Botox injections.

"Look at the parents' posture," continued Megan, pointing at the picture. "They're huddled together staring at our Miss Bones as if they're scared of her, but they look angry, too. Look at the mother's face. She's frowning at Miss Bones at the same time she's almost hiding behind her husband."

"Did you find another picture, one with the whole family standing beside the car and a woman just turning away?" I asked Randel.

"Of course he didn't," said Megan, still studying the picture. "Randel's great-grandfather gave it to Herb's grandfather. I'll bet there are no duplicates made. Am I wrong there, Randel? Did your great-grandfather ever make duplicates of his pictures?"

"Wait a minute. What's this about Herb?" asked Randel, sitting up in his recliner.

Megan explained about Herb and his family while I studied our murder victim, and I'm sure it was she. With her heels on she was taller than either parent and seems to be looming over them. She stood straight with her shoulders back and looked sure of herself and frankly arrogant. It was amazing what the photo revealed. I was going to be very careful from now on about being photographed, particularly with Megan. I'm afraid my body language would give away my feelings about her. Not that everybody except Megan didn't already know.

"So it probably wasn't Herb who broke in," said Randel. "And it wasn't the professor, because he has a couple of classes in the morning, so that leaves Ray. He's the only other man in the reading circle. But I don't understand why he wanted the picture."

"He didn't," said Megan emphatically. "He wanted the one that Herb is looking for, the one with the other woman, Herb's grandfather's mistress."

"Wait a minute! I never heard anything about a mistress," said Randel. "My great-grandfather could talk your leg off about the people he took pictures of, but he never said anything about Herb's grandfather and any mistress."

"Maybe he thought you were too young and innocent to hear about a mistress. His generation was more careful about talking about scandal and scarlet women around their young," I said. I couldn't resist picking on Randel.

"I was in my late teens, and I knew all about the birds and the bees, Professor," snapped Randel.

"Maybe he thought it was a bad idea to talk about Herb's family," said Candi. "Didn't you tell me that Herb was a nicer man than his grandfather and his father?"

"He is a nicer guy. It's hard to believe he came out of the same nest as the other two. They were tough as boot leather according to my great-grandfather. The grandfather once took his cane to the guy who owned the laundry — I guess I ought to say the guy who rented the laundry since you said Herb's grandfather bought it. Herb's father wouldn't dirty his hands fighting somebody; he'd just sue them over anything and everything. My great-grandfather said it was worth your life to cross the grandfather, and worth your property to cross the father."

"When did the grandfather cane the laundry man, and more particularly, why did he cane him?" asked Megan.

"My great-grandfather said it wasn't any of his business. The man didn't go to the police about it, that I know. I guess my great-grandfather figured if the guy wouldn't call the cops, then whatever happened, he and Herb's grandfather wanted it kept between themselves. That was probably good enough reason for Great-Granddad to stay out of it. As for when it happened, I think it was 1940, before the war anyway."

"I'll bet," I said, "that it was after Herb's grandfather bought the laundry, and the former owner would be out of a job if he went to the police. The Depression was still on, and losing your job was serious."

Nobody said anything. I think everyone was thinking about the former owner possibly threatened with being fired and having to live with that threat and Herb's grandfather. I decided that I didn't much like Herb's grandfather. He sounded like a good candidate to be the murderer.

"Did your great-grandfather ever talk about a woman who came to the filling station every day to buy a Coke?" asked Megan.

"Sure. I don't remember her name or even if my great-granddad ever mentioned it, but he did say that she worked at the laundry."

Megan and I looked at each other. We had the connection now between the woman, the laundry, and Herb's grandfather. But what about Ray?

"What about Ray?" I asked. "He's a retired cop. Surely he could search a house without leaving a trace."

"He's a man," said Candi. "And he doesn't know I have OCD. In anyone else's home I don't think they'd see a thing out of place, or if they did, they'd think they did it themselves."

Megan nodded and so did I. Candi's theory made sense.

"And you're both sure you didn't tell anybody about the Kodaks?" asked Megan.

Candi and Randel looked at each other, then shook their heads. "Nobody knew a blasted thing but the reading circle," said Randel.

"One of them might have told someone who wasn't a member of the circle," I suggested.

"I didn't tell anyone," said Megan. "Randel and Candi didn't. Herb spent his time worrying about that picture. You know that Agnes, Rosemary, and Lorene would never discuss an ongoing investigation to outsiders. They take their responsibility seriously.

That leaves Maria and Pearl. Any guesses which one might be your burglar?"

Candi and Randel didn't guess, and I already knew which Megan suspected, so I didn't guess either.

Megan held up the picture. "Anyone want to look at the picture and then guess?"

We crowded around Megan and all studied the picture. I concentrated on the two children, because of the adults, we suspected one of being Miss Bones, and the parents would be in their late eighties or even their nineties, too old to be breaking into houses. But the two kids would probably be in their seventies, and the girl was apparently still spry enough to search a house. Or maybe Megan was wrong. Maybe it was Maria after all. Maybe she was a great-granddaughter to the parents. Maybe she wanted the picture because — why? She didn't want a scandal attached to her family? Pretty lame motive I thought.

I looked at the picture again. It's hard to be absolutely sure of hair color in a black-and-white photo, but the kids and the mother looked to be blonds. And Maria had a head full of blond hair. But I still couldn't think of a good motive for her. As for Pearl, she was the right age to be the daughter, but she had grey hair. Then I thought of something Ray said. He said Pearl dyed her hair, that her roots were light.

"It's Pearl," I said. "She dyes her hair."

"That's true according to Ray," said Megan, a little impatient with us. "Look at the eyes, Ryan. The eyes of the mother and both children are so light a color that they almost look like a photographic negative. And look at the shape of their eyes, and think about Pearl. She has those light grey eyes with that same peculiar slant."

"By God, Megan, you win the brass right!" yelled Randel. "You're right, it's Pearl."

"But why would she want that picture you say Herb has?" asked Candi. "According to what you told us, and I think it sounds reasonable, Herb's grandfather's mistress killed Miss Bones. Pearl and her family went to California."

"But we don't know that," Megan pointed out. "They could have settled here in Amarillo. When did Pearl open her fortune telling business? Does anyone know?"

"I don't keep up with fortune tellers," said Randel, then had the decency to blush when Candi looked at him.

"But, Megan, what's her motive?" asked Candi.

Megan slipped the picture inside her purse. "Why don't we go ask her?"

14

They say murder is grave because ir-
revocable, because you can't bring life
back. Are the crimes not graver when, and
because, life goes on? When the consequences continue to ripple steadily out-
ward . . . distorting and destroying?

Nicolas Freeling's *Arlette,* 1981

TIME AND AGAIN BOOKSTORE — LATER THAT NIGHT

"Is the Skeleton Task Force ready for action?" asked Megan in the same enthusiastic
tone of voice a coach would use to pump
up his football team before the big game.

She had marched into Time and Again
like the quarterback leading his team onto
the field for the first play of the game, and
was sacked before she could hand off to the
running back. Brilliant lights clicked on and
hit her in the face. Blinded by the lights she
stopped abruptly and felt Ryan trod on her

heels. She stumbled backward, and Ryan caught her before she fell.

"Cut!" commanded an impatient voice, and the lights went off. "Can you make another entrance, Dr. Clark, and give us that same line? 'Is the Skeleton Task Force ready for action?' That's perfect. Our high-priced writers couldn't come up with a line that good." A short, thin man in jeans and a pink broadcloth shirt unbuttoned enough to show off a gold chain resting on his skinny chest, stepped from behind three television cameras and a number of spot-lights on poles. A sound man with head-phones on watched the positioning of micro-phones.

Trying to blink away the spots in front of her eyes, Megan focused on the short man. "Who are you? What is all this? Agnes, what is going on?"

The man slapped his chest lightly, his fingers splayed out, and bowed like the vil-lain in a melodrama. He would be perfect if his dirty blond hair was black and slicked back, instead of straggling to his narrow shoulders. A pair of designer sunglasses rested on top of his head. Sunglasses? It was dark as pitch outside. Megan thougth he looked like a caricature of what she thought a Hollywood director of a grade-B movie might look like.

"I am Otto Steven George, the director and producer of a documentary on Sixth Street during the Depression framed within your investigation into the identity of the skeleton and her murderer. Reality Cinema, Limited is the production company, of which I am CEO, that will be filming and distributing this documentary. I expect it to be a blockbuster."

Megan turned toward the checkout counter. "Agnes, what is going on? Did you give these people permission to sandbag me?"

Agnes nodded, but Megan noticed the bookseller had red splotches on her cheeks, which meant she had a mad going. "Mr. George or whatever your real name is before you stole from Otto Preminger, Steven Spielberg, and George Lucas, get your lights, cameras, and let's see a little action as you get off my property before I call the police and charge you with criminal trespass."

The little director/producer/fraud stood on his toes in mock outrage. "We have a contract, madam!"

Agnes picked up a document and waved it at him. "You mean this?"

"Of course, I do, you silly — I mean, Ms. Caldwell."

"I read your contract while we were waiting for Megan, Mr. George, and what's more, my attorney, Mr. Herbert Jackson the Third to read it. He was advising me when Megan arrived and you filmed her without explaining to her what you were doing. That was underhanded. The upshot is, Mr. George, that you have no signed contract. Mr. Jackson tells me that there are more snakes in this pond than he has seen in a contract since he began the practice of law. I consider you to have entered my business under false pretenses, so you may exit, and we will end our association on a civilized note."

The director grabbed at the contract, but Agnes jerked it out of his reach. "Give me that contract, you stupid woman, and I'll show you the paragraph that states the contract is in effect if a verbal agreement is witnessed. And we did have a verbal agreement. My soundman, James Gilley, witnessed it." He turned to call the soundman and stiffened. James Gilley was dismantling the sound equipment. Cameramen were already walking toward the door.

"Jimmy! What are you doing? You men get those cameras back in here! Jimmy, I need you to confirm that you witnessed a verbal agreement between me and this old woman." Megan stood back and waited for the explosion. No one crossed Agnes — and nobody called her old, either, unless they wanted to be banned from the bookstore forever.

The man called Jimmy picked up a case and headed for the door. He stopped in the doorway. "That old woman reminds me of my grandmother. Granny lived in Arizona in some old mining town in the middle of nowhere. She killed three different men who tried to break into her house. Each time she loaded the victim in her trunk and hauled him to the sheriff. It got to the point that the local undertaker staked out her house, and anytime Granny got into her car, he would follow her. If I were you I'd write this one off and leave. That's what I'm doing."

Otto Steven George jumped up and down like Rumplestiltskin, and Megan watched to see if he would split himself in two and disappear into a hole in the floor. As she recalled, that's how the fairy tale ended.

"I'll blackball you in the industry if you don't come back, Jimmy!" screamed the little man.

Jimmy grinned. "I don't think anyone

would pay any attention to you, but go ahead and try. I've had an offer from the film school at USC to teach next year. I've accepted. Maybe I can teach the film students more than how to spell ethics."

Ray Roberts walked over to the director. "Ms. Caldwell has asked you politely to leave her establishment. Are you going to go?"

Ray was in his seventies with grey hair and age lines gouged on his forehead and along each side of his mouth. The director looked him up and down and dismissed him as an old man. To his other faults Megan added terminal stupidity.

"Go back to your seat, old man. Ms. Caldwell and myself are conducting business."

Ray nodded and smiled, then picked up the director by the collar of his pink shirt and the waistband of his jeans. He walked to the front door and tossed the little director through it. He dusted off his hands and closed the door behind the last of the film crew and snapped the two bars across it. He walked to the checkout counter amid the applause of the Skeleton Task Force.

Ray leaned on the counter. "Herb, you suppose you could draw up a contract between Agnes and me that says I'm her security force. That way that little man can't charge me with assault."

"Who told them that we were investigating the skeleton?" asked Megan.

"You know Sixth Street, Megan. Probably everyone in the San Jacinto area knows," said Agnes.

"I think we should have let them film," said Maria, looking tired and discontented. "The skeleton makes a wonderful story, and we would have gotten so much publicity. He might of paid us, too. And it would have taken my mind off my grief."

"Has anyone seen them on Sixth Street before now?" asked Megan, looking as disgusted with Maria's claim of grief as she was with the producer.

"You can't turn around without falling over somebody toting a camera over his shoulder, or a microphone in his hand," said Barney. "I had six of 'em ask me today how the investigation was going. Our friend that Agnes just kicked out is one of the six. It'd be hard to miss Shorty in his pink shirt. He's been trolling Sixth Street all day, buttonholing people to interview and taking wide-angle shots of the street and buildings."

"I've had cable networks try to interview me," said Hazel Gilbert, "but I refused to let them in my store after one cameraman

288

knocked a very expensive decanter set on the floor and broke it. I made a claim on the network, but who knows if I'll be compensated for the loss. But I've not seen this person before. I don't know about his reputation, but his fashion sense is terrible."

Pearl Smith walked through the back door that led to the storage room, bathroom, and Agnes's apartment. "I take it that it's safe to come out now."

"My goodness, I forgot all about you, Pearl," said Agnes as she fed the film contracts into the shredder behind her desk.

"Were you hiding from our Hollywood dunce?" asked Megan, wondering why the fortune teller was — if she was.

"Yes, I was," said Pearl, pouring a cup of coffee at the refreshment table. "I may not care what people think of me, but I care what they think about my family. My son is a superior court judge in California. Imagine what would happen to his professional career if his mother is revealed as a Gypsy witch by a lurid documentary. My other son is a heart surgeon. I don't think his patients would be impressed if they knew of my second career. My daughter is an attorney in a very conservative law firm. The other partners wouldn't be pleased. And I have grandchildren trying to establish themselves in professional careers. I refuse to put them in jeopardy."

"Then why do it at all?" asked Megan. "Why the whole Gypsy fortune teller bit? Based on how successful your family is, I can't believe you're impoverished."

Pearl sipped her coffee before answering. Her unusual eyes stared without blinking at Megan. "Everyone has their own reasons for what they do, and mine are private."

"Does dying your blond hair grey have something to do with your private reasons?" asked Megan, determined to break through this woman's facade.

Pearl spilled coffee as she attempted to set the cup on its saucer. It was a clumsy move, and Megan had never noticed the woman being clumsy before.

"Have you ever seen a blond Gypsy?" she asked Megan, her face stiff.

"I don't think it would hurt your business much," said Megan. "By the way, I tried to call you this afternoon to make an appointment, but I didn't get an answer."

Pearl's cup clattered against the saucer. "I had some errands to run. I'm sorry I missed you."

"How long have you been living on Sixth Street and practicing — is that the right word?— your, uh, profession?" asked

Megan, stepping close to Pearl. Violating an American's private space always evoked a response. It was almost a visceral reaction. Pearl involuntarily took a step back, then realized what she had done and stood firm.

"What is the point of all these questions, Megan? Do you think I'm the Back Stabber?"

"Did you call on Randel and Candi this afternoon? They're sorry they missed you." Megan saw Randel and Candi move up beside her.

Pearl's nostrils flared, and Megan swore she saw fear in those grey eyes. "What are you accusing me of?"

"I think you know," said Megan softly as she took the old Kodak out of her notebook. "Is this what you're looking for? You can dye your hair, but you can't change the shape of your eyes."

Pearl's shoulders slumped, and her face aged as the vitality that had been Pearl Smith seeped away. "I've failed."

Megan felt like a bully. Pearl as much as admitted that she was the little girl in the car, but Megan didn't feel good about finding out. Brushing against wounded souls and secret pain and guilty secrets hadn't been a problem in her other investigations, because her suspects in other cases hadn't been her friends. Her cases were puzzles to be solved, board games where she moved people around like chess pieces, indifferent to their suffering except on a cerebral level. She had abhorred the hatred or the avarice or psychopathic selfishness that motivated the murderer, and felt a vague, distant pity for the victim, but the victims themselves had been so unpleasant or pathetic or caught in the consequences of their own choices that it was difficult — and downright impossible on occasions — to feel sadness or real empathy or fury at the injustice at their demise.

With sudden repugnance she recognized her responses up to now had resembled her mother's emotional involvement with her causes, which had robbed Megan of so much of her childhood: sincere, but abstract and not personal. Her mother saw people in the mass, not the individual in trouble. She didn't risk her heart.

This time it was as if Megan was hypersensitive; as if she was turned inside out, and she identified with the suffering of each of the victims and the sorrow of each of her friends involved, felt each individual's pain as if someone had touched her raw, exposed flesh with a live electrical wire. Her hands shook, and she felt overwhelmed with emotions. She wished for the return of her objectivity. It was well and good to say that it was better to have loved and lost than to never have loved at all, but it was a damned painful philosophy to practice.

She empathized with Pearl's sense of failure and led the old woman, and Pearl was suddenly old, through the bookstore's back door followed by Ryan, Candi, and Randel. She closed the door behind them, locking out the rest of the members. In silence she led them to Agnes's apartment and steered Pearl toward the living room couch.

"Candi, do you think you can manage to make us all some tea without your OCD going into overdrive at the sight of the clutter in Agnes's kitchen?"

Candi smiled and drew a deep breath and held it for several seconds. "I'll concentrate on remembering that it's not my environment."

Megan sat on one side of Pearl and motioned for Ryan to take the other. "Randel, find a tissue or handkerchief or something for Pearl."

Randel searched wildly for the requested materials. Over the sound of a tea kettle's whistle, Megan heard him open drawers and cabinet doors in the kitchen and finally come rushing back to Pearl with what was clearly a dishtowel. "It was all I could find," he said in a defensive voice.

Pearl smiled without that hint of arrogant amusement that had always irritated Megan. "Any port in a storm, Randel. Thank you."

"I believe that's from Shakespeare," he said, clearly unused to being appreciated by anyone but Candi.

Pearl smiled again. "It could be. Most really appropriate clichés originated with Shakespeare."

Candi carried in a cookie sheet with steaming mugs of tea and a sugar bowl. "No milk, and I couldn't find any sweetener."

"So you are the girl in the picture?" asked Megan as she watched Pearl wrap her hands around her mug. The woman must be freezing, because Megan's own mug was hot enough to fry an egg.

Pearl nodded. "I'm impressed that you are observant enough to notice my blond roots. I wear a red silk kerchief over my hair when I'm telling fortunes, and I forget about my roots."

Megan felt ashamed to admit that she was almost as good as Herb at avoiding noticing personal details about people. She dissected expressions and body language, but not a thing like hair roots until they were an inch long. "Ray noticed, not me. Why did you want the picture? So you wouldn't be recognized?"

"No, so no one would see that woman." She saw Megan open her mouth to ask another question, and shook her head. "Let me tell my story my way. I think everyone will understand why I'm in Amarillo disguised as a Gypsy fortune teller. I don't know all of what happened because I was so young, only four years old at the time. My brother told me some of what I know, but he was only six, so my story is how two children interpreted what they saw adults do, and children don't always correctly understand what they see. My brother died on some muddy hillside in Korea during the war, so we never discussed it as adults. And it seemed so far in the past anyway. How could it hurt us? Shows you how foolish children are.

"And I never asked my parents. My mother died of a massive heart attack in 1950, so I never had a relationship with her as an adult woman. My father died in 1980 at age 82, an advanced age for a man who suffered the starvation and desperation of the Great Depression. And we suffered. I remember him walking through the fields after a dust storm when the crops were buried under sand dunes. I remember that after we slaughtered our last cow, we sold up everything we had except one mattress. We sold the furniture, china my mother had inherited, her wedding dress that I was supposed to wear when I married, my father's watch that belonged to my grandfather, what machinery there was left. We didn't sell the farm because it was mortgaged. When the banker and the sheriff came out to evict us because the bank had foreclosed, we were all packed and ready to leave. I didn't look back; none of us did. You could smell the sense of failure from my father, but he didn't let his shoulders slump. He was always a proud man even when he had no reason to be."

Pearl look a long drink of tea. "I get thirsty just remembering how dry the land was. I don't think we had seen more than a few sprinkles since my birth. At least, I never remember seeing real rain until we drove through the mountains of New Mexico. Anyway, I remember Amarillo. It looked like a fairy tale city to me, because there were no boarded-up stores that I saw. Every store on Sixth Street was open, and people were actually buying things, food and clothes. The only ragged hungry people I saw were other Okies like us. We stopped at the filling station."

She stopped and her mouth trembled. When she spoke again, her voice was lower, her words widely spaced as if the past weighted each word down. "Men who worked at the station were smiling, some of them were even laughing. They lived in another world from ours. I had never seen my father laugh. My father bought gas, and as he paid he looked at my mother. I was only four, but I could read his expression: our money is almost gone. I don't know how my parents found the strength to drive on. When we ran out of gas again, there would be no money to buy more. I guess they didn't know what else to do but drive on. Then that woman — I remember thinking how pretty her clothes were — started talking to my parents. She took my father down the street a little ways, and they talked for what seemed like hours. My mother stayed in the car. I saw tears rolling down her cheeks, but she never made any noise. What was the use?"

Pearl drank more tea and stared into the distance. Megan didn't know what Pearl was visualizing, but she was glad the old woman didn't share her visions. Randel shuffled his feet, and Candi shushed him.

Eventually, Pearl continued talking but even more slowly now, her voice high-pitched like a child.

"The woman came back followed by my father. My mother got out of the car, and she and my father argued. Finally, my mother gave up. She didn't give in, she gave up. We followed the woman to a motel; at least, that's what we call a motor court now. My brother and I didn't understand. People like us didn't stay at motor courts. My mother sat on the bed holding on to my brother and I. She had been crying, and her eyes were all red. That woman and my father were at the other end of the cabin by the door. Nobody was saying much until someone knocked on the door. It was another woman who came in. She was wearing a faded housedress, but I still thought she was prettier than the tall, mean-looking one in the fancy clothes. My mother got off the bed and led us kids toward my father and the two women. My parents started arguing, and my father hit my mother. He had never hit her before, and he never hit her again. Then the tall woman said something, and the pretty woman pushed her out the door. At that point my brother and I ran back to the bed and hid under the covers and never saw anything else of what transpired until my father brought my mother back inside and put her in bed with us. Mother was crying, horrible loud sobs, and Daddy told my brother to lock the door behind him and watch over Mother.

"It was daylight when Daddy and the other woman, the pretty one, came back. We all got in the mean woman's fancy car and left. Mother had her purse — the mean woman's, I mean. There was money in the purse, a lot of money. There was enough for my father to buy an orange grove just outside of Los Angeles. That was the start of our prosperity.

"We never talked about Amarillo and the woman and what happened to her. Gradually, after my mother died and my brother was killed, the story became a bad memory, one I finally stopped thinking about — until after my father's death and I found the letter from Herbert Jackson the Second. It was dated 1973 and informed my father that Herbert Jackson had died, but he, Jackson the Second, had inherited the property and would hold it in the family until everyone who knew about the events was dead. I kept the letter secret from my family and subscribed to the Amarillo newspaper, so I would know if the body was found. If Herb the Second could trace my father, the police could, too. In the meanwhile, I prospered, and my children prospered, and I tried to put the whole matter out of my mind. I wasn't successful all the time, but successful enough that I could enjoy what I had."

"What changed to bring you to Amarillo?" asked Megan.

"As the years passed, I started worrying more and more. Herb Jackson the Second couldn't live forever, and I knew nothing about Herb the Third. I didn't know if he would honor his grandfather's and father's pledge. But I did know that you can't just ignore property. I had written Herb the Second, so I knew that the property was an old laundry. He never told me any specifics, but I guessed that the laundry and the mean woman of my memories were connected. I suspected her body was buried somewhere on the property. It had to be; that was the only logical conclusion. I didn't want that body found. I didn't want that nightmarish night dragged into the light. My family has a few contacts in the film industry, nobody important or well-known, but we're prominent enough otherwise that *National Enquirer* would feel it hit a bonanza. Finally, I moved to Amarillo four years ago and transformed myself into a Gypsy fortune teller, so I could watch over the property.

Then Herb the Second died, and Herb the Third put the property on the market. The worst has happened, and now I wait."

"The police aren't interested in investigating, Pearl. Your family is safe."

"But you want to know, don't you, Megan, and you're more dangerous than the police."

"I don't know what the argument between the woman and your parents was about, but your family had nothing to do with her death. You were in the wrong place at the wrong time. Your family might have precipitated the murder, but that's all, if even that. We don't know if there was any history between Herb the Original's mistress and the mean woman of your memories, but the mistress is the one who committed the deed."

Pearl searched Megan's eyes. "You're absolutely sure?"

Megan patted her hand. "Absolutely. You believed your father killed that woman, didn't you? That's why you wanted the picture, to erase any evidence that your father ever met Miss Bones? Well, the police just want to file the skeleton as a cold case. Besides, how could your father know about the false wall in the laundry? Your father probably helped bury our Miss Bones, so he must have thought the mistress was justified, and Herb the Original certainly did. But he's dead. You can't prosecute a dead man for interfering with a corpse or aiding the mistress. The police can't prosecute her; they have no evidence and no witnesses left alive. And you said you never saw what happened, so you can't testify. I just want to know the mistress's name and whereabouts, so I can reassure her if she's still alive. Between the discovery of Miss Bones, and all the garbage in the newspaper, she has to be really worried. She has to be an old, old, woman, and she doesn't need hassling by the police or the media for a murder she did to protect your family from whatever threat Miss Bones represented. And I believe from the body language of your parents in this picture that they were afraid of Miss Bones. I can't imagine any threat she made that could be as bad as what your parents were already enduring, but that's why I want to talk to the old woman. I want to know the motive, and I think you do, too."

Megan paused, drew a deep breath. Now was the time to ask her. "Pearl, do you remember a young woman drinking a Coke at the filling station, standing beside your car at one time?"

Pearl bowed her head and folded and refolded the dish towel as she thought. She lifted her head finally. "I don't remember any woman like that."

15

We often hear (almost invariably, however, from superficial observers) that guilt can look like innocence. I believe it to be infinitely the truer axiom of the two that innocence can look like guilt.

Franklin Blake in Wilkie Collins's
The Moonstone, 1868

TIME AND AGAIN BOOKSTORE — IMMEDIATELY LATER

I knew Megan was frustrated by Pearl's unexpected answer by the way she flung herself back against the couch. I felt a little frustrated, too, but there was no point in nagging Pearl about it. She had filled in some gaps for us, but we couldn't expect her to do all our work for us.

"Megan, we need to get back to the meeting. Everyone will want to hear Pearl's story, and everything else we found out today," I said, rising off the couch and stretching my back.

"Not Pearl's story," said Megan emphatically. "That stays with us. I trust the reading circle to keep the secret of Pearl's family's involvement, but Barney is liable to entertain his customers with the story. Hazel might tell the story at her next cocktail party when she's trolling for future customers. Or she might keep the secret and become Pearl's best friend and ardent supporter. Of course, she would try to convince you to improve your wardrobe first, Pearl."

Pearl smiled for the first time since before she told her story. I was glad to see it. "She'd be wrong. If you ever have to hide, hide in plain sight in as flamboyant a persona as possible. Who would look for the blond Los Angeles socialite in the person of a black-haired Gypsy fortune teller living in an old frame house painted yellow? By the way, Megan, you caught me unaware when I first visited the reading circle. I wear brown contacts when I tell fortunes. I took them out so I could wash off my garish makeup and failed to put them back in. Fortunes turn on trifles. If Ray hadn't noticed my blond roots, and if I hadn't forgotten my contacts, I don't think you would have guessed I was the little girl in the picture."

I could see Megan thinking about it for a moment. "Yes, I would have, because all the members who refused to help were keeping some secret connected to, or they thought was connected to, the skeleton. Ray is the last holdout, and I'll have to actually know the name of the mistress to shake him."

"Why would that be necessary?" asked Pearl.

"Because I believe Ray Roberts is related to the mistress, but I have to know her name to confront him."

"But what about Maria?" asked Randel. "I don't remember her volunteering to help."

"Randel!" gasped Candi. "Her husband had just been murdered! How can you expect her to be interested?" I was beginning to really like Candi. She might straighten out Randel in the end. I still think she could have chosen a better subject to reform, but maybe she wanted a challenge.

"Oh, yeah, I forgot." Seeing everyone looking at him, he flushed red and shrugged his shoulders. "Well, she's not exactly wearing widow's weeds, is she?" Leave it to Randel to point out the obvious.

"Just don't say anything like that to her, or she'll have hysterics again," said Candi, "and we'll waste another discussion period while Agnes, Rosemary, Lorene, and I try to calm Maria down. I feel so sorry for her. She said something to me last week about having to alternate sleeping on each side of the bed, or one side of her contour sheet would wear out and the other side wouldn't, because there would be no one to sleep on it. It sounds silly, but sad at the same time. There would only be one of everything to wear out. Don't you think that's sad, Megan?"

Megan glanced at me. We each had only one of everything: one pillow on the queen-sized bed; one glass, one plate, one serving of silver. Megan lived with her mother if you called her company, but I didn't have a queen in my queen-sized bed. Candi was right; it was sad.

Megan and I switched our gazes to opposite corners of the room. One of these days soon we were going to have to move from communicating visually to communicating verbally. A crisis in our relationship was approaching; I could feel it.

"Let's leave Maria and Ray out of our discussion for the time being," said Megan, her voice sounding a little husky, from, I hoped, shared fantasies our eyes revealed. Or maybe I didn't hope that. My fantasies were growing more explicit by the day. I didn't want her thinking I only wanted her body; her mind was on my top ten list, too.

I realized I must have missed part of the conversation while I was daydreaming. "— returning to Pearl and her story and who she should tell. I think Larry Spencer is impossible to predict. He might go to his grave with the secret, or he might tell the next person he sees."

Pearl kissed Megan's cheek. "Thank you, dear. After all these years protecting my family, I'm not entrusting strangers with my secret. I'll tell the reading circle when I decide it is the right time." I hoped she decided soon because my intuition told me time was running out.

We saw all the expectant faces when we stepped back in the bookstore. Megan held up her hands to stop the eager questions. "Pearl will tell her story later and so will Herb. Right now I'd like to hear what you all have found since the Skeleton Task Force last met." I decided by the quick smiles from everyone but Ray that members and merchants both liked Megan's name for the group.

"Rosemary, Lorene, what about the census records?"

Rosemary and Lorene nodded their heads

in unison. "Rosemary and I put away Dame Agatha and Dorothy L. to work on the census records. I brewed coffee in my twenty-cup pot each morning at eight o'clock, and we started work. We first made a list of everyone living within six blocks on either direction of Sixth Street in the 1930 census, then we checked the telephone books to see if there were any residents still living and had a phone number. The ones we found were for children who would have been too young in 1938 to be involved, but we called anyway. We wrote their answers by the names. We also checked each name from the census records on the Internet. We got some interesting results —"

"Terrific! Here's to the Terrible Twins!" said Megan, holding up her coffee cup in a toast. "Give me your results on the census and I'll study them. Please keep your conclusions to yourselves for the time being. I want to put all the results together to see which of my theories they support. Agnes, what did you find in your mother's sales receipts?" I wondered why Megan was so anxious to keep the twins' results a secret from the rest of us. And what theories was she talking about? She never mentioned any theories to me.

"Hers and mine. The search went more

quickly than I anticipated because I disregarded those slips for women I already knew were dead. There were only a few names from the thirties that appeared after 1980 and only one after 1990. Sarah Robertson, your mother, Ray. She was such an entertaining and lovely woman and didn't look anywhere near her real age. I have no receipts for her after 1995. That must have been when you moved her to a nursing home, Ray. She wasn't too happy with you as I recall."

"She was ninety years old!" Ray burst out. "She couldn't live by herself anymore. My wife was dying, and I needed to take care of her, and I couldn't take care of them both. After my wife died I left Mom where she was. She seemed content enough, and I wasn't any spring chicken myself. I couldn't take care of a woman her age, and she didn't want me to try. She only had a little while left, and she needed to be where she could have twenty-four-hour care. I felt guilty about it — afterwards."

Ray looked so miserable that I wished Megan would interrupt this conversation. I wouldn't want to talk about my mother either if she were deceased. Megan's face was completely expressionless. I couldn't believe she couldn't see Ray's misery as well as the rest of us. The twins were looking at her as if they couldn't understand why she was letting Agnes run, either.

"I'm sure you did the best you could for Sarah under the circumstances, Ray," said Agnes in a sympathetic voice. "I'm sorry I missed her funeral. I always check the obituaries, but I must have missed hers."

"It wasn't in the paper. There was no one left who knew her, so we had a private memorial service, just the family. I'm sorry I didn't think of you, Agnes. I was thinking of people her age, and just forgot that she was your customer for so many years," said Ray, his head bowed.

"Don't feel guilty, Ray. I remember her and that's enough."

"Thank you, Agnes. If I could have the sales receipts, please," said Megan, holding out her hand. There was that brusque voice again. I didn't even know that Megan could be brusque. Just when I thought I knew her as well as any man could, she surprised me.

"Candi, I'm sure you have a meticulously written report," said Megan with a smile, again holding out her hand.

"I didn't find anything I thought was helpful. I'm sorry," said Candi, wringing her hands.

"Don't worry about it, Candi," said

Megan. "Here's something else you can do if you have time." Megan wrote something in her spiral notebook, tore out the page, and gave it to Candi.

Candi read the note. "But, Megan, there's no reason to look this up —"

"You can share your results next week, Candi, not now."

Again that brusque voice cutting off Candi's words. What was Megan doing? She was moaning over everyone else's changed behavior, but she wasn't any better herself.

Herb stood up, a stoical expression on his face. "Megan, I think I owe it to the reading circle to confess my family's involvement in this morbid affair."

I felt sorry for Call Me Herb. This affair had scandal written all over it, and anal retentive Herb would rather have a case of herpes than be involved in a scandal. Personally, I didn't care as long as Megan wasn't hurt by it, although given her attitude tonight, I might reconsider that position.

"Later, Herb. Did you look through your father's papers?"

"Yes, and I have canceled checks, but I'm afraid there is some confusion about —"

"For now let's keep names to ourselves, Herb. In fact, don't go into anything you found among your father's papers. There is a privacy issue that I have to clear up first. No one knows enough by themselves to violate privacy, but if we lay it all out, then we will be harming someone who doesn't deserve it. Next week I will satisfy everyone's curiosity — if I have permission to do so."

Megan gathered all the papers from her researchers and dropped them in her Peruvian woven bag. Everyone eyed the bag as if they wanted to steal it. Nothing spikes curiosity like being told you have to wait. And speaking of waiting, I can hardly wait to get Megan alone and wring the secrets out of her.

"Wait a minute," said Barney, trying to pull his pants and belt over his belly as he stood up. It was a temporary fix before his belt begin to slide down his belly's overhang. "Before Herb starts talking I think we all ought to be here. Larry ain't here yet, and he didn't answer his phone when I called. I looked out the door, and his lights in the store are still on, which I can't figure out. Since the Back Stabber has been running loose, he's been closing at five or before. Maybe he bought some more memorabilia today and thinks he ought to get it displayed before he closes, but I'm tired of waiting for him. Larry's gonna make the undertaker wait to embalm him."

"Ryan and I'll go get him, Barney. The rest of you get a cup of coffee."

Megan and I walked down Sixth Street toward Larry's store.

"You were in a hurry to get out of there, Megan. What's wrong? And what's all this secrecy? What are you planning that you don't want me to know about?" I asked.

Megan held out her hand, and I clasped my fingers around it. Her hand was freezing. "These two cases are horrible. People will be hurt, and there is nothing I can do about it except try to limit the damage as much as I can. I hurt inside from all the stories we've heard today, Ryan, and I've never felt that way before. And I hurt even more from Pearl's lies."

I tugged on her hand. "Stop right there, honey. We've heard so many evasions, exaggerations, and fibs in the last week or so, that I think you're seeing lies where there aren't any. I thought Pearl's story was straightforward. I believed her. What part didn't you believe?"

"Ryan, how could she miss seeing the mistress? According to what Randel's great-grandfather said, the mistress was there every day, drinking her Coke and laughing with the help. And she had been by the car, probably talking to the parents. We know that because we have the picture. Why is she lying about noticing the woman? It doesn't make sense."

"Megan, honey, maybe she really didn't notice. She was a little girl, remember. Just four years old."

"Pearl would have noticed her, Ryan. I was a four-year-old girl once."

"Honey, you were an unusual four-year-old girl. I remember. You were the sharpest knife in anybody's drawer." I stopped, remembering that I was a grown man with two kids and a wife pregnant with twins when Megan was four. Suddenly, I was aware of the gap in our ages. What was I doing pretending that Megan and I had any future together? When she reached my age, I might have removable teeth and be worrying about my prostate.

She didn't notice my stricken look. "There was something else that shocked me. When I talked about the mistress being alive, she wasn't surprised. She already knew it. What is going on, Ryan? Pearl is telling most of the truth but not all. Ray isn't telling any of the truth because he's not talking at all."

"Calm down, Megan. You'll learn the truth before it's over. You always do."

"I know most of it now; I just can't prove all of it, and it all hurts." She stretched up on her toes and kissed me. "I'm so glad I've got you."

Her kiss undid me. I wrapped my arms around her and pulled her tightly against my chest, tighter and closer than I had ever held her before, until every firm inch of her body pressed against mine. You couldn't have pushed a toothpick between us. I rested my chin on the top of her head. "Do you know what you do to me when you say things like that?"

I could feel her blush right through my sweater where her cheek rested against me. "I know one thing," she stuttered.

I rushed to reassure her. "That's minor —" I started to say, my voice so hoarse I had trouble speaking.

"— Feels pretty major to me."

I don't know what I would have said or done next, but a light stunned us, so I never had a chance to find out. Anything major or minor shrank into insignificance.

"That's good, Doc. Kiss her again. A little sex will liven up the film. Investigators Indulge in Affair While a Back-Stabbing Killer Roams Sixth Street."

Megan and I sprang apart like two magnets repelling each other. "It's that jackass director!" I said, starting toward him with the premeditated malice of a sexually frustrated male. "I'm going to punch his lights out, stomp on his head, and smash that damn camera."

"Now, Doc, keep your pants on," said Otto Steven George as he backed up and took shelter behind his much taller cameraman.

Megan caught my arm. "Don't hit him, Ryan. That's what he wants. Come on, here's Larry's store. Let's find him and go out the back door and circle around through the alleys to the bookstore."

I was still growling when I let myself be pulled to the store. "When I find out who sicced him on us, I'm going to kick his butt up between his shoulder blades."

"You think someone deliberately persuaded him to come to Sixth Street?"

"No, I think he originally came on his own like the rest of the vultures, but why is he suddenly concentrating on us, Agnes's bookstore, Barney, taking panoramic shots of the street and building? He's been waiting outside the building for more than thirty minutes. Why? To take shots of the book club members? Why does he think his documentary is going to be a blockbuster? It smells, and not of coincidence. Somebody is setting us up, but I don't know who or why."

"To either distract us or discredit us," said Megan, wrinkling up her forehead as she thought. "Those are the only two motives I can think of."

"But why would anyone want to do that, and if they did, why did they have to bring in such a jackass as Otto Steven George?"

"Because we're getting too close to the truth, or someone thinks we are," replied Megan. She paused, gazing at the producer and his crew. She smiled, then started laughing. "I should have thought of it before."

"What truth? We already know the truth about Miss Bones even if the reading circle doesn't know it yet. That leaves the Back Stabber, and we don't have a clue as to who he is."

Megan didn't answer, and a sudden chill ran down my spine. She knows or suspects the truth. Before I could confront her with my suspicions, she anticipated me. "Who told us that she had a few contacts in the film industry, and who didn't want us learning anything about Miss Bones, and who might have wanted to distract us?"

"Pearl?" I guessed in horror.

"I'm sure she'll call the little jerk off now

that we know. She was pretty clever though. I've decided I like Pearl a lot. I wish she'd stay in Amarillo, but I suppose she'll move back to California now that the skeleton is out of the closet — or laundry wall."

Megan pushed on Larry's door. It swung open, and a tiny bell rang. "He must be here. The door's unlocked. Larry, where are you? Everyone's waiting for you, and Barney wants to skin you alive for holding up the meeting."

There was no answer, and I heard Megan draw a deep breath in frustration. Then she froze. So did I. We both smelled an odor that was becoming all too familiar: a sweetish, copper odor that tightened my stomach and started my head spinning.

"Stay here, Ryan," she said, letting go of my arm. I couldn't have moved if I had wanted to — and I didn't want to.

I watched Megan look up and down the aisles of memorabilia, then walk toward the sales counter. I knew what she would find before she rounded the chest-high counter, and I squatted down and put my head between my knees and breathed deeply and slowly.

"Ryan, use your cell phone to call 911. Tell the dispatcher to send Special Crimes. I've found another body. While I diddled around with a 70-year-old skeleton and waited for proof so I could tie up all the loose ends like I was Hercule Poirot, the Back Stabber struck again."

16

You call subjecting an innocent man to the business of a murder trial justice? That is law, not justice.

> Bella Bartholomew in Douglas Clark's
> *Poacher's Bag,* 1980

ROUTE 66 GIFT SHOP, SIXTH STREET — AN HOUR LATER

The elderly African-American Justice of the Peace had come and gone, leaving behind one very pissed off lieutenant and an equally pissed off sergeant. There is nothing that pissed off cops more than being told that a civilian sleuth was a smarter investigator than they were. Jenner was enjoying Schroder's and Lieutenant Carr's humiliation as much as he was able, but he figured it would just make them come down harder on Megan Clark when they got the chance, which dampened his enjoyment somewhat. The JP may have thought he was clearing the air between Megan and Lieutenant Carr and Schroder by reaming them out for not letting her study the marks on the victims' foreheads, which she had convinced him were the signature of a serial killer, but all he did was add more pollution to the atmosphere.

The evidence techs, on the other hand, respected Megan and liked her. She always watched them collect evidence and asked questions that allowed them to show off, that is, when Carr and Schroder didn't throw her off the crime scene. Evidence techs weren't dummies, though. They felt the tension in the air and recognized the lieutenant's and Schroder's red faces and narrowed eyes as boding no good for Megan Clark. Occasionally, one of the white figures in their disposable suits and paper booties would wink at Megan in sympathy behind their mighty leaders' backs. Not that sympathy would help Megan; nothing would unless she managed to magically disappear.

Jenner figured Megan was right on the money about there being a serial killer loose in the neighborhood, and if she said those marks weren't meaningless cuts, he believed her. If Carr and Schroder didn't, then they were cutting off their noses to spite their faces and delaying justice just like the JP said. He would run interference for Megan if he could figure out how, because Schroder couldn't get past the idea that anyone who found as many bodies as Megan Clark had must be guilty of something. It was only a matter of time before the burly sergeant came up with a charge. Then he'd get a search warrant and take apart Megan's house, truck, garage, dog house, and dog feces looking for proof she was involved in the Back Stabber murders. She wasn't, though. Why couldn't Schroder see that?

Jenner looked around the gift store while Schroder and Lieutenant Carr engaged in a staring contest with Megan Clark. When somebody finally said something, he'd listen. Meanwhile, he'd take a gander through the store. There was memorabilia everywhere: postcards of famous sights along Route 66 in a rack by the counter; battered and dented Route 66 road signs that looked authentic — maybe they were and maybe they weren't — a series of Burma-Shave signs hanging on the wall behind the counter; cheap plaster replicas of landmarks — a café shaped like an Indian tipi, an art deco restaurant with rounded corners inset with glass block windows; a really cool replica of Sixth Street as it looked in 1940. Jenner examined it more closely. There was the laundry that held the body, already two years old in 1940, that turned up as a skeleton last week. Across the street was a miniature of a filling station. Down the street a block away was Time and Again Bookstore looking exactly the way it did tonight, except there were no planters filled with flowers out front, no narrow border of bricks along the edge of the sidewalk, and no newly planted trees. The planters, trees, and brick border had been added to the length of Sixth Street after the area was declared a historical district. Jenner could remember when the street was mostly used furniture stores and junk shops before the city and the State Historical Society realized that Sixth Street was one of the very few locations on Route 66 that had remained relatively unchanged since the historic road had been built. Most of the original buildings were still in existence, although their function had changed. Now the street was lined with antique stores, gift shops, trendy little restaurants that featured live music at night, and Barney Benson's B&B Blues Bar. Barney's bar and Time and Again Bookstore were the only businesses whose existence stretched back to the thirties. They were both still owned by the same families that first opened them, although

Agnes Caldwell wasn't a family exactly; she was a spinster who probably also stretched back to the thirties. Jenner wondered what would happen to the store when Agnes passed on to that bookstore in the sky.

"Tell us how you happened to find another body, Dr. Clark?" asked Schroder in that low rumble that passed as a voice. Jenner unobtrusively moved to stand behind the sergeant and Lieutenant Carr, but not too close. Schroder and Carr were going to grill Megan Clark, and Jenner didn't want to be part of the group. He liked Megan. She was smart, knew her field, and was cute as a little red wagon. Especially tonight. She was wearing a V-necked, orange sweater that fit her like a glove, a multicolored velvet skirt with swirls of orange and gold and brown with splotches of turquoise. The skirt was a couple of inches shy of her knees and left well-shaped calves and narrow ankles bare to be admired. She even wore velvety-looking high heels without backs — he thought his wife called them mules — instead of hiking boots. She was a well-packaged female, and it was no wonder that Professor Stevens hung around her like a slobbering dog ready for a tummy rub. Lieutenant Carr wasn't much better, but he'd be a lot closer to a doggy treat if he'd stop threatening to arrest her every time they met over a dead body. Particularly when Jenner knew she was as innocent as an angel in Heaven.

"I was looking for him, Sergeant. I don't mean his body; I mean him. Alive. He wasn't at the meeting, so Ryan and I walked down to hurry him up," said Megan, gesturing with her hands. Jenner thought she looked a little pale and not quite on track. Finding as many bodies as she had in three weeks' time would do that to you.

"Where's Professor Stevens?" asked Schroder. "I didn't have to step over his unconscious body tonight."

The store's front windows lit up like someone had set off fireworks, and Jerry Carr turned around. His eyes went first to the windows, then to Jenner. His face was red. "Jenner, get out there and move that cameraman and the short guy with the microphone out of here. Tell him to keep his skinny butt and camera on the sidewalk across the street. If he doesn't want to move, tell a couple of the uniforms standing around outside with their fingers up their noses to pick him up and move him. If he resists, arrest him for assault on a peace officer. He damn near stuck that microphone down my throat when I got out of my car.

I'm out of patience with the press. They're crawling all over Sixth Street and Special Crimes like cockroaches crawling from behind the baseboards at midnight, and I've had a belly full. We're not the only town with a serial killer on the loose. Let them go occupy some other city."

"So you finally admit it's a serial killer!" said Megan. "I was right all along, and you wouldn't listen."

"It's the skeleton that did it, Lieutenant."

"What are you saying, Jenner?" asked the lieutenant in an ominous voice.

Jenner wished he'd kept his opinion to himself. "We've got a serial killer *and* a skeleton buried between the walls of an old laundry. I can't think of another city with that combination."

Jerry Carr looked tired of hearing about the skeleton. "Jenner, go chase that jackass back across the street like I told you to."

Jenner went.

The little skinny guy with the microphone wore a pink shirt. Jenner didn't remember seeing anybody in Amarillo wearing a pink shirt who wasn't female or thought he was. There was a transvestite on Amarillo Boulevard who always wore pink, but Cookie wore dresses. He was generally a nice guy once you got past the protruding Adam's apple and five o'clock shadow. Cookie had a heavy beard and needed to shave twice a day.

"Sir, you need to move across the street. You're interfering with public servants in pursuance of their official duties," said Jenner, trying to ignore the pink shirt.

"The press have a right to report the news," said Otto Steven George, bristling like a bandy rooster.

"I know that, sir, and you can report the news just as well from across the street."

"I need close-ups, and I can't get close-ups from that distance," retorted George.

Jenner scratched his head. "Sir, you try to get any more close-ups of Lieutenant Carr, you'll get free room and board at our downtown facilities."

"Are you threatening me?" demanded George, standing on his toes and sticking his face as close to Jenner's as his height allowed.

Jenner turned his head. The little guy had been eating enough garlic to ward off a platoon of vampires. "No, sir, I'm not threatening you. I'm just telling you that the lieutenant is a little impatient tonight. I wouldn't wait around until he's a *lot* impatient."

George was quiet a moment, then he

smiled. Jenner's blood ran cold. "How about I trade something the lieutenant would like to have for permission to stay here?"

Jenner's heart sank to his stomach. He didn't like this. This little scumbag was trying to pull something. "What do you have the lieutenant might be interested in?"

Otto Steven George danced on his little feet. "How about a copy of a tape of the discovery of the body from the time Clark and that professor locked lips, to the time the lieutenant pulled her from behind the counter? Very hot stuff!"

Jenner wanted to stuff the tape down the peckerwood's throat, but that wouldn't help Megan Clark. "Let me have the tape, and I'll go see if the lieutenant wants to make a deal."

"Oh, no. I'm from Hollywood; I know better than to make a deal without money up front. The lieutenant gives his permission, then I give him the tape."

"He can always get a warrant for the tape, then you don't get anything."

"And a camera can always malfunction, and the lieutenant gets a blank tape."

Jenner felt the slats of the barrel he was over. "I'll go tell the lieutenant."

Jenner went back in the store, walking as

slowly as he could without coming to a complete standstill. The three main characters were all red-faced. He thought he'd wait awhile before giving the lieutenant Hollywood Hannah's message. He didn't want to interrupt, and there was always the chance an eighteen-wheeler would barrel down Sixth Street and squash Skinny Butt, tape and all.

"Tell me again why you and Ryan came looking for Mr. Spencer?" asked Lieutenant Carr.

Megan's face turned a shade redder. "Are you suffering a loss of short-term memory, Jerry? I've already told you three times. Larry hadn't shown up for the meeting, so Ryan and I came to find him."

"Whose idea was it to come looking?"

"It was mine!"

"What did you do when you found the body?"

Megan sighed like a long-suffering mother questioning her teenage son about the *Playboy* magazines she found under his bed. "I sent Ryan outside to call 911, then sent him back to the bookstore. Ryan's not good around dead bodies if they're bleeding or seeping."

"Was the body bleeding?"

"No, Jerry, he was dead! The body doesn't

bleed after death unless by means of gravity, because the heart stops beating."

"Thanks for the lesson in basic forensics, Megan. What did you do next?"

"I checked his carotid artery for a pulse. There wasn't one."

"Then I suppose you turned him over?"

"There wasn't any need to. He was posed just like the others, and he had the marks on his forehead. These were like the other marks on the other victims: similar but different. I think they're letters of the same alphabet, but I don't know what alphabet. I need to study them, but other developments have kept me busy."

"Like the skeleton?"

Megan nodded. "Like the skeleton among other things."

"Jenner, you've been monitoring Megan's interference in that case. What have you found?" asked Jerry.

Megan interrupted before Jenner could answer. "We know it must have been somebody who worked in the laundry."

"Well, duh, Megan. A first grader could have guessed that. I had hoped that playing around with that case would keep you out of trouble, but it hasn't. You're still stumbling over dead bodies. Three so far and one seventy-year-old skeleton. An objective observer would not accept coincidence as a reason."

The blood drained from her face, then rushed back, leaving her flushed with what Jenner suspected was anger unless it was scarlet fever, which wasn't likely. He could practically see steam rising from her head. "Are you accusing me of *murder?*" She sounded outraged, and Jenner didn't blame her. The lieutenant was way out of line.

Carr rubbed at his hair. "I don't want to, but even you have to admit that circumstances look dicey, Megan. Where were you this afternoon from four o'clock on?"

"Ryan, Rosemary Pittman, and I were visiting Herb Jackson at his office until nearly five o'clock, then Ryan and I went home and changed clothes and went to dinner at a Mexican restaurant."

"How long did it take you to change clothes?"

"For God's sake, Jerry, I didn't use a stopwatch! Okay, let me think. Three minutes to wash my face; five minutes for eye shadow, mascara, lipstick; ten minutes for sweater, skirt, panty hose, heels, and to finger-comb my hair; two minutes to walk next door to Ryan's. That makes twenty minutes. Ask Rosemary, Herb, and Ryan if I wasn't in sight of one or all of them all afternoon and this evening except for personal grooming."

Carr shook his head. "I'll ask them, of course, or Sergeant Schroder will, but Megan, we won't put much credence in their statements. That reading circle would stretch the truth for you at the very least, and Ryan Stevens would do more than that: he would lie, cheat, or steal for you."

"Ryan is *not* a liar! Why would he do that anyway?" Jenner saw Megan's hands curl into fists. He figured she was about one accusation away from punching the lieutenant's lights out.

Carr laughed, but Jenner thought it was the saddest laugh he had ever heard. "Megan, he's a middle-aged man, a widower who's lonely, and a beautiful, sexy young woman hangs out with him every chance she gets. You're his lifeline to youth. With you hanging on his arm he feels like a young stallion again."

"Ryan's my friend!" Megan said desperately. Jenner felt like he was eavesdropping on a very private conversation, and he thought the lieutenant was alienating Megan Clark with every word he said.

"Ryan Stevens thinks he's in love with you. Like every man having a midlife crisis he's making a fool of himself, only this fool would commit perjury if he thought it would keep you out of jail. I wouldn't believe him if he swore on a stack of Bibles!"

Megan looked as if someone had sucker punched her. "Ryan has never given me any indication he was in love with me!"

In all her statements she had made tonight, Jenner figured this one was her only lie.

"*Thinks* he's in love with you!"

Jenner couldn't decide if the lieutenant was lying, or he really didn't believe Ryan was in love with Megan Clark. Either way Jenner figured the only fool in this conversation was Jerry Carr. He hoped the lieutenant was head over heels with this girl he took to dinner the night Old Ben was murdered, because he for sure would never get through Megan's front door again.

Megan's face was pale again, and Jenner thought her lips were trembling. "You ought to be out questioning witnesses and investigating Larry's background. He might have enemies or business rivals."

"The same enemies as our first victim, the homeless wino? The same enemies as Police Officer Damian Constantine?"

Megan rubbed her temples. "No, I guess not. But serial killers have a pattern, Jerry. What's his pattern?"

"I can say something to that," said Schroder, clearing his throat. "His pattern is he kills every time you're on Sixth Street meeting with your book club. Like I said before, he works on your schedule."

"So of all the members, you're picking on me? I suppose you've eliminated everyone else. Can you imagine Agnes or Rosemary or Lorene killing someone? No!"

"Agnes Caldwell is short enough," said Schroder. "The autopsy report said three of the stab wounds were low on Old Ben's back from a slight downward angle, slicing through both kidneys and his liver. The other ten were after he had fallen and the perp was standing maybe a foot from his head. The first of the ten according to the pathologist's best guess was to the heart. Of the first three stab wounds on Officer Constantine's back, all were low on his back, two through the kidneys and one between his vertebrae that sliced his spinal column in two. If he had lived he would have been a cripple. Of the other ten stab wounds, the first one was to his heart. All stab wounds were from the same angles as Old Ben, and again according to the pathologist, the same knife or one exactly like it was used. Ms. Caldwell was short enough to fit the perp, but she's an old woman.

Probably too weak for these killings. These wounds were deep, almost through the body. The human body is a lot harder to cut than most people think."

"I wouldn't know, Sergeant! I've never stabbed anyone!"

Schroder ignored her. "It took somebody younger and stronger than Ms. Caldwell. Ms. Pittman and Ms. Getz are too tall to stab the victims at the right angle in the lower back, and again, are too old and too weak. Besides, they all had solid alibis.

"Same with Professor Anderson and his girlfriend: solid alibis. Herb Jackson ought to change cleaners to the one Ms. Constantine uses. The lab could still pick up traces of coffee on his vest, but Ms. Constantine's blouse checked out like it was brand new except for a couple of light spots where she said she wasn't careful and spilled a little bleach when she tried to wash it herself. Anyway, Herb Jackson —"

"You found nothing on Maria Constantine's blouse? Nothing at all?" demanded Megan.

"I told you, just two bleach spots. Now, as I was saying —"

"Where were the bleach marks?" asked Megan, interrupting again.

"Two little spots in the front near the

336

hem." Schroder's face was turning a little redder with each interruption. "As I was saying, Herb Jackson had an alibi. He stayed late at his office to see a client. The custodian saw him leave his building at six thirty, and he was here at the bookstore a little before seven. The lieutenant and me drove between Jackson's office and the bookstore five times. Jackson didn't have time to kill Old Ben and get to the bookstore when Ms. Caldwell said he did. Of course, she could be lying."

"Agnes wouldn't lie!" said Megan. Jenner thought that if her face got much lighter, she'd look like a ghost with red hair. There was no doubt in his mind that she was having trouble holding it together. It was like she was paying attention with only half her mind; the other half was out in left field.

Schroder slipped an unlighted cigarette in the corner of his mouth. He never smoked at a crime scene, but Jenner had once watched him slobber his way through a whole pack at the scene of a mass murder.

"I arrested a little old lady about Ms. Caldwell's age for poisoning five different husbands — arsenic in their rice pudding. She had the kindest face you ever saw, taught Sunday school, and baked cookies for the neighborhood kids. I ain't turned my back on a sweet-faced old lady since then."

"What about Maria?" asked Megan. Jenner noticed her voice sounding weaker each time she spoke.

"Officer Constantine worked days that week and was home about five thirty. He said his wife didn't leave the house until six thirty, and Ms. Caldwell said she got to the bookstore about ten 'til seven. Again she didn't have time to kill Old Ben. Ms. Smith was defrauding the public with her palm reading until nearly six thirty, then she had to change out of her Gypsy witch duds. She got to the bookstore about the same time as Mrs. Constantine: ten 'til seven.

"So you see, Clark, the only two people who was late, and the only two who alibied each other, was the professor and you. Seeing as how you two are as close as you are, I ain't willing to take your word for it, or his either, 'cause all he knows is what you told him. The way —"

"Just a minute, Schroder," said Megan in a cold voice. Jenner could practically see her breath in the air. "You won't take mine and Ryan's word because you say we're too *close,* but you took Damian Constantine's alibi for Maria, and he's her *husband!* Wouldn't you say he was too close to her

338

not to lie? And who alibied her last week? Her *husband* was dead under a pile of leaves!"

Schroder's mouth hung open, then snapped shut like a mousetrap. Jenner watched him snort air through his nose before the sergeant answered. "Damian Constantine was a police officer."

"He was Maria's *husband!* Why wouldn't he lie for her?"

"The way I see it is you drove to Sixth Street about six o'clock when it's nice and dark, killed Old Ben, drove back home and told the professor your truck wouldn't start. Now you get your mechanic that fixed it to swear that it wouldn't run, that would go a long way toward convincing me that maybe I'm jumping on you too quick."

Jenner noticed that Schroder was addressing Megan by her last name instead of calling her professor or Ms. That was a bad sign.

"I didn't take my truck to a mechanic! I fixed it myself. You think just because I'm a woman that I can't fix my own truck?"

"She's got her own tool kit, Schroder," said Jerry Carr.

"And I know how to use every tool in it," said Megan defiantly. Jenner saw her standing straighter, and her voice sounded stronger, so he figured she was getting her spirit back.

Schroder rolled his cigarette to the other corner of his mouth. "That's real interesting, Clark, and it might help you if you didn't have some other problems. You claim to be a paleopathologist —"

"— I don't *claim* to be one. I *am* a paleopathologist. Do you want to see my graduation diploma?"

"So I figure that you know where to stab a man to hit just what you want to hit. And you're short and probably strong, so you could stab a man nearly clean through."

"And why would I want to kill Old Ben? Why would I want to kill anybody, Schroder?" demanded Megan. She was calling Schroder by his last name, and Jenner didn't think that was a good sign either. She sounded pissed.

"I got an idea about that, too. You stumbled over Lisa Heredia's body last year and played detective. You got your name in the paper, and everybody in Amarillo was talking about you. Then you found another dead body at that hotel, played detective, and got your name in the paper again. Then Mr. Gorman hired you to find out who killed his grandson's wife. I think you liked playing detective by then. Then there was that case in September in Palo Duro Canyon. Know what I think?"

"I'm holding my breath, Schroder," said Megan as she began to pace back and forth in front of them.

"I think you got to liking the attention you got when you found a body and played detective so much, that you decided to keep on doing it. When no more bodies showed up the last few weeks, you decided to furnish your own. I think you got a new kind of Munchausen syndrome by proxy. Instead of making kids sick or killing them to get attention from doctors and nurses, you murder people, then try to solve the murders to get attention."

"You're crazy, Schroder!" shouted Megan, stopping in front of him, than taking a few steps backward.

Sworn to uphold the law as he was, Jenner figured it was his duty to mention to Schroder that there was an open back door to the right of the sales counter and about four feet behind Megan Clark. And he would get around to mentioning it as soon as it was convenient.

Megan Clark kept moving backward. "You're so anxious to solve these murders that you're making things up. You can't redefine Munchausen syndrome by proxy to make it fit me —"

"Then I'll call it Ted Bundy syndrome by proxy," said Schroder.

"You're not even trying to find the real murderer, Schroder. You're trying to twist the facts to fit your theory. What about those marks on the victims' foreheads? Have you even tried to decipher what they mean?" She pulled slips of paper out of her skirt pocket. "Here are copies of the marks. I've been keeping copies, but I haven't had a chance to really study them. Just look at them. Let me put them in order for you."

Jenner watched her fumble with the slips of paper with shaking fingers. "Damn it, I dropped them. Schroder, you've made me so angry that my hands are shaking."

She knelt down to pick up the slips, and Jenner saw her freeze. When she stood up, her eyes were wide with surprise. "Oh, my God," she said, her voice shaking. "Oh, my God. It's the Phoenician alphabet. The murderer wrote it while he was kneeling at the victims' foreheads, but I, all of us, looked at the bodies while standing by their feet, so the letters were upside down. That's why I thought the marks looked familiar but never recognized them."

No one said anything except Megan as she pointed out each letter. Jenner saw

Schroder's eyes light up and felt nauseous. He could guess what was about to happen.

"Know anybody who speaks Phoenician, Clark?" asked Schroder.

"No one speaks it, Schroder; it's a dead language. We don't know how it was pronounced. I can read and translate it, though, and these marks are Phoenician."

"I suppose you can write it, too," asked Schroder. Jenner noticed that Jerry Carr had covered his face with his hands.

"Of course I can, Schroder. I can't believe I was so stupid as to not recognize it before. The alphabet! The ABCs! This explains everything. It's the missing puzzle piece. Oh, my God, I've been so stupid! How could I let myself be fooled so badly?"

"How many folks in town do you suppose can write Phoenician?" asked Schroder, taking his damp, limp cigarette out of his mouth and dropping it in his pocket.

"No one that I know of in Amarillo has a degree in anthropology-slash-archaeology with the concentration for my master's being Middle Eastern archaeology. I learned to read Phoenician, Egyptian hieroglyphs, Hebrew, and Greek, but anyone with an Internet connection can copy down the Phoenician alphabet; you don't need a degree. Schroder, this is an important clue. You see, the killer copied the Phoenician alphabet off the Internet, or from the *American Heritage Dictionary* for a specific reason. It's a red herring that points to me because the Back Stabber knows I'm an archaeologist. Combine that fact with others I've found, and you have a viable suspect."

Megan got up and held out the slips to Schroder. Jenner held his breath. Schroder had to see that Megan Clark must be innocent. She just told him where anyone with a computer could copy the Phoenician alphabet. The knowledge wasn't exclusive to Megan Clark. Anybody could copy those marks on the victims' foreheads. Schroder needed to get off Megan's case.

"So I need to find somebody with no alibi, who's on Sixth Street at the right time, is probably short but strong, knows anatomy, and can write Phoenician. Why do I need to look for a viable suspect? I already got you," said Schroder, pulling his copy of the Miranda warnings out of his pocket.

"Sergeant Schroder, listen to me! Jerry, listen and think a minute! These murders are patterned after those in a book: *The ABC Murders* by Agatha Christie. In the book a railway guide called the *ABC Guide* is left by each victim. We don't have such a guide in Amarillo, so the murderer wrote the Phoenician alphabet on the victims' foreheads instead. In the book the murderer killed a number of people, but he really had a specific target. The rest of the victims were to hide that fact, so our murderer is choosing random victims to hide the real target. They are killed on my schedule because I'm vulnerable. I've found too many bodies, so you're naturally suspicious of me. My schedule is also the murderer's schedule. I'm being framed! But I know who the killer is. One of you has to come to the bookstore, and I'll unmask the murderer. I'll provide you with solid evidence, not just the circumstantial I have now."

"If I had a nickel for every killer who screamed he had been framed, I could retire rich. But I'll listen to you. Who's your suspect?"

"Oh, no, Sergeant Schroder, we'll do this my way, so I'm sure you hear the confession and find the proof. A conventional investigation will only give warning and this psychopath will walk. You can fit me with a wire if you want. Jerry, you believe me, don't you?"

Jenner had never seen a man so conflicted as Jerry Carr. Would he follow his heart and risk his career? Or would he let his sense of duty rule?

"Megan, I have to go where the evidence leads."

"What evidence? Where's the weapon? What's my motive, and don't quote Schroder's psychobabble. You can't prove me guilty beyond a reasonable doubt. The DA probably won't even take the case, Jerry."

"He will. Schroder has already talked to Maximum Miller at the DA's office." The lieutenant stepped back, and Jenner saw how shiny his eyes were. "Why did you do it, Megan? Why?"

"I didn't kill anybody!" screamed Megan.

The store's front door banged open, and they all turned to look. Except Megan. Out of the corner of his eye Jenner saw her dart through the open back door behind the counter. He turned his head to look directly at the front door where a skinny man in a pink shirt stood.

"Hey, Mr. Lieutenant, you gonna take my deal or not? I got the networks and cable guys waiting to buy copies. I can get a higher bid if you're gonna use the tape as evidence."

Jenner cleared his throat. "Hey, Schroder! Did you happen to notice that door behind the counter?"

17

From any crime to its author there is a trail. It may be . . . obscure; but, since matter cannot move without disturbing other matter along its path, there always is — there must be — a trail of some sort. And finding and following such trails is what a detective is paid to do.

"House Dick" in Dashiell Hammett's
Dead Yellow Women, 1947

ROUTE 66 GIFT SHOP, TIME AND AGAIN BOOKSTORE — THE SAME NIGHT

Megan lay on her belly in the semidarkness of the Route 66 Gift Shop roof. Without the streetlights that reflected off the low cloud cover she would be lying in darkness, only her, the heating and air-conditioning units, and the bird poop. She tried to bring her breathing under control, not that she thought anyone could hear it over the pounding of her heart. Not until now could she truly appreciate what an adrenaline rush really felt like. She had barely made it up the drain pipe and over the foot-high brick wall that bordered the roof before Jerry Carr and Sergeant Schroder rushed out the back door. If she hadn't tripped up Schroder and Jerry Carr by tipping over several shipping boxes of Route 66 memorabilia from Taiwan, China, and Japan as she ran through the store's back room, she would be sitting in the backseat of a patrol car on her way to an interview room at Special Crimes. Or, if Jerry and Schroder had been thinking in three dimensions instead of two dimensions, one or the other would have thought to check the roof, and she might well be under arrest, handcuffed, and on her way downtown to enjoy the amenities of the city jail in the same cell with one of Amarillo Boulevard's working girls. She'd be sure not to drink after her.

She would be photographed holding a sign with her very own number on it and fingerprinted on little white cards where each finger got its own space. Then she'd be given a new outfit, a unisex jumpsuit — well, not new, it had probably been recycled several dozen times — a one-piece garment of durable material, no belt, and Potter County Jail stenciled on the back in case she forgot where she was. Sometime during the processing procedure she would be strip-searched by a female deputy without a nursing degree. Then when she was feeling humbled, humiliated, and homogenized, she would be escorted to an interrogation room with dirty paint and the smell of other people's fear. Then that jackass, Jerry Carr, and his sidekick jackass, Sergeant Schroder, would read her rights to her for the fourth or fifth time — which she would refuse to sign for the fourth or fifth time, and consequently piss them both off.

But none of those scenarios was happening. Instead, she was relaxing in the bird poop on the cold, hard, tar paper and asphalt roof of Larry Spencer's Route 66 Gift Shop, wondering how she would get across the street and one block down to the bookstore without being seen by one of the ten million cops blanketing Sixth Street and the San Jacinto area. And she was going to have to do it without a coat or shoes in forty degree weather with a strong wind. She really hated discarding her shoes in the back room when she escaped, but heels weren't compatible with a drain pipe. She had only bought those heels last week, along with the sweater and skirt she wore tonight, both now covered in bird poop. What did the old-time cowboys say? She had been "all feathered out" like a male peacock spreading his tail to entice the female when she had knocked on Ryan's back door. She wasn't a male peacock, but from the look in Ryan's eyes tonight, he'd wanted to check out her tail feathers. God, she was pitiful. Using sex to entice a man to — what? Well, Scarlett, girlfriend, she'd think about that tomorrow. Tomorrow was another day — if she wasn't in jail. She wouldn't be, though. She had all the pieces now, or all that were necessary for an arrest warrant for capital murder, and she had a logical explanation for the ones that weren't necessary. Now that Schroder and Jerry Carr had decided it was a serial killer after all, they would be red-faced to learn that it wasn't.

She wondered if she would be arrested for fleeing from the police after all this was over. She didn't think so because she had not actually been arrested yet, had not been charged, had not been indicted. But what did she know? Was she actually better off running so she wouldn't be arrested? Hell, yes! There is no bail for multiple murders, so she would be in jail until she had to be in court, and if she was in jail, she couldn't uncover the real murderer. It was as simple as that. Jail or be a fugitive. Two lousy options, but being a fugitive was infinitely better than being in jail, no matter what society might think.

She heard footsteps in the alley and a man whistling. She flattened herself even closer to the roof and belly-crawled into the shadow cast by the short brick wall that extended a foot above the roof's surface. She couldn't dare a look over the little wall. What if the cop — and it surely was a cop — happened to look up and see her head outlined against the clouds? She heard him talking and thought there were two cops returning to the scene of her crime. She bit her lip to focus her mind on something besides her mind-numbing, nausea-evoking fear, and realized that whoever was in the alley wasn't talking to another cop. He was talking to himself.

"Schroder, Lieutenant Carr, this is Jenner," he said in a low, conversational voice. "I'm in the alley behind the Route 66 store. I thought I might hang here awhile in case Megan Clark decides to circle back. Can you hear me, Schroder, Lieutenant? Guess not. My cell phone must be dead, so, Jenner, you're on your own. So where do I go from here? I guess I ought to ask what would Schroder do, then do the opposite. That's easy. I didn't want a hand in arresting Megan Clark anyway because I think she's innocent. Schroder's got a hair caught crossways about her, because she's always finding bodies. He thinks she must be a killer because everybody else he's ever questioned who finds more than their quota of bodies, is generally guilty of supplying them first."

Megan covered her mouth to hold in the laughter, then felt her eyes brimming with tears. The sergeant wasn't talking to himself; he was talking to her. He knew she was up here and was trying to tell her what to do. Next to Ryan, Sergeant Jenner had to be the bravest, kindest man in the universe. He was risking his career and maybe even arrest to help someone he believed was innocent. Could there be a better policeman than Sergeant Jenner? She wiped her eyes on a spot on her skirt that wasn't polluted, and listened to Jenner.

"Part of Megan Clark's problem is she needs to stay out of dark alleys. You never find anything good in a dark alley. Her finding a body? It was coincidence. But Schroder doesn't believe in coincidence. I do sometimes. Everybody in town knows her reputation for finding bodies, so the killer left his victims where she was liable to find them. I call that my theory of victim placement. You might even say that Megan Clark herself is a victim of her own reputation. I'd help her prove it if I could do it without violating my sworn oath to uphold the law.

"I guess I better head down this alley, check out the other end. I'll leave my car parked at this end. It isn't locked, but I won't worry about that. There's a thousand cops on Sixth Street tonight. Who's gonna be stupid enough to steal my car? What would be, I guess you'd say ironic, is if Megan Clark crawled under that blanket in my back seat and rode down to the bookstore without my knowing it. I gotta talk to the uniform who's guarding the front door. I want to see if he's thought to check the cars in the bookstore parking lot. Probably better call in the licence plates while we're at it. Since my cell phone's out, we'll use his radio after he moves his patrol car down the alley to that dumpster where Old Ben's body was found. That way we'll block off that cross alley where Megan Clark's dog found Damian Constantine's body. Don't want to take the chance that Megan Clark might slip into the back door to the bookstore from those two alleys."

Whistling, Jenner sauntered down the alley.

Megan slid down the drain pipe and on

bare feet ran silently to Jenner's car.

The first person Megan saw once she slipped through the door of Time and Again was Ryan. The first person to reach her was Ryan.

"Oh God, Megan," he whispered, wrapping his arms around her and bowing his head to rub his cheek against her hair. "I thought I'd lost you. I thought your luck had run out just like I'd warned you would happen if you kept playing Sherlock Holmes. Promise me you won't get involved again."

"I wasn't playing Sherlock Holmes!" she protested not very fiercely. She didn't want to bicker with him, she just wanted to stay exactly where she was and let him stroke her back and feel his warm breath stirring her curls.

"I know you weren't, sweetheart; that's why it was so dangerous. Playing detective is one thing; the police can laugh at you, and the newspaper can make fun of you. When you're serious and show up the police, then they stop laughing. They focus on you instead of likely suspects, and all the little anomalies, like your constantly finding bodies, start to look suspicious. Schroder, who Ray tells me is really a good detective, starts following the numbers, and when they all add up to you, then you become 'a person of interest.' That's why Jerry Carr is always warning you off — and you don't know how hard it is to give him credit — because he knows how easy it can be to start twisting the facts to fit the theory instead of twisting the theory to fit the facts. It's a temptation every detective has to watch out for, and this time Sergeant Schroder succumbed to it. But he finally faced up to his mistakes and let you go before he went too far."

He tipped her face up and kissed her. When he finally let her up for air, her head was spinning. He wrapped her up in his arms again. "God, Megan, I was so scared! Don't ever do this to me again — to us again."

"Ryan," she said to the front of his sweater. "Schroder and Jerry didn't let me go. I escaped."

He went absolutely still. She thought his heart even stopped beating. Then he freed her, but grasped her arms and looked into her face, a disbelieving expression on his own. "What did you say?"

"Schroder and Jerry didn't let me go. I escaped."

"I thought that I had misunderstood, but

you cleared up my confusion. So you're a fugitive, and Schroder will probably send in the SWAT team."

"I hadn't actually been arrested yet, but Schroder was pulling out the card with the Miranda warning printed on it, so I thought I'd leave before he could read it to me."

Ryan nodded — and kept nodding. "I'm glad you cleared that up."

"If I'm in jail, then I couldn't uncover the real murderer."

"I knew you'd have a rational explanation for evading arrest, and risking the SWAT team pulling up out front and shooting the hell out of Agnes's BOOKSTORE!" His voice got louder and louder until he was shouting. "Don't you know this is the first place Schroder, Jerry Carr, and that clown Jenner will look?"

"Don't call Sergeant Jenner a clown! I rode here in his backseat, and he distracted the officer outside so I could run inside. See, he told me the plan while I was on the roof, and he was pretending to be talking to himself, so we have to pretend he didn't know I was in his backseat under a blanket. He's risking his job, so the least we can do is lie for him." She looked up at Ryan. He had a strange expression on his face that made her feel anxious.

"You were on the roof?"

"Of the Route 66 Gift Shop. That's where the bird poop smell came from."

"I wondered about that."

"I smell a little rank, but I didn't have a choice. Bird poop was everywhere, some of it from condors I think."

Ryan was nodding his head again. She wondered if she ought to be concerned. She stood on her toes and pulled his head down so she could whisper in his ear. "Go outside and bring Sergeant Jenner back here. I've finally put the pieces together, and I think Sergeant Jenner ought to be the one to make the arrest, don't you, since he's the only cop who believed from the git-go that I was innocent."

Ryan's eyes showed a flicker of interest. "You know who the murderer is?" he whispered.

"Yes, and I'll explain everything when you get back with Sergeant Jenner. Now, go."

Megan turned to the reading circle whose members were gathered around her, but at a distance. Apparently no one liked *eau de perfume bird poop.* She had to admit that its acidic earthiness took getting used to. "Rosemary, may I speak to you a moment? Privately," she added moving to the sales counter.

Rosemary walked to the sales counter, but to the other side it. She took a dainty handkerchief and a small bottle of perfume from her purse and sprinkled the handkerchief with the perfume. A light, flowery scent wafted from the soft linen, which Rosemary held to her nose like some eighteenth century courtier might do to counteract the smells of the common man.

"I'm sorry, Megan, I don't mean to offend you, but you smell terrible!"

"Bird poop."

"So I heard. I may never feel the same about birds again. But what is it you wanted to talk to me about?"

Megan pulled the three slips of paper from her pocket and spread them on the counter. "The Phoenician alphabet, nine letters in all, three on the foreheads of each of the Back Stabber's victims. All three were purposely posed on their backs even though they were stabbed in the back and fell face down. Do you agree they were posed that way so the marks would be seen?"

"The alphabet? Oh, dear, that's horrible, but I do agree with you. I can think of no other logical reason. And they would be heavy, wouldn't they? Because they were dead. I've read that the dead seem heavier than the living when you try to move them, so it wasn't easy, I imagine, so the murderer would have to have a very strong reason. But why Phoenician? Why not English so everyone would immediately recognize them?"

"Who in this group would be likely to recognize Phoenician and have an unsavory reputation with the police for finding bodies?"

Rosemary looked up from the slips, an expression of realization and anger in her eyes. "You would. And the police would think — oh, Megan, this is an ugly person. Bad enough to kill three men, but deliberately to implicate you is despicable!"

"So you think that is the intent? That the letters are not trying to convey another message? That the alphabet is a red herring?"

"Oh, Megan, no! Surely not!" Rosemary bowed her head. "I feel so guilty! I thought my program was such a good idea, educational and fun at the same time. I never thought it would lead to this. To *murder!*"

Megan patted the old woman's shoulder. "I didn't mean to upset you, I just wanted to make sure I wasn't reading something into these marks that wasn't there. And by using the alphabet the murderer is taunting me. 'Yes, I'm here. Now find me.' You're the authority, and I wanted your opinion. I was so caught up by the skeleton that I never studied those marks the way I should have. I only recognized them as the Phoenician alphabet by accident tonight, and of course, Sergeant Schroder jumped on recognition as the last piece he needed to arrest me on probable cause of committing murder. Then, of course, I had to think about the Back Stabber and put all the pieces together, and almost immediately I recognized the pattern and that we were not hunting a serial killer as I first thought. We're hunting a psychopath, all right, but not one who kills because he likes it, although maybe that's true, too, but a murderer who kills for a specific reason and covers up the crime with more bodies. I wanted to interview Ray and Maria, but I can't now that I'm a fugitive. I have to wrap up the Back Stabber case tonight or risk being caught. Besides, weren't there four bodies in *The ABC Murders*?"

"Yes, dear, there were."

"We don't want four murders, do we?" asked Megan somberly.

"Absolutely not! I won't sleep well at night with three murders, but four! Good heavens, I'd never sleep again."

"There won't be four. I can promise you that," said Megan, turning around at the sound of the door opening. "Here's our policeman now. Sergeant Jenner, are you surprised to see me?"

Jenner grinned. "So you were on the roof? I thought so. I was the last one out of the store. Schroder and the lieutenant were long gone, but I had tripped on one of those boxes, so I was checking to see if I had twisted my ankle. While I was sitting on the floor in that storage room, I heard a scuffling sound on the roof. It wasn't a loud sound, but it was enough to give you away, Dr. Clark. I figured you'd want to come to the bookstore, so I arranged a way for you to get here. I think you're innocent, and I figured you'd prove it one way or the other."

Megan straightened her shoulders. "I'm prepared to do just that, so have a seat."

She waited until everyone was seated, closed her eyes for a moment to arrange the items of proof in her mind, and crossed her fingers that her guess about the weapon was right, or she was going to look like a fool. She opened her eyes and looked at Ryan. He smiled and held up his thumb. "Go, girl," he mouthed at her.

"Go, girl," she said to herself under her breath. "I'm a fugitive from justice as you all heard when I told Ryan. I'm a fugitive because I stood at the feet of the Back Stabber's victims, so I didn't receive the murderer's message until tonight. That's when I recognized the marks as the Phoenician alphabet. That's when I realized that those marks were a red herring meant to mislead the police into suspecting me. The thirteen stab wounds and the posed bodies were meant to suggest that our killer was a serial killer. In fact, if the murderer could have resisted the need to taunt me by using the Phoenician alphabet, I and the police would believe we were still hunting a serial killer. But for that one act the killer might have escaped capture. As it is, though, I accept the challenge of unmasking you."

"What kind of challenge are you talking about?" asked Ray.

"The alphabet on the forehead served two purposes: first, it cast suspicion on me because I can read and write using the Phoenician alphabet. The second purpose is that it taunted me to solve the crime and catch the murderer. The murderer is one of us, and the murders are patterned on the The ABC Murders by Agatha Christie."

"My God!" said Ray Roberts. "You're right, Megan. Without the alphabet, the murderer would have walked. Stupid bastard."

"So if the murderer is following the pattern laid out in Christie's book, then who is the intended victim, and who are the red herrings? We have an alcoholic homeless man, the cop, and the merchant. How are they dissimilar? Old Ben and Larry Spencer live in the San Jacinto area; Damian Constantine does not. Old Ben and Larry have no family; Damian is married. Old Ben and Larry are older men; Damian is thirty at most. Therefore, Damian Constantine is the odd man out."

"Somebody murdered Damian on purpose!" cried Maria Constantine. "Who hated him that much? It's not true."

Agnes and the twins immediately went to Maria with tissue and sympathy. Candi, Megan noticed, quietly slipped out the back door. Megan figured Candi was taking a potty break.

Clearing her throat, Megan continued, "The murderer had to be familiar with Damian's patrol route, which would indicate that he lived on Sixth Street or the San Jacinto area. On the other hand, the murderer probably escaped in the truck that Barney Benson heard, which indicates he lived out of this area. Otherwise, he would have disappeared into his own home, cleaned up, and not reappeared until the body was found. By driving a truck to the place where he plans to murder someone, he risks the truck being seen and described. But what if the murderer is also driving to Sixth Street for an innocent reason — attending a meeting of Murder by the Yard Reading Circle. Sergeant Schroder said once that the murders were committed according to my schedule. Actually, they were committed according to the book club schedule, which suited the murderer because I would also be attending, so in addition to being familiar with Phoenician, I was also in the right place at the right time. The stab wounds were all in the back, and according to the pathologist, the first three were rather low, below the midpoint of the back. Therefore, the murderer was short; the last ten were struck after the victim was down. As you may have noticed before now, I'm short."

The members, Jenner, Hazel Gilbert, and Barney Benson dutifully laughed, but it was nervous laughter that relieved tension, not laughter at a comic comment.

Megan closed her eyes and took several deep breaths to calm herself, then opened her eyes to look at the murderer. "In a way it is a very clever murder; on the other hand, it is so transparent once you disregard the alphabet — which you should do because the letters were a private message to me written on the flesh of dead men. Letters of the alphabet, letters to Poirot. There is a certain symbolism. Imagine the fearlessness of this person: kneeling on the ground within a foot of their heads, the one place where there was no blood, and scratching those letters on the foreheads of the victims, witnessed only by their eyes blinded by death."

The murderer sat without flinching or reacting, and Megan wondered how any human being could remain so composed in the face of such accusations. "So what do we know about this murderer? Who lives across town, but is still very familiar with Sixth Street? Who knows Damian Constantine? Who would Damian Constantine agree to meet in a dark alley? Who would Damian Constantine, a cop, turn his back on without fear? Who is familiar with *The ABC Murders*? I think the murderer was clever to think of using a fictional murder as a pattern, but unimaginative in strictly following the book. When you murder by the book, you become predictable. Isn't that right, Maria?"

Jenner stood up and took out his handcuffs, but before he had a chance to say the four magical words, "You are under arrest," Maria Constantine laughed. "That was a suspenseful story, Megan, very imaginative, but it could fit a number of us besides the one person in this room who has lost the most: her husband!" she cried as she reached down by her chair and lifted her purse onto her lap.

"Sergeant Schroder told me that the tests on your blouse came back negative, Maria. The test should have found the coffee as it did with Herb's vest. How could that happen? Because they tested a different blouse from the one you wore that night. Therefore I theorize that you destroyed your blouse with the blood and coffee on it and bought another identical to it and gave that one to the police for checking. I'm sure the sergeant can verify that by interviewing the clerks at Dillard's. You're very distinctive looking, so I'm sure the clerks will remember."

"I spilled bleach on the blouse, and I bought another one," said Maria.

"Thank you for telling me that in front of witnesses, Maria. The jury will have no problem believing you gave the wrong blouse to the police."

"Wait a minute," said Jenner, still standing in front of the couch with his handcuffs. "Where did she hide the knife when we searched the house after Damian was killed?"

"I have two answers for that," said Megan. "The knife was either in a drawer with all the other knives, or she was using it while you were searching."

Jenner looked embarrassed. "She was peeling potatoes."

"As Edgar Allan Poe did in 'The Purloined Letter,' hide it in plain sight," said Agnes.

"As for where it is now," said Megan, "if you look in her purse, I think you'll find a blood-stained knife. There's enough room in that purse to hide a dozen knives."

Suddenly, Maria pulled a double-edged knife with an eight-inch blade out of her purse. "Everyone stay back or I'll cut her," she said, circling around and placing the knife against Agnes's throat. "Get up very carefully, Agnes, and stand in front of me."

"Put the knife down, Mrs. Constantine," said Jenner, his hand on his gun. "You're under arrest for the murder of Damian Constantine."

"Leave your gun in its holster and raise your hands, Jenner. If you don't, I'll stab her in the back. It won't be a fatal stab, but it will bleed, and it will hurt."

Jenner raised his hands. "You won't escape, Maria, and you don't want another charge laid against you. Injury to an Elderly

Person is a felony."

"What will one more charge matter when I've already committed three murders?" asked Maria, nudging Agnes toward the door.

Over Maria's shoulder, Megan saw Candi in the mystery aisle. Candi pulled a hardback off one of the shelves and began creeping up behind Maria, her expression both scared and determined. Megan began praying silently. "Lord, if Candi hits her, let it be hard."

Ryan got up and took a step toward Maria. "Come on, Maria. Give it up before you hurt somebody. There must be ten thousand cops on Sixth Street. You can't get away from them all."

"Can't I? You just hide and watch me."

Maria backed up a step, pulling Agnes with her, and Megan saw Candi raise the book and bring it down hard on Maria's elbow. Maria screamed and dropped the knife from her suddenly paralyzed arm. Jenner ran to her and jerked first one arm, then the other behind her back and cuffed her. Everybody else sat frozen, staring at Candi.

Candi lifted a hardback copy of *The ABC Murders.* "I was afraid I'd hurt her if I hit her in the head, so I hit her ulnar nerve."

18

Circumstantial evidence, that wonderful fabric which is built out of straws collected at every point of the compass, and which is yet strong enough to hang a man. Upon what infinitesimal trifles may sometimes hang the whole secret of some wicked mystery.

Robert Audley in Mary Elizabeth Braddon's
Lady Audley's Secret, 1887

THE WILLOWS RETIREMENT AND CONVALESCENCE HOME

When I read in the newspaper about the discovery of the old car in Wild Horse Lake, I figured the law wouldn't bother much with it. But when I read of the discovery at the old dry cleaner's and that Megan Clark was investigating, I figured it was only a matter of time before I heard a knock on the door. What did you say, Megan? I'm going to call you Megan because I'm your senior by so many decades that you're just a child, and you generally call a child by her given name. You thought it was a laundry? Well, it was, but the dry cleaning was such a much bigger part of the business that I always called it a dry cleaner's.

It wasn't until the skeleton turned up that Ray told me that he followed me that night. Only six years old! I'd have blistered his backside for being out by himself that late at night if I'd known about it. Of course, he didn't see everything that happened, so he didn't know for sure that the old car in Wild Horse Lake was "the car." But when they started tearing down the old dry cleaners and found the body — I still can't think of it as a skeleton — Ray was pretty sure the car and the body were connected and I was the — what did he it call it?— the intersection point of the events.

Anyhow, it doesn't matter how Megan tracked me down. I'm lying in this nursing home waiting to die, and since my people are long-lived, I reckon I'll hang on a few more years whether I want to or not. So long as I'm on this side of the grave I welcome company, especially company like Megan and the reading club, even Mr. Policeman there as long as he doesn't stir up mud in the bottom of the pond. Sometimes it's better to leave the mud alone. Now, you folks, Megan in particular, want to ask me if I recall an incident on Sixth Street? I remember it like it happened yesterday instead of nearly seventy years ago. An old woman's memory is like that: you remember what you saw and heard and felt years ago better than you remember what your granddaughter told you last week. I always thought time was kind in that way, letting you remember things that happened when your sight and hearing and smell were fresh and sharp. Nowadays, if I misplace my glasses I can't see beyond the end of my nose, and folks sound like they're swallowing half their syllables when they talk, and as for smell, a person can forget that and just as well, too, Otherwise you might smell your own aging, that musty odor you can't ever quite bathe away.

But I'm getting sidetracked, another trait of an old woman, although men are worse about it in my opinion. I was saying how I remembered what happened just as clear as could be with none of the details gone from my mind. "Imprinting" my granddaughter calls it. (See, I did remember something she said on her last visit). According to her, and she's got some fancy degree from college — got that instead of a husband and family —

incidents that evoke strong emotion burn themselves into our memories. Sounded a lot like branding cattle to me, but I didn't say that to her. Besides having a face that looks like five miles of hard road, my granddaughter doesn't have much in the way of a sense of humor. Of course, being close to the change of life like she is doesn't help, but she never had one even as a youngster. Have you ever noticed how folks dedicated to good works and holding the best of intentions toward others always seem to rub some folks the wrong way?

I see. Some of you have and some of you haven't.

Well, I have. Noticed it nearly seventy years ago, and I noticed it last week when my granddaughter visited me. Is it the Bible that says the path to Hell is paved with good intentions? I'm not so closely acquainted with the Holy Scripture as most women of my generation, but around here religion is in the air, and a body picks up odds and ends of scripture whether you have much formal Sunday school or not — and I don't. My daddy's place was so far out in the sticks that we never got to town for church but about every six months. That was before everybody had a car, and besides, there weren't any roads worthy of the name.

But just because I didn't go to Sunday school doesn't mean I don't know right from wrong. My daddy taught us the difference with a razor strap. He was a hard man, my daddy, and a little too fond of that razor strap. Looking back, I wonder if I would have done what I did if I hadn't heard another razor strap whistling through the air and seen the red welt rise up on that poor girl's thin little arm. I don't know, and there's no way to sort out the might-have-beens now. Likely it wouldn't have made any difference.

Megan, I see you shifting on that chair like it was a red-ant bed. You just have some patience like these other folks and listen to what I'm saying. I'm getting to where you wanted me to start, but like most young-sters, you don't give enough credit to what went on before and what came afterwards. Nothing in this life ever happens without a before and after. You keep that in mind and you'll be a better archaeologist.

To get back to my story, it was 1938, a Saturday in late March. I don't remember the exact date because the days were all alike for me except Saturdays were busier and the next day was Sunday, and I could rest up from ironing starched shirts and pressing pants and suits and breathing the fumes of cleaning fluids. I used to sit in my front yard on Sunday mornings and just breathe the clean air. Then on Monday morning I'd go back to work. You know, I can still close my eyes and remember how that dry cleaner's smelled? The bleach was worst of all. The stink of strong bleach will bring tears to your eyes, not to mention what a touch of it will do. And the moist heat smell of freshly ironed shirts. Yes, sir, I was one who thought permanent press was a gift straight from God, and so did every woman who ever lifted a heavy iron or used a pressing machine. And of course you know that Sixth Street is old Route 66, and that the Mother Road is part of the story. Might not have even been a story without 66. You might even say that if time or place or people had been different, there wouldn't be a story or — what did you call it?— incident on Sixth Street. But once everything came together and all the pieces rubbed up against one another, there was no stopping what happened.

I'll start with the time — or maybe I should say times. It was still hard times in 1938, the Great Depression with capital letters, and it had the whole country in a headlock. Except for here in Amarillo, it wasn't so bad as elsewhere. We never had any banks go bust for instance, and our breadlines were a whole lot shorter than the ones you saw in pictures of New York and Chicago. That doesn't mean everything was rosy in the Panhandle of Texas — it wasn't — but it could have been a lot worse. We never saw dozens of our neighbors tying their mattresses and box springs on top of their cars and piling the kids in the backseat and driving off down Route 66 into the setting sun. Mind you, there were some who left, some who couldn't wait it out until the rains came instead of the wind. I'm not blaming those who couldn't stick it out. Some folks have more grit than others. A black duster will show what a body is made of fast enough. But most of you are too young to have lived through one. Lord, but they were awful, the air so full of dirt that the sun couldn't shine through. It would be blacker than the devil's heart at midday, and a person couldn't see his hand before his face. I remember hanging wet sheets over the windows and stuffing rags under the doors to keep out the dirt. And I'd dip a handkerchief in water and tie it over my mouth and nose so I could breathe. In a couple of hours, less if I went outside, that wet hanky would be caked with mud. It was a sight to behold, those clouds of black dust that reached up into the sky to block out the sun. It was a sight I could have done without. I lost my youngest boy, Ray's brother, after the black duster of 1936. He was always a sickly child, and hanging a wet sheet over his crib didn't save him. He died of what we common folks called dust pneumonia in those days. I don't know what they call it now. Probably nothing, since we don't have black dusters anymore, thank the Lord.

The country wasn't out of the woods in 1938 despite Roosevelt and CCC camps. In a certain way it might have been the worst year of all for some folks, the ones who had held on through all that came before and thought they would make it. But when the weather and the banks and the markets don't cooperate, and you've got a family to feed and clothe and house, and there's no money for shoes in the winter, nor seed for crops in the spring, and once you slaughter that last calf for food, then you got your back to the wall. You have to get out or starve.

The dry cleaner's had a big front window, and while I worked, I watched the caravans of Okies and Arkies and Texies in their beat-up old cars loaded with all they owned — and it was a light load — go driving down Route 66 in search of better times.

But the saddest ones, the most pitiful of those caravans were at the tag end of the Great Migration as they called it, when you thought it was over. In 1938 the cars were older, the tires looking like round checkerboards from being patched so many times, and the faces — Lord, but the faces were gaunt. Did you ever see pictures of the Okies, Megan, the ones Steinbeck wrote about in *The Grapes of Wrath*? Surprised that I read that book, are you, an old woman with not much schooling? You shouldn't be. It was about my times and the people I saw drive down 66. But it's not the book I'm asking you about, it's the people. The gauntest faces I saw during the Depression were in 1938, and it wasn't starvation that melted the flesh off the bones — although most didn't have enough to eat — it was hope. Hope betrayed them. They held on until they thought they saw the end in sight, and then they lost. To lose from the beginning is one thing, but to see victory so close you can almost touch it, that's giving yourself over to hope. When you lose then, it's a cruel loss that cuts the heart right out of a person.

Those were the times as best I can describe them to youngsters who never lived through them and won't ever live through anything like them, and you better hope you don't. Now for the road — the Mother Road, the Main Street of America some called it —'cause 66 played its part, maybe the main part of this story.

Route 66 was more than just a ribbon concrete running from Chicago to California; it was the Highway of Dreams. It was Route 66 to a second chance, a new beginning. It was the route you took to start over. It was DX service stations and motels built in the shape of Indian tepees; rattlesnake farms and roadside zoos, and curio shops that sold genuine Indian moccasins made in foreign countries. It was fantastic sights and outlandish shops and diners that sold fried chicken like Mamma made. It was the road to freedom and adventure even if you didn't have more than a dollar in your pocket and ate peanut butter sandwiches all the way to California. But most of all, Route 66 was hope, even to those last Okies who had already been betrayed once. And they were afraid to trust hope again — you could see it in their eyes — but they didn't have any choice. Hope was all that was left to them. Hope or just give up and die — and those folks were too tough to die.

And now I come to the people. There's me, of course. I worked at the dry cleaner's and lived just north of Sixth Street in a frame house my first husband bought the one and only time he was flush with money. When he died, he left me the house, a worn-out Buick, and two boys, not counting the one who died. I went to work at the dry cleaner's because hard work was all I was educated to do, and I was lucky to get the job. Opal Bannister was the young girl with the skinny arms, and she sat by her husband, a fellow by the name of Leroy, in the front seat of a Ford that was at least ten years old if it was a day, with bald tires and a slate off an apple crate in place of a passenger-side window. A mattress was doubled over and strapped on top of the car, and a couple of canvas water bottles were tied to the radiator cap and hung down in front of the radiator. That was back when radiators were in the very front of the car and you didn't have to open up the hood to get to them. That's where hood ornaments came from, you know, radiator caps, because everybody had as fancy an ornament on the cap as they could afford. There were cupids and eagles and about everything else you could imagine, and if you were rich, why then your ornament might be bronze or maybe even silver or gold.

I saw you nearly jump out of your chair

when I mentioned the radiator cap, but don't interrupt me to ask about it. I'll get around to it soon enough and in my own way. Now, where was I before I got side-tracked on radiator caps? Oh, yes, the water bottles. Most folks carried them because car radiators in those days were liable to boil when the engine overheated — which they did regularly. Also, the folks driving the cars needed to drink a lot of water. Remember, the only air-conditioning those cars had came from leaving the windows open.

There was something else you ought to know about 1938. It was the year of the dedication ceremony of Route 66 by the Will Rogers Memorial Highway Association, whose headquarters was right here in Amarillo. Sixty-six was finally paved from Chicago to Los Angeles, and you had all kinds of motorcades starting from one city or the other. There were lots of ordinary folks driving the distance before and after the ceremony, too, folks who weren't Stein-beck's people or part of the motorcades, but just wanted to share in the celebration and had the wherewithal to do it. Adele Davis was one of those folks, and it was just bad luck that she drove into Amarillo right behind the Bannisters.

In those days there was a filling station right across the street from the dry cleaner's, a Phillips 66 I think it was, or maybe it wasn't, and I used to go over there on my lunch hour and buy a cold Coke. I was sitting inside the garage, kidding with the mechanics while I drank my Coke and smoked a cigarette, when this old Ford drove in. Lord, but I thought I had seen some wrecks before, but this car was held together with spit and bailing wire. The only fancy thing about it was that radiator cap, a woman dressed up in one of those Roman outfits — togas, I think they're called — pointing a sword toward heaven. Yes, it looks like the one you got in that plastic baggie. I reckon it's the same one or you wouldn't be showing it to me. But to get back to my story, a tall, thin man climbed out of that Ford, a young man aged beyond his years, wearing overalls and a checked shirt that had been washed until it was nearly worn out. It was probably the only shirt he owned besides his Sunday one, and I would have bet my Coke that he was saving that one for job hunting when he got to California. He was an Okie. I could tell the minute he opened his mouth. After years of hearing folks on the Great Migration talk, I could tell an Okie from an Arkie or a Texie. If I hadn't been born poor and the wrong sex besides, I might have gone to school and been what my granddaughter calls "a linguist." I tell you that just so you know I'm in the way of being an expert in where folks originate.

"I need some gas," Leroy Bannister said to the attendant, Elmer I recall his name was. "And you got any kerosene for sale? I got my own can."

"I got kerosene for sale. About how much would you be wanting?"

"I need a gallon of gas, and five gallons of kerosene," Leroy answered, taking a can from the trunk of his car.

Elmer filled up the can with kerosene — filling stations kept a supply in those days — and put a gallon of gas in the old Ford. "That will be nineteen cents for the gas and forty-nine cents for the kerosene."

Leroy nodded his thanks and pulled a ragged leather coin purse from the hip pocket of his overalls. With cracked and calloused fingers, he carefully counted out two quarters, a dime, and eight pennies. I know because I'd finished my Coke and was walking by the old Ford on my way back to work. I also know there wasn't much money left that I could see in that coin purse.

Elmer took the money, gave the windshield a last wipe, and smiled at the two white-haired children, a boy and a girl, in the backseat. "You have a good trip now," said Elmer, "and thanks for stopping by."

I tarried a minute, pretending to study the gas pump like I'd never seen one before, while I tried to get a good look at the passengers. I couldn't tell you even now why I was so curious about the Bannisters when I'd seen so many Okies just like them driving down 66, except that there was something noble about that particular family. Whether it was Leroy's clean shirt, or the hole in the little girl's sweater that had been so skillfully darned with thread almost but not quite the right color, or just the way Leroy asked for gas. Everything from clothes to car shouted out defeat, but Leroy still stood tall with his shoulders back. If he had been flat broke, he would have offered to trade labor for gas. His kind never asked for charity. My daddy was the same way.

Leroy drove a half block down the street and stopped the car. He got out with the five-gallon can of kerosene and walked to the gas tank. Elmer nudged me about that time. "Watch what he does now. He's going to pour that kerosene in his gas tank. I knew he was going to do it when I sold it to him, but as long as he's not on the premises when he does, then I haven't broken the law. I'm not allowed to sell kerosene for cars, but a lot of these Okies use it when they run low on money for gas, and they're mostly always low on money. Old cars like that will run on kerosene so long as you start them up on gasoline and keep the engine warm."

"Isn't that dangerous?" asked a well-dressed woman who stepped out of a brand new Cadillac.

Elmer and I had been so busy watching Leroy Bannister that we had missed seeing Adele Davis drive up. According to what Leroy told me on that long dark night that was to come, she was a rich oil man's widow from Oklahoma City who didn't mind telling you how well-off she was. To me that meant she married above herself, because the only folks I know who tell you what everything they own cost are the ones who started out poor as church mice and haven't adjusted to their new circumstances. The old rich never mention cost, probably because they grew up never having to ask the price.

Elmer snapped to attention like he was still in the trenches in France and an officer had just walked by. "I don't think so, ma'am, not in these low compression engines like that Ford. Can I fill you up?" he asked with a smile while he wet his sponge and began to wash her windshield.

"Of course, that's why I stopped," she replied while watching Leroy pour the kerosene into his gas tank. "But now that I have, I believe I'll step over there and have a word with that young man. Mixing kerosene and gasoline might be dangerous, and he has young children in the car. His kind are often ignorant of the danger their actions cause to others. Makes you wonder why God gives children to them and not to the more deserving."

There was something about Adele Davis that went all over me — probably the way she dismissed Leroy Bannister as "his kind." At any rate, I put in my two cents' worth. "Elmer said it wasn't dangerous, and I don't see as how you have any call to be saying different. Besides, I figure that man has enough worries for two men without you adding to his troubles."

"You know him?" she asked, raising her plucked eyebrows. Women used to pluck their eyebrows into a narrow little line, like a pencil streak above their eyes.

"No, but I know his kind," I said, dragging out the last two words just so she would know I caught her meaning.

She looked me up and down like I smelled bad — which I probably did, sweating like sixty working in the cleaners all morning. "I don't believe you need to concern yourself about the young man. You hardly look like you can care for your own needs, much less worry about his."

Honest to God, Megan, that's exactly what she said in that Okie accent that wasn't any better than Leroy's. She just used fancier words, is all. Well, if I'd been mad before, I was like a rabid dog now. I reached out to grab her by the lapels of her suit — imagine wearing a suit to drive from Oklahoma City in those days — but Elmer stepped between us. "I reckon it's time you went back to work," he said to me, frowning to beat the band.

I stood there a minute, feeling hot and shamed and not about to take Elmer's advice. It wasn't any of my business one way or another, but I couldn't seem to let go of it. "You don't know anything about me — or about him," I said to Adele.

"I don't know you personally, of course, but since my husband passed away I've had the privilege of sitting on many charity boards, and I have a great deal of experience helping people do what's best for themselves and their families. You, for example, should improve your grooming and personal hygiene if you want to better yourself. After I speak to the young man, I'll jot down a few suggestions for you and leave them with this gentleman. You may pick up the list at your convenience, and I hope you find it helpful."

She patted her felt hat with the narrow brim that turned up all around her face. It was attractive on her, and I'm sure she dazzled poor Leroy upon first acquaintance. Opal she intimidated until right up to the last. The children she frightened, but then the very young have good instincts about predators.

I watched her walk up to Leroy, then went back to work, and I watched out the front window. That's how I knew that Adele Davis and Leroy stood together talking for more than two hours. Or rather Adele talked and pointed to the children, and Leroy nodded his head every once and a while. Occasionally he would sneak a glance at his children, and I knew Adele was giving him what for on the subject of what was best for the youngsters. She never did appreciate that he was doing his best.

Finally, around four o'clock, Opal got out of the car. She was more than thin. She was skinny, her hip bones jutting against the worn cotton dress when the wind blew the fabric tight to her form. Her hair was pinned up in a knot on the back of her head and was just as white blond as her children's, but a few locks straggled down her neck. I saw Adele pull a comb out of her purse and hand it to Opal, gesturing all the while. I figured she was giving Opal pointers on personal grooming. Opal just bowed her head and took the comb. I could see her white skin turn red from where I stood in front of the cleaner's.

When work was over I sprinted across the street to the filling station. "Elmer, what happened to the Okies and the rich widow?"

He frowned at me. "I don't see that it's any of your business — or mine, either."

"Come on, Elmer. Don't you want to know the end of the story? I'll tell you when I find out."

I never did, of course.

Elmer finally told me that he heard Adele persuade the Bannisters to go with her to a travel court farther down Sixth Street past Georgia. Travel courts are what we used to call motels, and even a cheap one was way out of the Bannisters' reach, and this one wasn't particularly cheap. It was shiny white frame cabins all connected together in the shape of a U. The building's still there, only it's not a travel court anymore. Anyhow, I couldn't imagine what Adele had in mind for Leroy and Opal, but I knew Leroy, or rather I knew men like him. He would never admit to a woman like Adele that he was too poor to pay his own way. That's how men like him get themselves into messes. Like the Bible says, pride goes before a fall.

I went chasing down Sixth Street to the travel court like the Devil himself was chasing me — and maybe he caught up — maybe he caught up with all of us. That time of the year in Amarillo it got dark about seven o'clock, but by the time I got to the travel court it was already good and dark what with the clouds and the wind blowing grit through the air. It was chilly, too; windy and chilly. I kept thinking of that ragged sweater the little girl wore, and how it wouldn't keep her warm in a car with one window boarded up.

I found the battered old Ford with its apple crate window glass parked in front of a cabin, and Adele Davis's new Cadillac in front of the one next to it. I don't know what possessed me to hammer on the Bannisters' door. Maybe it was an accumulation of all the years of watching folks like them drive by the cleaner's on the Highway of Dreams, knowing that what they were fleeing to was nearly as bad as what they were fleeing from. I read the papers. I've always been what you call a well-informed person. I knew California didn't want the Okies and the Arkies and the Texies. The state didn't have enough jobs for their own citizens, much less the thousands that crossed its borders every month. I knew the migrants ended up in tent cities, living on handouts and being treated like dirt, working for pennies a day when they could find work. In 1938 all we had was hope and each other. That was what struck me the most as I watched the Great Migration through the front window of the cleaners. It was families — families holding together despite defeat and misery, families like the Bannisters. It was parents sacrificing so their children would have a chance for a better life.

That's what Adele Davis counted on, you see.

Leroy opened the door and peered at me, his forehead wrinkled up like he was trying to remember where he'd seen me before — which he probably was. He had his overalls on without a shirt, like he'd been in the middle of shucking off his clothes when I knocked. The two white-haired children — towheads, we used to call them — were sitting on the bed, cuddled next to their mother like two frightened puppies. Opal had an arm around each child and didn't look much bigger or stronger than her offspring. Mother and children had red puffy eyes, and Opal's mouth looked loose and quivered every now and then, as a woman's does when she'd been crying desperate tears. It's the desperate tears that make you sick to your stomach and give you such an ache round your heart that it's a wonder you don't die of it.

"Yes, ma'am?" asked Leroy, which goes to show you what kind of man he was. He didn't ask who the devil I was, and why was I knocking on his door. Not Leroy Bannister. His mama raised him right, be polite to women, even strange women who knock on the door at night.

Suddenly Adele Davis appeared at his shoulder. She must have been sitting on the room's one chair against the wall next to the door because I didn't see her when I first looked in. "Did you follow us here, young woman? I saw you staring at me all afternoon, and I didn't know if I should be flattered or afraid. Financial hard times bring out the worst in certain people, you know."

"I know. I have a good example right in front of me," I said.

She put her hand on Leroy's bare arm, just rested it until looking at it sent the shivers up my back. "You misunderstood me. I wasn't speaking of Leroy."

Was it a sexual touch, did you say, Megan? No, that wasn't the way of it between those two. Not at all. She thought she was calming him, like you might rest your hand on a toddler's head to reassure him when a stranger comes to the house. Come to think of it, that's a fair comparison. She didn't think much more of Leroy Bannister's smarts than she would of a toddler's. They could both be calmed and talked into doing what you wanted them to — which goes to show that Adele Davis never had kids of her own, or else she would know that there's no more stubborn mortal in the world than a toddler.

There we were — The Bannisters, Adele Davis, and me — frozen in place like we were subjects in one of Elmer's old Kodak photographs. Maybe if Adele hadn't insinuated that I either admired or threatened her — both ideas set me off like a volcano — I might have backed away from that door and gone home. Not that my leaving would have changed anything in the long run. Sooner or later, either on Sixth Street or further down Route 66, murder would have been done. I just wouldn't have disposed of the body.

"I wasn't staring at you because I admire your kind" — bearing down on those last two words — "or because I was planning to steal from you. My mama raised an honest woman, and I don't like you thinking otherwise. I was watching you because I was curious. I couldn't figure out what you wanted with these folks, and anybody who knows me can testify that when I'm curious, I'm like a dog with a bone. I don't give up without a fight. You want something, and these folks are in such a fix that I don't think they can turn you down if there's money to be had. I don't like the smell of this business, Mrs. High and Mighty. For all me and these folks know, you could be a gangster's moll."

Oh, I was so mad, I was bristling, but I wasn't as outlandish as I sound now. Bonnie and Clyde, Pretty Boy Floyd, Machine Gun Kelly, gangsters like them got all the headlines in those days. Of course, they were mostly dead by 1938, but they all escaped from the cops at some point by driving down Route 66.

"It's none of your business, and if you don't leave now, I intend to call the manager and have you thrown off the premises," said

Adele before Leroy had a chance to do more than open his mouth.

"Mrs. Davis will be taking our children to raise," said Opal. She had the most soft, musical voice I've ever heard, soothing is what it was, but her words struck me dumb. "They'll have good food to eat and nice clothes to wear — shoes and each one will have a coat when it's cold. Leroy has tried his best to provide, but we don't have a home anymore and no money, and my babies are hungry all the time. Mrs. Davis says it's best that she take them — at least until we get on our feet again."

I finally found my voice and indignation to go along with it. "They won't ever be on their feet enough to suit you, will they?" I asked. I looked at Adele Davis and she didn't even have the decency to blush. That's the kind of woman she was.

"Leroy and Opal agree that the children would be better off with me. I would provide them with the best money could buy, and they would have a chance to better themselves."

"If you're so filled with the milk of human kindness, why don't you provide the *parents* with the best money could buy, and they could better themselves so they could take care of their own children?" She didn't like me questioning her good intentions because her face turned red just over the cheekbones.

"By the time they bettered themselves it would be too late. Their attitudes are too ingrained to change quickly. No, the best solution is to save the children."

"I ain't going to do it," said Leroy, suddenly coming to life and shaking off Adele's hand. "I ain't giving up my children. I'll find some kind of work when we get to California. I'll provide."

Opal came off the bed at his remark. "But we said we wanted the best for the children. I can't stand to see them go hungry again, Leroy. I'd rather give them up than see them starve."

She took each child by the hand and walked toward Adele Davis. Just when she came even with Leroy, he grabbed her arm. "I told you we ain't giving our children away. They ain't puppies, Opal, they're our babies, and nobody can love them like we do. Just have a little faith in me. We'll manage."

"I don't have any faith left, Leroy. Mrs. Davis made me see how foolish I've been. She says this is the best way, and that we owe it to the children."

Tears were rolling down Opal's cheeks like

rivers, and the children were hanging back, scared half to death but not crying. Kids raised during the Depression lived through too much to do much crying. They learned the hard way that crying didn't put fried chicken on the table, or shoes without holes on their feet. ·

"Please don't do this, Opal," said Leroy, tears of his own streaking down his cheeks. "I'll stop you if I have to, and I don't want to hurt you. I've never hurt you, but I will this time if that's what it takes."

The tears just rolled faster out of Opal's eyes as she pulled away from Leroy. That's when he did it — grabbed the razor strap and brought it down on his wife's arm. She gasped and dropped her son's hand to cover her arm where a huge red welt swelled up before any of us could draw breath. Leroy fell to his knees and pressed his face against her legs, but I could still hear him crying, sobbing really, and that's when I knew for a fact that no good could come from Adele's intentions.

I did what I wanted to do at the filling station. I grabbed Adele by her lapels and whirled her away from Leroy and Opal and shoved her out the door where she landed on her behind in the dirt. I never felt such satisfaction in my life.

"Can't you leave them alone?" I asked in what sounded to me more like a hiss than a voice. "They seem to be decent people, and they're going to kill each other over an idea you put in their heads. Don't you have any idea of the harm you're doing?"

She dusted over her behind and glared at me. "I see the harm that vicious bully did his wife. The very idea — hitting her like that. The best thing that could happen to those children is if I took them away from those people."

"Leroy may have hit her — and I bet it was the first time ever — but you pushed him into it, putting him and his wife at odds over their children. You're standing in judgment when this mess is as much of your making as theirs."

She ignored me like I was a piece of trash she had to walk around, and climbed the step in front of the door. "Bring the children out here, Opal. I'll put them to bed in my cabin."

Opal twisted her skirt out of Leroy's grasping fingers and walked outside, closing the door behind her. It was probably close to nine o'clock and very dark, the sky black with clouds and the wind whipping the dirt through the air. The only light was what leaked out around the edges of the blinds on all the cabin windows. I couldn't see Opal's face and could barely hear that soft voice over the wind and the sound of the occasional car driving down Route 66 in front of the travel court.

"I've changed my mind, Mrs. Davis. I can't give up my children. I can't hurt Leroy like that. He'd never forgive me for doing it or himself for not providing better."

I was close enough to Adele Davis to feel her turn stiff as a fence post. She and Opal were practically nose-to-nose on that little step, and it didn't take a second for Adele to recover. "Don't be ridiculous, Opal. You and that brute you're married to can't take care of yourselves, much less helpless children."

I don't know whether it was Adele's calling Leroy a brute, or her insinuation that neither one of them was up to the job of being parents, or both remarks, but Opal slapped her. You could hear the crack of Opal's palm against Adele's cheek as clear as anything — or maybe it sounded louder than it was because it was such a shock. Frail little Opal didn't look like she could stand up for herself, but it turned out she could give as good as she got.

Adele stumbled backward off that step, same as she did when I shoved her, but this time she swung her arms around like a windmill trying to keep her balance. She staggered backward another couple of steps, until she fell against the Bannisters' old Ford. She was a tall woman, and her heart matched up perfectly with the radiator cap. If she had been shorter, she would have lived. As it was, that sword the lady in the toga was holding went right through Adele. She didn't make much sound, just kind of a whoosh when the breath left her.

Leroy, being a decent man, wanted to call the police, but I persuaded him that since we were two of a kind — that kind — that we had better handle this ourselves. Otherwise, Opal was going to serve some hard time. Or rather Leroy, since he was planning on taking the blame. We put Opal to bed with the kids and piled all the blankets we could find on her. When we left, Opal was sobbing, and the two kids were patting her. It was a sad picture.

Leroy and I lifted Adele off the radiator, and I guess you already know all about how we buried her in a grave between the walls. At the last minute I ran out and broke off the radiator cap and threw it in the grave. Don't ask me why I did that because I don't know. It just seemed fitting that Adele be buried with the instrument of death.

The hardest part of the evening after we repaired the wall and moved that industrial dryer back in front of it, was dumping bleach on Adele's shiny new Cadillac. Have you ever noticed that when people see a car with its paint peeling, they automatically think it's an old car even if it isn't? Well, they do. Tie a couple of canvas water bags on the radiator, and you've got a beaten down Okie in a beat-up car. Worked like a charm. Then Leroy helped me push the old Ford into Wild Horse Lake, and we drove the Cadillac back to the travel court.

I cleaned Adele's belongings out of her cabin, and put all the cash — and there was a considerable amount — into Adele's purse and gave it to Opal. I didn't figure she would shrink from using it since she suffered enough heartache to earn it, but I never heard one way or the other. A few months later I visited Harold and his wife, Maude, who owned the travel court. I managed to tear out the page in the register with Adele's and the Bannisters' names on it while he had his back turned and Maude was fixing coffee. By the way, Bannister is just a name I made up, so you couldn't hunt them down. It wasn't their real name at all.

I think justice was done about as well as a judge and a jury could do it. Those nights I can't sleep for thinking about what happened, I remind myself that nothing I could have done would have brought Adele back, and that I made the best of a tragic situation. Never sacrifice a living family for a dead busybody. You remember that, Megan.

Epilogue

The one thing you learn, if you're capable of learning anything, is that you can't know everything.

Professor Mandrake in John and Emery Bonett's *Dead Lion,* 1949

The Willows Retirement and Convalescence Home — Later That Day

"So Sarah was protecting your family rather than the other way around?" Megan asked Pearl as we were walking to our cars outside the retirement home. "I was wrong about that. I was so sure that she had killed Adele Davis."

"And I was so sure that Daddy had killed her," said Pearl.

"How did you know that Sarah Robertson was still alive?" asked Candi. "You gave me that note with her name on it, so I could look up her obituary."

"Herb's father's will gave me a strong hint when it mentioned that Herb the Second and Herb the Original had taken care of a long-term obligation, but I wanted to be sure. Everyone has to have a death certificate, and death certificates have to be filed with the county clerk. But once Agnes started talking about Ray's mother, and Ray looked so distressed, I was sure she was alive. Why else would Ray be so adamant about not helping? If his mother was dead, she was safe, and I don't think Ray would have worried about scandal. He's too practical. But if his mother was alive, then she would be a suspect, and Ray didn't want to take a chance on that. Am I right about that, Ray?"

"I didn't know for sure what had happened, because when I saw my mother shove Mrs. Snooty Pants out the door, I got scared and ran home. I'd never seen her act violent before, and I didn't want her catching me as mad as she was," said Ray.

"She's quite a character," I said, holding Megan's hand. "I like your mother."

"She likes you, too, Ryan. I tell her all about the book club when I visit her, and she always asks questions about you." Ray suddenly avoided my eyes, and I wondered why he was nervous.

"What kind of questions?" I asked.

Ray flashed a quick look at Megan, and I knew. Even a hundred-year-old woman realized I loved Megan. Why couldn't she?

"She just asks one thing or another. I can't remember exactly," replied Ray.

"Do we know yet why Maria killed her husband?" asked Rosemary.

We reached my Ford Ranger, and Megan leaned against a fender. I leaned next to her, our shoulders touching. Until she tells me not to, I'm going to touch whenever and however I can.

"She lawyered up and isn't saying anything, but Jenner said that she persuaded Damian to up his county insurance to one-hundred-thousand dollars. Murder is always about sex or money, and this time it was money," said Megan. "Also, I believe she's a psychopath. She wanted out of her marriage with a little money. Murder is the way she chose. You have to remember that killing Damian wouldn't bother her because psychopaths have no conscience. But she didn't want to get caught, that wasn't part of her plan, so she decided to set me up for the blame. Then she read *The ABC Murders* and decided to follow Dame Agatha's plot.

"I'm furious that she used Dame Agatha for her plan," said Rosemary. "That's just despicable." I wasn't sure but what Rosemary wasn't as angry about Maria's disrespect for Agatha Christie as she was that Maria killed three innocent men.

"I can't believe she was so stupid as to buy another blouse," said Lorene.

"I can't believe the police were too stupid to check," said Megan. "It was one of the first things I thought of when Schroder mentioned it the first time. I would have mentioned it except I was afraid I might be wrong."

"When did you first suspect her, Megan?" asked Randel.

"I was suspicious that something wasn't kosher when she came to the book club right after we found Damian's body. If someone I loved were murdered, I'd stay in my room and grieve until I was old and grey," said Megan. She turned her head and looked at me, and my heart speeded up at what I saw in her eyes.

Call Me Herb frowned as he asked his question. "Why did my father leave all those canceled checks to The Willows with Sarah's name on the memo line? He never said a word about her or the obligation and affection he and my grandfather felt toward her, but they kept all those canceled checks. I don't understand it."

"I think they wanted you to know if you absolutely had to, but if you didn't, well, it was their secret and Sarah's. What did she whisper to you when we were leaving?" asked Megan.

Call Me Herb smiled. "She told me that I looked just like my grandfather, and that it made her feel young and feisty again. I'm not sure what she meant." Poor Herb. He didn't have a clue about anything really important.

"Hey, Professor!" yelled Randel from his car. "It was *Love's Labor's Lost,* wasn't it?"

"No fair guessing, Randel," I answered, and closed my door. Megan scooted next to me and laid her head on my shoulder. I put my arm around her shoulders and pulled her a little closer. It was a good thing the Ford had automatic transmission, because I didn't have a spare hand to shift gears.

We hope you have enjoyed this Large Print book. Other Thorndike, Wheeler, and Chivers Press Large Print books are available at your library or directly from the publishers.

For information about current and upcoming titles, please call or write, without obligation, to:

Publisher
Thorndike Press
295 Kennedy Memorial Drive
Waterville, ME 04901
Tel. (800) 223-1244

or visit our Web site at:

www.gale.com/thorndike
www.gale.com/wheeler

OR

Chivers Large Print
published by BBC Audiobooks Ltd
St James House, The Square
Lower Bristol Road
Bath BA2 3SB
England
Tel. +44(0) 800 136919
email: bbcaudiobooks@bbc.co.uk
www.bbcaudiobooks.co.uk

All our Large Print titles are designed for easy reading, and all our books are made to last.